SALVAGE

SALVAGE

keren david

www.atombooks.net

ATOM

First published in Great Britain in 2014 by Atom

Hardback ISBN 978-0-349-00137-1
C-format ISBN 978-0-349-00191-3

Typeset in Palatino by M Rules
Printed and bound in Great Britain by
Clays Ltd, St Ives plc

Papers used by Atom are from well-managed forests
and other responsible sources.

MIX
Paper from
responsible sources
FSC® C104740

Atom
An imprint of
Little, Brown Book Group
100 Victoria Embankment
London EC4Y 0DY

An Hachette UK Company
www.hachette.co.uk

www.atombooks.net

For my son, Judah.
A constant inspiration.

1: CASS

Pretty much everyone in town knew my name, although not because there was anything special about me. That was fine, or, at least, I was used to it.

But the day I met Will it wasn't fine at all. It hadn't been fine for exactly twelve days. Dad was still hanging in there as a government minister, but was better known as 'Olly with the Dolly'. Or 'Monty in a Muddle'. Oliver Montgomery MP was having an affair – and a baby – with his intern, and now everyone didn't just know my name: they stared, pointed and whispered, too.

Even before Dad was on the front page of all the papers, day after day, I was always careful. I could never get away with being one of those girls who hitched up their skirts to flirt with the grammar school boys on the bus. We lived in a small town, and all the busybodies who knew my parents from the Conservative Party would certainly gossip if they saw me step out of line. It wasn't worth rebelling. It'd be too embarrassing.

SALVAGE

Mostly I didn't bother with the bus, and walked instead. When I did get it (if it was raining, or I was in a hurry to get home before youth choir or county orchestra or a Conservative Future meeting or whatever), I made sure I sat at the back, kept away from the crowd, pulled out a book, plugged in my headphones and enjoyed twenty minutes of peace and quiet.

That day I was sitting near the back next to a large elderly lady, whose cat hissed and spat from a closed basket on her knee. The basket jiggled against my thigh, which was annoying. I'd have preferred to sit next to the window, tracking the raindrops as they dribbled down the glass.

I hardly noticed when Will spoke to me: he touched my shoulder to get my attention, and I jumped and squeaked.

'What? What is it?' My voice sounded high and panicky, and it was all his stupid fault.

'Um, sorry,' he said, whipping his hand away as though I'd burned it. 'It's just ... you're Cass Montgomery, aren't you?'

I'd seen this boy around before, but I'd never spoken to him. He wasn't in choir or orchestra, although I'd seen him once or twice at the inter-school debating competitions. He'd done a good job last time, opposing a motion about school uniform promoting discipline.

I knew about him, though. I knew his name was Will Hughes and I knew he was in the sixth form, and I knew he was incredibly popular and supposedly funny and bright. I knew all about which girls had been out with him and which girls wanted to. I knew these things the same way that people knew I was head-girl material and heading for Oxford. He had a reputation: a more interesting one than mine.

2

He was a local landmark, like the art deco cinema. He was massively tall, all gawky limbs, but strangely graceful – he floated like a daddy long legs. His afro sprung loud and proud around his head, and he wore ludicrous, outsized tortoiseshell-rimmed specs.

I knew he went to Bonny's, which is short for Bonnington's School. It's where you go if you don't get into the grammar schools but your parents have enough money to avoid the comprehensive.

My brother, Ben, had started at Bonny's in September. We were all worried because Ben doesn't do disruption very well, which Dad should have thought of before he ... but I didn't want to think about Dad.

'Why do you want to know?' I didn't mean to sound aggressive, but I also didn't want to encourage him. Couldn't he respect my privacy?

'My name's Will. Will Hughes. I want to discuss something with you.'

The back seat was full of Bonny's sixth formers, with Will in the middle. I knew one of them, Jordan Strachan, as he played the bassoon in the county youth orchestra. They were all in hoodies and jeans, but Will had on a tweed jacket, indigo cord trousers and a bright orange shirt. His bag was a neon pink *Dora the Explorer* rucksack, meant for a six-year-old girl. He was like a flamingo among pigeons – attractive, sure, but totally out of place. Except you never saw him without a huge flock of pigeons.

I really wasn't in the mood to talk to exotic, attention-seeking strangers. 'You haven't picked a great location,' I said, in my politest brush-off voice.

He didn't get the message. 'I thought we could go for a coffee.'

'Oh, did you?' I was aiming for sarcastic, but realised too late that I sounded potentially interested.

'You're Ben's sister, aren't you? I mean, I know you are. I wanted to talk about Ben.'

'You've done your homework.' Surely the sarcasm was biting enough this time?

'I'm his form's peer buddy,' he said. 'We're like a sixth-form emergency squad – there to help if kids in the lower years need individual attention, that sort of thing. I've been keeping an eye on Ben.'

Obviously Ben needed special attention. He always did. He struggled with some academic stuff, and he totally lacked any ability to make friends. You'd have thought he would have been used to it by the age of eleven, found coping techniques, accepted his fate as a loner, identified just one person to hang out with, but every day it was as though he'd only just realised that no one liked him. It broke my heart, so I tried not to think about it too much.

'Oh, well, thanks for that,' I said, looking away. Couldn't he see that I didn't want to talk to him? Especially about Ben. Especially right now.

'I just thought, perhaps we could talk about what might help him? I mean, obviously you know him better than I do.'

OK, this was too much. Talk about intrusive. He was using my brother, using my family's situation, to ask me out. On the bus, with Jordan Strachan and all his friends listening. What an insensitive idiot.

Luckily Grace wasn't next to me: she'd have accepted on my behalf as soon as he spoke. She was at the front of the bus, the giggling centre of a group of grammar boys. She'd been late out of school, detained by Miss Graham, head of the sixth form, for one of their ritual chats about skirt length and leggings. Grace thought I was tragic and frigid and sad, and her mission in life was to make me more like her.

I refused to fall into her trap. She might be able to turn out A* essays, do loads of extra-curricular activities and have an active love life, but I didn't think I could. Instead, I purposely kept my make-up minimal and my clothes functional, so I wouldn't attract unwelcome attention. It wasn't just the fear of gossip: I didn't want my future messed up by some stupid teenage romance.

Not that Will Hughes was even a suitable candidate for romance, with me, anyway. I'd seen him on the bus before, holding hands or more with various girls including Daisy Travers-Manning, whom I remembered from Brownies, and Ruby Thomas, who was in my year but none of the top sets. He had a type, and that was blonde and curvy and giggly. I wasn't his type.

I didn't have a type, but if I had, he wouldn't be it.

'What do you think?' he asked, and one of his friends sniggered.

'I'm busy.'

'It needn't take long. We could get off at the high street. We don't have to go to Starbucks. It's just that I think Ben's not very happy right now and maybe I could help.'

How dare he even begin to discuss my family in public? I opened my mouth to tell him what I thought of him. Then I shut it again.

I didn't want some sort of scene. Especially scenes that outsiders could construct as racism, or worse (is there worse?). It wouldn't look good, especially when the entire British media was already running stories on my family.

'Maybe another day,' I told him. He grinned, much more pleased than he had any right to be.

'Look, give me a call, or drop me a text or something,' he said, presenting me with a business card – a business card! What sixth former has a business card? What a poser!

I shoved it into my pocket, looked back at my book. We were nearly at the high street. Usually Grace got off here, headed for Starbucks for coffee and flirting. I never bothered. I actually had no idea how she got any homework done at all.

The bus lurched to a stop, the cat basket crashed onto my knee and I went flying off my seat, cannoning into weirdo Will as he and his mates filed towards the door. For a second I clutched at his scratchy tweed jacket, breathed in his surprisingly sweet smell.

'Oof!' he said, clutching his stomach, as I scrambled back into my seat, hot-faced with embarrassment. His friends howled with laughter. The cat lady glared at us. I wished I could just disappear.

'Bye, Cass!' he yelled back at me, just as he got off the bus. How could he laugh at me in front of everyone? I crumpled his card in my pocket and tossed it onto the seat next to me, but the stupid cat woman said, 'I think you've dropped something,' and handed it back to me. I was too humiliated to disagree, so I shoved it back in my pocket again.

2: CASS

Grace sank into the seat in front of me. 'What was all that about?'

'All what about?' I snapped, and she said, 'Oh, come off it, Cass! Why was that boy shouting goodbye to you? Will Hughes? The one with the hair and the clothes and the bag and the glasses? He's *gorgeous*. Ruby was *devastated* when he dumped her.'

'It wasn't him,' I said. 'It was Jordan Strachan. He plays in the county orchestra. We'd been discussing Mozart.'

Grace grimaced. She thought orchestra was hopelessly boring, but she admitted it would look good on my university application form.

'Why aren't you in Starbucks with all your admirers?' I asked.

'Because I wanted to see that you were all right, of course. I'm going to come back to your house and make you hot chocolate and you can tell me how things are going. I feel so bad for you, and we haven't talked at all, and I want to be there for you, Cass. After all, you're my best friend.'

Grace and I decided we were best friends when we were six. I liked her because she had a pet rabbit and she liked my orange hair. But recently I'd been feeling that our bond was based on a shared history of Brownies and summer camps, parties and prep school and, to be honest, we had hardly anything in common any more. I'd been looking forward to going to university and making new friends more like me. Quieter. Serious. Not given to asking personal questions.

'That's so nice of you,' I told her, 'but you know, I've got that history essay to finish, and then there's youth choir. I haven't really got time tonight.'

Grace pouted, but she didn't argue. She'd done her bit. My friends were being very supportive, but in a competitive way. I put it down to the general ethos of high achievement: we put the 'best' into the phrase, 'Best Friends Forever'.

Grace, Victoria, Megan and Alice kept picking away at my nicely frozen numbness, like Arctic explorers tackling a glacier, and I really didn't want it to start cracking or melting somewhere inappropriate, like a history lesson or during senior orchestra. Or even somewhere appropriate, like my bedroom or the girls' toilet. I needed to maintain a personal Ice Age, and I had to avoid the global-warming effect of concerned sympathy.

I knew I'd made a good decision when I got home and found Mum sobbing over a pile of photo albums on the kitchen table.

'Mum! What are you doing?'

She looked up at me and I was shocked. Her hair lay flat

8

against her head, limp and greasy. Her skin was blotchy and her eyes red-rimmed. I knew she was upset, obviously she was upset, but seeing my smart, confident Mum unravel like this ... well, anything could happen. A hurricane could lift our house and blow it away. An oil tanker could smash into our front garden. Mum always wore make-up; she went to the hair-dresser every week: 'An MP's wife has to look the part,' she'd say. Who was this stranger?

I hated Dad for destroying her like this.

'We were a happy family, Cass, weren't we? I'm not making it up?'

I sat down beside her, moved her wineglass out of reach. 'Of course we were happy,' I told her. 'We had everything. Of course we were.'

Together we looked at the pictures. Holidays: Tuscany, Vancouver, Devon. The house in France. Mum, wearing a big sunhat, waving at the camera. Dad, in sunglasses, reading the *Daily Telegraph*. My stomach clenched when I saw him. What was he thinking, getting involved with an intern? He was actually old enough to be her father. It was disgusting. He was disgusting.

More photos. Cass with her swimming certificates, her oboe, in the choir. Christmas. Christmas. Christmas. Ben's christening. Baby Ben, big eyed and serious. Me, all dressed up for my first day at prep school, ginger plaits and a straw hat. Thank goodness my hair has darkened a bit since then. I still have the freckles, though.

'Of course we were happy,' I told her. 'Look, no one's died. Lots of people's parents split up. We'll be fine.'

'We've let you down,' she said. 'It's not the same as if ... we took you on, we promised you a proper family … I feel so bad.'

Oh God. The guilt of an adoptive parent. It's always there, unspoken mostly, but lurking in the background. They're trying to make it up to you, because everyone knows they really would have preferred to make a family the normal way. The home-grown way. Although, mind you, Ben is their biological son and he's as unlike them as it's possible to be. We'd make a fabulous nature versus nurture case study for some scientist.

In my opinion, nurture wins out. What did I inherit from my birth parents? Freckles and red hair. What did I get from Mum and Dad? A whole long list of stuff, everything from religion (C of E), politics, education, aspirations, the way I speak, the way I write, the way I cope with stuff: I put on a brave face and I get on with life. Which is what Mum should have been doing, and what I fully expected her to get on with.

I wondered how Dad's new baby would turn out. The one he'd made with Annabel's nice fresh eggs. Granny Matilda (that's Dad's mum) suggested once that maybe Ben's problems were due to Mum being forty-two when he was conceived. Granny Matilda is famously tactless. When I was ten she told me that it was very fortunate I'd turned out so well, 'because I don't think your real family were nice people at all'. And I've heard her telling Mum they'd have to watch me when I got to sixteen because that's how old my birth mum was when she had her first child; she was eighteen when I came along. 'Don't be silly,' Mum had replied, but Granny Matilda said, 'Blood will out. The mother was clearly promiscuous.' I think Mum agreed with her because I'd had all the lectures about contraception a million times, even though at 16 I'd never even had a serious boyfriend. Or a non-serious boyfriend, come to that.

Anyway, as it turned out, Granny Matilda was the one who brought up a son who wasn't able to be faithful.

Mum gave a huge sniff, ruffled her hair and said, 'I look like a fright. I must pull myself together. So sorry, darling.'

I shoved the tissues at her. 'Mum, none of this is your fault.'

'Oh, Cass, sweetie. Thank you.'

'If Dad hadn't been so ... if the Party Chairman people hadn't made him decide so quickly ...'

'The press had got hold of it,' Mum said, blowing her nose. 'The same thing happened to Rosemary Hayes, do you remember? David Hayes got the call that the press had got wind of his affair, and he announced he was leaving while they were watching *Last Night of the Proms.*'

David Hayes used to be Foreign Secretary. His wife, Rosemary, was one of Mum's friends. She'd been furious when Rosemary didn't even get to come to the Party Conference any more. 'So unfair,' I remember her saying. 'Don't they realise how much work the wives do on the home front? They should get some sort of a redundancy package when their husbands leave.'

Now Mum was in the same position. Annabel would go to Conference. Annabel would open the summer fête. Annabel would have to make friends with all the local Party workers – most of whom were Mum's best friends. I felt an uncomfortable and entirely unwelcome glimmer of sympathy for Annabel, which I stifled right away.

'You should call Rosemary,' I told her.

'I can't bear it. She's become a born-again evangelist of

divorce. "You should have done it years ago," she'll say. "I'm having the time of my life!"'

I didn't see that this would do Mum any harm at all, but I gathered she wasn't ready yet.

'What about, you know, those counsellors you can go to?' One of my biggest shocks had been discovering that Mum hadn't actually been all that surprised about the affair. 'Why didn't you try that?'

'Oh, don't be silly, darling. Have everyone in the world know our business?' Mum pulled out her compact and powdered her nose, with short, sharp stabbing movements. 'I just hoped he'd be, you know ... discreet. After all, he had his own flat in London. There was no need to ... to ...' A big gulp of wine.

'To get her pregnant?'

'He was still deciding what to do about that. It wasn't too late. No, the real mistake was taking the job as minister for families. It made him a sitting target for the press. And once it's out in the open ... well, the spin doctors believe in quick decisions. And he chose her.'

'Do you hate them?' My voice trembled shamefully. 'Do you hate him?'

She managed a tight smile. 'I'm so wet, darling – I can't bring myself to blame him. I mean, you know, an MP's life is difficult. They work such long hours, spend so much time alone in a flat. I suppose ... well, to be honest ... I turned a blind eye. I didn't ask questions. But I thought he'd be satisfied with that. I didn't think he'd ever break up the family.'

All these years I swallowed the lie that my parents were blissfully in love; I never even thought to question it. And actually he was probably having loads of affairs. No wonder he insisted on having his own flat near the House of Commons, even though his constituency is only thirty minutes from central London by train.

If she didn't want to hate him, that left it up to me. I surprised myself how much hate I could generate all by myself.

'Mum, I'm going to make you a coffee. Have you had anything to eat?'

'I didn't really fancy any lunch.'

Mum had lost about a stone in the last few weeks. Normally dropping a dress size would be a reason for great celebration for her. Now, she'd hardly noticed.

I rummaged in the freezer, looking for something to warm up for her. It was full of homemade stuff, packed into foil boxes. Macaroni cheese, Irish stew, shepherd's pie ... oh God, not shepherd's pie.

Mum had just taken a shepherd's pie out of the oven when it happened. Dad's phone rang, and he accidentally put it on speakerphone. So we all heard his personal assistant say, 'Jesus, Oliver, you're in big trouble. The *Sunday Mirror* has got hold of a story that you've got your intern pregnant.'

Dad dropped his phone onto the red-tiled kitchen floor. The screen smashed, but Gareth kept on crackling into our silence. 'Oliver? Are you there? Sorry to hit you with this, but this is a crisis.'

Dad trod on his phone – his brand new iPhone – and Gareth shut up, but we knew it was true. If it hadn't been true, Dad would have laughed and said, 'Whatever will the journalists think of next?' and started dictating some sort of denial, or calling his lawyer. Instead, he stamped on a perfectly good phone. His face went pink and his mouth opened and closed, goldfish-like

When Gareth's voice finally stopped, all Dad could do was look around the table at us – at all of us, but mostly at Mum, standing in her oven gloves, clutching the steaming dish of pie – and he said, 'I'm sorry. I'm so sorry. I didn't mean it to happen. I didn't mean you to find out like this.'

'But we did,' said Mum, in a strange, far-away, un-Mumlike voice, which jolted me as much as the time in Italy when I drank an iced triple espresso in one, just to see what it was like. Then she dropped the shepherd's pie with an enormous *bang*, globs of mince and mashed potato exploded everywhere, and our family was over, just like that.

We all stared at the mess, the meat and potato all over the floor and the walls and the table. Then Ben made a little noise in his throat and ran from the room, and Mum went after him.

My hand was on my glass of water, and I couldn't let go. My muscles seemed to be in spasm. Just for a moment I imagined lifting the glass, throwing it at Dad. Not just the ice and water, splashing his smooth face, but the heavy glass, too. Would it smash? Would it damage him? Just for that moment I scared myself. Then my hand went limp and I could move again and I got a wad of kitchen roll and started furiously scooping up shepherd's pie from the floor.

Dad tried to talk to me, but the sounds coming out of his mouth weren't anything like his usual smooth fluency. He was blustering and stuttering and I hated seeing him like that. 'Go away!' I hissed at him. 'Go and see that Ben's all right!'

I wiped and scrubbed and tried to eliminate all the random splodges of mashed potato. If the kitchen was clean again, then there was hope that our family could survive. But even if we did stay together, I knew I could never clean away this memory. We were stained and spoiled for ever.

Since then, Dad had told us that he was staying with Annabel, but he hadn't actually moved his stuff out yet. He was everywhere: his papers, *The Economist* – the house even smelled of his expensive aftershave. I kept meaning to buy some air freshener, just to eliminate him from one of my senses.

Right then, bent over the freezer, I felt weary and old and sad. There was no way that I was going to be able to sing that evening. As I warmed up macaroni cheese for Mum and Ben and me, I texted the choir director, told him I wouldn't make it to rehearsal. Two minutes later, I sent another text quitting altogether. I was only doing it for the personal statement that was going to get me a place at Oxford, after all. Singing didn't seem to fit in my life any more.

Over supper, I worked hard to get Mum and Ben talking about neutral things, like television programmes and books, and what to buy Granny for Christmas. I did my economics essay, helped Ben with his geography. Then I kissed Mum goodnight – she was watching a box set of *Downton Abbey* and seemed reasonably stable – went into my room and checked Facebook.

Twenty messages, and a friend request from Will Hughes. It would look snooty to refuse, and I don't put much on Facebook anyway, so I accepted him. Then I scrolled through the messages. Friends and acquaintances checking how I was, sending me love, poking their noses into my business. Fake, fake, fake, I thought as I scanned them.

And then I froze. There was a name I knew and yet I didn't know.

Aidan Jones.

I swear my heart almost jumped out of my chest. I opened the message. I felt sick.

'Cass,' I read. 'I think I might be your brother.'

3: AIDAN

The waiting room is pretty full, which is crap, but normal for our local hospital at midnight on a Monday. I've been here with Rich a few times before. People come and go. Some wait for hours. Some – like Rich – get rushed off on a stretcher. We got here three hours ago and Rich is the only one who got the stretcher treatment, though half of them look nearly dead.

There's nothing to do. Most people have someone to talk to, or a newspaper at least, but I'm just sitting, trying to block out all the times I've seen Rich in a state – pills gone, vodka bottle empty, or once, in the children's home, blood every-where, like he'd had a bath in it. A blood-bath. Ha-bloody-ha.

I could do with a drink, but you can't get much in the A&E waiting room – just crisps and chocolate and coffee. I haven't got any money on me anyway. I don't know where it all goes. I'll have to walk home, it's only about a mile. I owe Holly a tenner.

An old lady says, 'Call this a health service? It's a disgrace.'

She's talking to me, because the old man with her is snoring. I nod and smile.

'Two hours, we've been waiting.'

The old man doesn't seem hurt like some do – no blood, no bruises – but he leans against her, head on her shoulder, and his breathing makes a rattling noise. If he was a car, his exhaust would be about to drop off.

'How long have you been waiting, love?'

For ever, I want to say. Even being with Holly doesn't stop, it just makes it much, much easier than it used to be. Sometimes I forget that I'm waiting at all.

'Ages,' I say. 'They took my friend in hours ago. I'm just hanging on to see if he's OK.'

'Very bad, was he?' asks the old lady, perking up a bit. 'Must be, if you've been waiting for hours.'

'Pretty bad. He tried to do himself in.'

'Ooh, that's terrible. Overdose, was it?'

'Pills and booze. It's not the first time. He just gets sad.'

'Oh, the poor lad. Did you find him?'

'Yeah.' I shiver, thinking of it. Rich sprawled over his bed. His lips the same colour as his skin, the same grey-white as the sheets. I thought he'd done it right this time, ended it for good, but I'd hit him round the face anyway. When his still body moved, I jumped a mile and yelled, and he gagged and retched and drooled. Then he puked, which probably saved his life.

'Has he done this before?' the paramedic asked, collecting up the empty bottles next to the bed, and when I nodded, she said, 'You'd better come along for the ride.'

A nurse calls 'Albert Brown?' and the old lady says, 'Thank heavens, at last,' and nudges Albert awake.

'I hope your friend is OK,' she says as they stand up. 'Here, have my paper. It's no good sitting here worrying, with nothing to do.'

Normally I'd have made some excuse, but it's quicker and easier to thank her and take her newspaper. It's not as though she's going to watch me read it.

Reading's not my thing, although I can do it if I need to. As long as the words aren't too long and I'm not stressed or tired.

My phone's buzzing in my pocket. You're meant to turn them off in the hospital. I stick the newspaper under my arm and go outside. Walking from the muggy waiting room into the freezing cold car park is like a slap in the face.

'Hey, babe,' I breathe into the phone.

Holly never sounds angry. She's all sweetness and heart, my girl, she's kind and good and she'd never hurt anyone. But I know that anger doesn't always show itself. It can lurk underneath the niceness. It's only a matter of time before Holly kicks me out. I'm waiting for it.

Sometimes I think it'd be easier if she got angry.

'Aidan! Where are you? You forgot to pick up Finn!'

Oh God. This is it.

'I'm sorry, really sorry, Holly.'

'What happened? This is the second time in a fortnight!'

My mind lurches away from the idea of Finn waiting hopefully for me, his eyes teary, his mouth trembling. Not to mention Poppy, our child-minder. We've been trying to keep her sweet. And then there's Holly, worried and disappointed, having to rush out from work because I've let her down.

It's worse because I'd offered to pick Finn up, to make up for the last time that I forgot, which was only last Wednesday. I promised the little guy I'd be there on time today.

'I know ... I'm sorry ...'

Silence from Holly. I know it's the end for us.

'Look, if you want me to move out ...'

'Do you want to move out?' Holly's voice is all wobbly like she might be about to cry.

I did that. I can't bear it.

'Of course not ... I just forgot ... I'm at the hospital.'

'Oh my God, Aidan! Are you all right?'

'Yeah, I'm fine. It's Rich. He's taken an overdose.'

'Not again! Is he OK?'

'I don't know, they're treating him. He can't help it, Holly. He's just programmed to self-destruct.'

'Poor Rich,' she says. 'Poor you. Did you find him?'

'Who else was going to?'

'I know,' she says. 'He needs a proper support network.'

'You sound like a social worker,' I tell her, which is kind of a joke, but also true. Since Holly started working in reception for a GP practice, she's picked up all the jargon. Or maybe it's since she started living with me.

Anyway, when Holly talks about a support network, it makes me want to laugh. Holly has two parents – even if her dad's living in Marbella – a step-mother, two sisters, four grandparents, three uncles, hundreds of friends and aunts and cousins and even one great-grandmother who is still alive aged 101 in a nursing home in Eastbourne. Holly tries hard to understand what it's like being Rich or me. She doesn't always get there.

Rich actually has it worse than me, because both his parents are dead, which is why he ended up in the system. I have a mum and I see her once in a while, even if we don't really get on. And I have siblings, although I never see them at all. Rich has me, and that's about it. I don't count his social worker. She's always off with stress.

Holly's totally forgotten to be annoyed with me. I love how caring she is. 'Are you OK, love? You must have had a shock.'

She doesn't really get that every time I go round to Rich's, I'm half expecting to find him dead. Or expecting to find him half dead. Like today.

'I'm fine. Tell Finn I'm sorry.'

'He's asleep. You'll see him in the morning, you can explain.'

'I'll try.'

'Aidan? You will be back by the morning?'

It's bitter cold, sleet scratching and biting my skin. My hands are numb. But Holly's voice has the power to warm me up, hot and sweet, like the drink of honey and lemon that she made me that time, just because my throat was sore. The best drink ever, I swear.

'I'll be back when I can. I *promise* I will. They're pumping his stomach. I just need to wait and find out whether he's all right.'

'I miss you,' she says. 'It's cold in bed without you.'

'I'll try and be as quick as possible,' I say. 'I will come back, Holly, I promise.'

'Love you,' she says, and I know it's true. I don't deserve her. One day she'll realise.

Back in the waiting room I glance at the paper that the old lady gave me. There's a big picture on the front page. A man and a girl. A girl with dark red hair, the colour of dried blood. A girl with a heart-shaped face and dark eyebrows and eyes that might have been green or they might have been grey.

Something deep inside my memory rustles and stirs, like a bear waking up in its cave, sniffing spring air after a long, cold winter. Finn and I watch nature programmes together sometimes and we saw a bear like that. Finn loved the bear. I thought it looked vicious.

I let my eye move to the black and white columns of whirling letters. I force myself to focus, to try and catch the right ones, squash them into a word, that word I remember. I used to write it on my hand every day until I got sent to Auntie Betty's and she had a thing about hand washing.

Cass.

The curve of the big C, the snaky s's.

She looks like Cass might now, and I'm almost certain that is her name underneath the photo. *Cass*.

My heart is beating fast and loud, and I feel hot and clammy and suddenly dizzy, and I know the signs, so I bend right down, head to my knees, because I don't want to faint in a hospital waiting room. They'd rush me off to some cubicle, when I really need to try and work out the rest of the article, find out why Cass, *my* Cass – it must be – is on the front page of the *Daily Express*.

Letters swim out of the page at me, but I'm too panicky to make them into words. M. D. L. They make no sense. I try to think who can help me. Rich, obviously, but who knew when he'd be in a fit state?

Holly. She'd be happy. She'd understand. Or would she insist that I showed it to my social worker? I'm pretty sure he'd say that I'm not allowed to even try and find Cass. That's what they've all said before.

I could show it to Mum, but that would be like throwing a grenade into an intensive care unit.

'Are you all right?' asks a nurse. She's brought me a drink of water. 'It shouldn't be long now. Your friend is OK. They're going to transfer him to a ward, keep him in overnight. I'll have the details soon, and you can go home, then come back and see him in the morning.'

It's quieter now in the waiting room. I gulp the water and wonder what to do. Normally I wouldn't ask for help. Generally, if people know you find reading difficult, they think you're stupid, and then they take advantage. I can actually read, it's just that the font has to be right, and I need the time to concentrate, and mostly I don't bother. It doesn't make much difference to my life, most of the time, and I can write my name and address and important stuff like that.

I look up at the nurse. She's not that old, about Holly's age, and she's dark and pretty. Girls like her are generally happy to talk to me. I think it's because I've got big brown eyes and I'm good at smiling and, like Holly said – the night we went from being landlady and lodger to something more – 'You look like someone who'd make love like he meant it.'

With Holly, I always mean it. Not with anyone else, though.

I say, 'Thanks for the water. How long are you on duty?' I fix my eyes on hers and I smile my best smile, and I see it reflected in her sudden grin.

We talk a bit about night shifts and being a nurse and missing her family back in the Philippines. Luckily no one interrupts us.

'I know it sounds crazy,' I say, 'but can you just read this article to me? I need glasses to read, and I've forgotten them.'

She looks at the paper. 'It's about the minister. You know. The one who's been having the affair.'

'He's been having an affair with her?' I stare at the photograph. The man – frowning, grey-haired, posh suit – looks way older than Cass. I feel sick.

'Not her, that's his daughter. It says she's called Cass.'

'Read it, please. I think I've found someone I used to know.'

She reads it. The man – Cass's dad – is a government minister. He's been screwing some girl from his office and she's pregnant. He says it was, 'an unfortunate personal error of judgment'. He wants to be left alone to repair the damage he's done.

'Mr and Mrs Montgomery have two children,' says the *Daily Express*. 'Mr Montgomery was photographed yesterday arriving at his constituency home with daughter, Cass.'

'Not nice for the family,' says the nurse, handing me back the paper. 'Not nice for the girl, either.'

'No,' I say, 'not nice.' Then she has to see to some prat who's fallen over drunk and is bleeding from a massive cut on his forehead.

I stare at Cass, and it is her, it is. His daughter. My sister.

And I'm thinking, Thank you, Mr Montgomery, for not keeping your trousers on. Thank you, secretary, for fancying an old man. Thank you, nosy newspapers, stalker photographers. Thank you, kind old lady, nurse with time to talk.

Thank you for helping me find Cass.

4: AIDAN

Rich has to spend the night in hospital but basically he's fine. Out of danger. 'It's a good thing you found him when you did,' says the doctor, 'because otherwise anything could have happened. Do you have any idea why he did it?'

I shrug. All Rich ever wanted was peace and love. Once upon a time he had a nan, who told him all about heaven and angels and forgiveness. Sometimes he tries to go and find her. I didn't blame him, really.

Maybe he'd have been better off if I didn't have a key to his bedsit, didn't know to go and check on him when he rang me, crying his eyes out. But if he'd really wanted his nan and the angels enough, would he have rung at all? This isn't the first time that I've been sitting in a hospital waiting room wondering if I've saved Rich's life or if I've let him down.

They tell me he'll be kept in until he can see a psychologist, so I should come back tomorrow. Not sure how I'll manage that, I'm meant to be at work, but I'll sort something out.

SALVAGE

It's late, so when I get back to the flat Holly and Finn are both asleep. I've gone beyond tired, and I'm starving, so I make myself some toast and switch on the TV with the sound down low.

Is it possible to be in love with a building? I love our flat. It's got incredibly high ceilings, which are decorated with curls and twirls – like a really fancy birthday cake. The floors are shiny and polished. When it's light, the room is bright and friendly. Our furniture doesn't match, it's all bits and pieces, mostly from the shop downstairs, but it's funny how a candy pink sofa, a swimming-pool blue rug and acid green chairs can look good together. At night, we draw the dark, wine-coloured velvet curtains and sometimes Holly lights candles. She buys things from the market too, so we've got old china plates and bent silver forks and a set of green glass tumblers. It's nothing like the plastic plates and tinny cutlery at the children's home.

I've lived in so many places before that they all get muddled in my mind, and sometimes I have nightmares where I'm lost in a house I can only half-remember. Now I wake up every morning and see our stuff and feel at home.

Just saying that I have a home is something new.

I have a job too, and I only have to go downstairs to get to it. Everything's gone right in my life since I started working with Clive Norman, salvage king of London. It's almost like magic. The only thing that spoils it is waiting for the magic to end.

Jon, my social worker, put me in touch with Clive after I left the children's home and he got me settled into a bedsit. 'Further education isn't for you, is it, Aidan?' Jon said. 'And it's not so easy to get onto an apprenticeship now. We could try the construction industry, but I think Clive might be looking for someone. I've placed quite a few care leavers with him. He was a Barnardo's boy himself, believes in giving kids like you a chance.'

I didn't like Jon much. He was one of those young ones who pretend they care but never deliver. Jon had a wife and baby twins and he used to talk about them all the time, like I was interested. He'd been my social worker for two years, and never found me a foster home. It was alright for him, he could go home at night. I couldn't.

Anyway, he left soon enough and now I have some other guy, but we don't have much to do with each other.

I was dead nervous, until I got to the shop where we were meeting Clive. Then I forgot to be scared because I fell in love right away. With the shop, obviously, not Clive.

Imagine a shop for everything, chairs and tables, sofas and rugs, dolls and teddies, games and footballs, plaster angels, huge china vases, gold-framed mirrors, kids' bikes, soft wool blankets, designer jeans, Nike trainers, suede jackets, sunglasses ...

'You'll be working a lot in the shop,' said Clive, who was shorter and wider than me, and wearing a leather jacket that kind of made you notice his grey hairs more than if he'd just worn a jumper. 'Also in the yard, schlepping boxes, unpacking the van. Can you drive?'

'He's only just turned sixteen,' Jon told him.

Clive grunted and said, 'They chuck them out much too young. Mind you, he looks older. If you do OK here, Aidan, I'll pay for some driving lessons when you're old enough, OK?'

I nodded, too dazzled by the shop to say anything, and he said, '"Thank you" wouldn't go amiss. I suppose you don't learn manners in that home of yours.'

'Thank you, Mr Norman,' I said, in a rush, and he said, 'That's more like it. You can call me Clive.'

The yard was just as interesting as the shop: a muddle of metal and stone. Piles of bricks. 'London domestic,' Clive told me. 'People want them for restoration jobs.' Slabs of marble. A mountain of kitchen cupboards. 'Mostly I buy stuff that's been written off by an insurance company. Fire or flood damaged, but still absolutely fine. The original owner can't sell it on, so they sell it to me. Then there's the stuff that comes from building sites. And I do house clearances. Bankrupt stock, too. I take anything that people don't need. Give them a fair price and sell it on. It's 100 per cent above board. I don't take stolen goods, and everyone knows it.'

I'd kind of assumed that some of the stuff must be knock-off, but I believed him because he looked at me hard and said, 'If you do one thing to screw up my reputation, you'll be out on your ear, do we understand each other?'

So I said, 'Yes, Mr Norman, I mean Clive, thank you, Mr Norman', and he said he'd see me on Monday morning, 9 a.m. and don't be late.

I didn't trust him, of course, but then I never trust anyone. It didn't make any difference when Jon told me all about how Clive had made a small fortune and how he lived in a detached house in Hadley Wood with his wife and three daughters. Sometimes the married ones are the worst.

At first I was jittery as hell whenever we had to be alone together, in the van or the yard or the shop. He put his hand on my arm once, and I nearly jumped through the roof. But he's OK, Clive. He didn't mean anything by it. He keeps his hands to himself. He's never asked me to do anything that I didn't want to do. If I turn up on time and keep my fingers out the till, do all the jobs I'm asked and don't complain, then he's happy enough. Mostly that's what I do.

Holly's laptop is on the table, so I switch it on and have a look. I carefully copy Cass's name from the newspaper. And here she is.

Her dad is a Tory MP and a government minister.

He's left home to live with a girl called Annabel who worked in his office. She's having his baby.

It made my head hurt just reading this much, so I switched to Facebook. Maybe I could find her there.

Cass Mont-gom-ery.

I'd looked for 'Cass Jones' before. I'd looked for 'Cass Mackinnon', which was Mac's name. When I turned eighteen, I'd asked my new social worker to find out who had adopted Cass, what her name was. He told me there was nothing he could do. A closed adoption. Cass needed to find me when she was eighteen. If she wanted to.

Cass Montgomery is an unusual name. Only three on Facebook. One from Australia, a grandmother of six. One with no details at all, not even a photo. And then her. Cass. My sister, Cass.

She has 270 friends. She goes to some posh school. She's in a netball team – there's a picture of her holding a silver cup up high, like she's won the Champions' League. She sings in a choir. She's not a party girl – no pictures of her snogging boys or getting wasted or showing off her legs or cleavage. She seems younger than sixteen in her pictures – no make-up, hair long and wavy, pulled back from her face in most of the pictures. Massive grey eyes. Freckles splattered on her nose.

I haven't got any pictures of when we were little. I did have some, once, I used to have a whole Life Book, but I lost it. Maybe it's at Mum's house. I left there in a bit of a hurry, so that's the most likely thing.

There's not much to read on Cass's profile page, not even any pictures of kittens or funny cartoons, all that Facebook crap. But one photo album is of her family at Christmas. The government minister dad. Her mum looks like a TV newsreader, all highlights and lipstick, sleek and scary. I just about remember them.

Cass's parents. The people who took my sister away from me. I get all shivery, just looking at them.

But of course I don't remember the little brother, who you can just tell is a total geek, although maybe I'm judging too much from his glasses and sticky-up hair and chemistry set.

Cass has a brother. Of course she has. How screwed up is it that it's him and not me?

'Aidan?' Holly is standing at the door, eyes half-closed, hair sticking up. 'Aidan? Come to bed, honey, it's really late ...'

'I'm coming in a minute,' I say. She plods back to bed. I open up a Word document. They were good on IT at the referral unit I got sent to when I dropped out of mainstream school, we did a lot of computer stuff.

I write what I want to write, spell-check it two or three times. Then back to Facebook, open message, copy, paste.

Cass. I think I might be your brother.

There doesn't seem to be anything else to say and I'm

dog-tired now, so I press 'send' and shut the computer down and switch off the lights. I walk out of the living room and across the hallway and into our bedroom. So much space! Sometimes I just walk from room to room, enjoying that feeling of having a different area for different things.

Our bedroom has got the same high ceilings as the rest of the flat. I found a chandelier in the shop once, and asked Clive if I could have it. He thought it was a good idea. 'That flat'll have to be sold one day, so it needs to look good. Don't look like that, lad, it's an investment. I'm letting you and Holly live there while she gets on her feet. It's not for ever.'

Clive doesn't really approve of me and Holly being together, partly because she's his niece and partly because we're a bit of an unlikely couple. Not that he put it like that. 'I'm not being funny, but I don't like it when the girl's older. Call me traditional, but it's not natural. Mind you, the baby does need some sort of a dad, even if you're just a kid yourself. Think you're up to it?' When I nodded, he patted me on the shoulder and said, 'Good lad.'

At least he's nice about it, not like Holly's mum.

Finn has a mobile hanging over his cot – a rocket and some stars – and this chandelier is like my version. It looks like diamonds, falling from a golden frame. I just lie and stare at it sometimes, jewels sparkling in the sunlight, hardly believing that I'm lucky enough to live here.

I peel off my clothes and get into bed. Holly cuddles up to me.

'How's Rich?' she murmurs.

I'd forgotten all about him. 'He's going to be fine. Same old.'

'Do you think we should offer to have him to stay?'

We've had Rich to stay quite a few times. He stinks out the flat with his roll-ups. He eats all the food. He cuts up in the living room. Holly spent ages last time trying to get the blood-stains out of the cushion covers.

'No,' I say, and then, 'Maybe. The bedsit gets him down.'

'He should talk to his social worker. Get moved.'

'His social worker's off with stress. He's meant to be getting floating support. I don't think they're going to help.'

Her arms go around me. 'I don't really want him staying here.'

'I know. Nor do I. It's just difficult.'

'You're really good to him.'

I try and explain for the millionth time. 'It's just that for a long time he was all I had and I was all he had.'

'Now you've got me. And Finn.'

I kiss her, slowly, hungrily, happy that I'm her special project. Kissing is easier than talking sometimes. It's easier than explaining that Rich has been my friend for ages – six years now – which is the longest that anyone's ever stuck around for me. Holly and I have been together for nearly two years. That's ages. I'm sure I'm going to mess it up soon.

When we make love, all I want is for her to enjoy it. She talks sometimes about how I'm different from other guys, how selfless I am, how she's never met anyone like me. That's good. She seems to have no idea how bad sex can be, even though she's older than I am, and I never want her to find out.

'You're beautiful,' I tell her. Holly is beautiful, but not in an obvious magazine kind of way. Her figure is kind of lumpy around the middle, and she's got thin, flat, light brown hair, a round face and tiny little blue eyes. When she first came in the shop I hardly noticed her. But now I love the way her body is so soft and comfortable, and I love her smell and her smile and her little snubby nose … I wouldn't change anything about her. I like that she's older than me, too. I like that no one thinks we're together until they find out that we are.

'Oh, Aidan,' she says. 'You're … oh, Aidan.'

Then Finn starts yelling. We freeze in the darkness, hoping it's a blip, hoping he'll go back to sleep.

'Mummy! Aidy!'

He's awake.

5: CASS

I read it again and again. Aidan. Aidan Jones. What was this? Was it a journalist trying to trick me? Trying to find out secrets about our family? Or could it be true?

Aidan Jones was my brother. He was right there in my earliest memory. I remember crying for Aidan, missing him, running through the house searching for him. But I couldn't really remember his face. I couldn't remember talking to him or playing with him. He was just a gap, an absence, a missing person.

That's what it's like, being adopted. It's probably different if it happened when you were just a baby, but I was four when some social workers and a judge decided to reassign me from my useless set of original parents to my bright and shiny new ones.

Some of my memories are just undeveloped ideas of people and places that I can't ask anyone about. They hang around in the corner of my mind like faceless ghosts. Aidan is my brother, but I wouldn't know him if he walked past me on the street. I used to worry about that sometimes. What if we saw each other? We'd never know.

I clicked on the Facebook profile. Aidan Jones joined Facebook last year. He's in a relationship with Holly Norman. He's not very active on Facebook. He only has ten friends. He hadn't bothered with a cover photo. His profile picture shows the back of his head. Dark hair. A white T-shirt. A tattoo on the back of his neck. 'Hope', it said, in swirly writing.

I stare at the photo, as though it's suddenly going to animate itself, so Aidan will turn around and smile at me. It stays stubbornly still.

I click on Holly Norman's profile, but it doesn't say much. There's a cover picture of Camden Market, and a profile picture, but she's wearing sunglasses and a big sunhat. Her pictures, her wall: all private. In a relationship with Aidan Jones. Lives in Camden.

Back to Aidan's message. What should I do? I knew my birth family weren't meant to contact me. There are rules, laws. Social workers say it's best to keep away until you're eighteen. Then it's up to me whether I wanted to trace them or not, and it'd be done with counsellors and support. My birth family had no right to contact me.

I only had a year and a half to wait because I was turning seventeen in April, and I hadn't even thought about whether I'd do it or not. I'd wait, probably, because I wouldn't want to be distracted from my exams.

But Aidan hadn't waited. He hadn't kept the rules. He'd found me on Facebook. He must need me back in his life, I thought. It was extraordinary how happy that made me feel.

SALVAGE

I'd looked for Aidan on Facebook a few times, but there are loads of people called Aidan Jones and none of them seemed right, and how can you tell anyway? He probably wasn't living in America, or Ireland – or was he? He definitely wasn't black, although he was darker than me, skin and hair and eyes.

I'd always assumed that he'd got a new family, so he wouldn't be called Jones anyway. But here he was. Aidan Jones. Maybe he'd been adopted by another Jones family: it was a common enough name. Maybe he'd changed his name back when he got to be eighteen. I calculated. He'd be nearly nineteen now.

I clicked 'reply'. I'd be careful, I decided – I wouldn't give anything away. I'd try and find out who this person was, if he was genuine, or if he was really a journalist trying to get the dirt on Dad and his affair.

'Hello,' I wrote, 'why do you think that?'

I wasn't expecting a reply. But the chat box opened up right away. It took ages for him to write something, though.

- *yr name is the saym & u hv the saym red hair.*

- *What do you remember about me?*

Long pause. Then:

- *u liked red jelly & horsis*

- *Go on.*

- *u wear scarred of dark & u had a lite*

If this is Aidan, I thought, he can't spell at all. Maybe he was dyslexic.

- *Lots of people are scared of the dark.*

- *the lite had a cat onit.*

I thought and thought. I had no memory of a cat light. I did like jelly though, and raspberry was my favourite. And I'd always been scared of the dark. What else could I ask him?

- *What's our mum called?*

- *janette*

- *What about our dad?*

Another long pause. A few minutes. I thought he'd gone. Then:

- *mac.*

- *Do you remember when my birthday was?*

- *april 15*

He *is* Aidan, I thought, or someone who has access to my adoption file. Or someone who knows me – but none of my friends had any idea that I had a brother called Aidan. Some friend of my parents? Someone who thinks this is an appropriate time to mess with my emotions?

- *Are you really Aidan?*

- *yes*

- *How did you find me?*

Another pause. I waited, trying to work out how I felt. A little bit scared, an awful lot excited. One thing was for sure: I wasn't thinking about my parents any more.

- *i sor yr foto in a paper*

Oh. My excitement faded. Here we were again. Oliver Montgomery, shamed minister, with his daughter Cass outside their £1 million constituency home.

- *u had the saym red heyr & the saym naym & i thort it must b u.*

- *I don't like being in the paper* I wrote, and sent it, and then I leaned my head against the screen and wondered why I'd written such a thing.

- *i bet. sorry*

- *That's OK.*

- *i wish i cd c u becos I mised u.*

- *I missed you too* I wrote, before I thought about whether it was really true. Can you miss someone you can't remember?

- *id lik to c u maybe 1 day.* He added a confused face to his message, and although I usually despise emoticons, I found myself smiling.

- *Maybe. Let me get over the surprise.*

- *sure.*

- *Are you in touch with our parents?*

A pause. Five whole minutes. Again I think he's gone. Then I see the magic words: 'Aidan is typing.'

- *mum a bit not mac.*

I wondered, for the first time, whether we actually had the same father. Perhaps Mac was just mine. Perhaps he wasn't really dad to either of us. Aidan could tell me. Did I want to know?

- *Sorry. Was Mac not your dad?*

- *No prob myn ded.*

- *I'm sorry.*

- *long tiym ago.*

- *I'm sorry.*

- *r u OK with yr dad & al that shit?*

OK, this was the first time I really thought he might be a journalist.

- *I'd rather not talk about that.*

- *sure. sorry.*

Parents didn't seem to be a great subject.

- *Where do you live? Are you at school?*

- *london camden u no it? I hv a job*

Not one that involved writing, I thought, and then felt mean and nasty. I wondered what sort of school Aidan had gone to. Not a private grammar school, that was obvious.

- *I go to Camden Market sometimes.*

- *maybe i sor u*

- *I don't think I'd know you. Sorry.*

- *u dont hv 2 say sorry*

This time I sent the confused face emoticon. He responded with a smile. I sent a smile back. I began to see the attractions of talking without words.

- *Aidan, how do I know it is you? Have you got a photo or anything?*

One minute. Two minutes.

- *maybe i can get a foto*

- *Can you send it to me? A copy?*

- *sure*

- *Thanks.*

It was midnight. I tried to imagine Aidan typing into a phone or a laptop. Was his bedroom as big as mine, as nice? What sort of place did he live in?

- *I'd better go. I've got school in the morning.*

- *I hv work*

- *What do you do?*

- *its a shop and a yard 4 salvage*

- *What sort of salvage?*

Mum got the fireplace in our living room from an architectural salvage yard. I imagined Aidan surrounded by Victorian tiles and original features.

- *stuf from fiyrs and fluds my boss bys it after. he sells on the gud 1s. we get allsorts, toyz, furnytur n stuf*

Aidan's spelling was so random that it would almost be funny if he wasn't my older brother and if every mangled word wasn't making me cringe.

- *Oh, sounds fun.*

- *its OK*

I want to ask him about Holly, but I don't want to look as though I've been nosing around his profile.

- *Do you live with your family?*

- *my girlfrend*

- *That's nice.*

Actually, I think he's incredibly young to be actually living with a partner.

- *shes called Holly. i want u 2 meet her*

Steady on, I thought, and then winced. That was one of Dad's expressions. I was never going to get used to him not living with us any more.

- *Maybe one day.*

- *i hope so*

Mum was moving around outside my room. I quickly minimised the chat box. My door opened.

'Bit late, darling. You've got to be in school early tomorrow.'

I did, too. Every week the headmistress had a meeting with the prefects. As I was on target to be head girl next year, I'd been incredibly conscientious about never missing a week ever since the beginning of sixth form. I was due to take over in May if all went well, as soon as Eleanor Butterworth, the current incumbent, started her exams. I had all sorts of ideas about things I wanted to do; a homework club for Year Sevens, a nutrition advisory committee for school dinners. They all seemed a bit unimportant now.

'I'm just going to bed.'

Mum came over and kissed me on the forehead. She'd brushed her hair, I noticed, put on some lipstick.

'I'm sorry about before. I'm still in shock, I think. I had no idea about this particular girl – and the baby – but you don't need to hear this. I'm here for you, darling Cass. Computer off now, you need your sleep.'

'OK, I'll just finish off,' I say.

'Five minutes! I'm going to check on you.'

She closed the door. I clicked the chat box.

- *Cass?*

- *Cass?*

- *Hv u gon? Cass?*

- *Sorry!* I wrote. *I had to talk to someone!*

But Aidan was off-line.

6: CASS

I couldn't sleep after talking to Aidan, so after I was sure that Mum and Ben were asleep, I turned on my light again. I knew I had photos of Aidan in my Life Book, but I had to climb up to get it – I had so many books that Mum and Dad had fitted floor-to ceiling shelves to one wall of my bedroom.

The album was on the top shelf , and I tried to shake the dust off before dropping the book onto my bed. Then I climbed down and carefully wiped away the rest of the grime and cobwebs, brushing the stray dust off my white duvet cover, before I opened the book.

It was just a normal photo album, big and blue with a label on the front that said 'My Life Book'. I used to look at it with Mum sometimes, when I was really little.

There he was on page three. Aidan and Cass. A wiry boy with dark curls over his eyes, and a big smile. Sweet brown eyes, staring at the baby – me – on his lap. I'm pale and white, his skin is darker. Now it seems obvious that Aidan and I must have different fathers, that we come from different ethnic backgrounds, but there's nothing in the book to say so.

Then the two of us again on the same big, brown sofa. The caption underneath, written in - I assume - a social worker's neat handwriting reads: 'Aidan and Cass in Gran's front room.'

I tried to remember sitting there with Aidan, tried to conjure up the smell and feel of that sofa. Was it lumpy or soft? Was the brown fabric furry or velvety? What did it smell like? There was nothing there. Just the memory of *looking* at the pictures – sitting on our sofa, soft blue with giant cushions, a sunny summer evening, with Mum smelling of the garden and macaroni cheese, saying in her steadiest voice, 'Your gran had been looking after you, but she was getting on a bit and she wasn't coping very well. Aidan was your big brother, and he loved you very much. We wanted to adopt him as well, but the social workers thought he'd be better off if they found him a family who could look after just him, all on his own. So he'd get loads of love and attention.'

'Lucky him,' I'd said once, because I was fed up with Ben crying and crying and getting all the attention, and Mum looked hurt behind her smile, so I had to explain that I didn't really mean it and I couldn't be happier to be adopted by her.

There were lots of people in the Life Book that I didn't remember. Birth mum: Janette Jones, young, pale as an empty exam paper, flaming ginger hair rippling past her shoulders. Birth dad: Mac, no surname, older, bulkier, red nose, moustache. Mac couldn't cope with having a family, according to the captions, and he got into trouble with the police. Janette had gone back to live with her mum: Mrs Anne Jones, grey and fierce and badly in need of an eyebrow shape, but then they argued and Janette got ill, and mixed with unsafe people, and Gran couldn't cope and gave us back to Janette, and she couldn't cope either, and asked social services to find us nice new families who could look after us better than they could. People who could cope.

Then there were the foster parents, Kath and Kevin (six weeks), Jan and Phil (nine months), and then – my favourite pages – Mum and Dad. Lots and lots of pictures. In the garden, on the trampoline. School uniform. Birthday parties. Holidays. Ben. It was the ultimate happy-ever-after book, because I was living it. So I didn't need to read it. Up on the shelf it went.

Looking at it again for the first time for years, I'm surprised to see that Aidan obviously visited me a lot when I first came to live here. There's a picture of him with me and Mum and Dad lighting candles for my birthday. He's the only one not smiling. It must have been hard for him to come and see me so loved and happy in such a nice house. Now I could ask him how he'd felt when I was adopted. Now I could find out what happened to him. Why hadn't I asked right away? I felt uneasy, and turned the page quickly.

All my best friends knew I was adopted, although it wasn't something that we shouted about as a family. 'It's no one's business,' according to Mum, but I think it was because Dad was high profile and they didn't want my birth parents tracing me.

My friends knew because they remembered me arriving. 'You were so quiet in those days,' Grace told me once. 'It was like you were learning how to speak English.' She thought it was romantic and exciting to be adopted, and would ask me if I'd ever thought of tracking down my birth family. 'No, never,' I'd say completely truthfully. My birth family wasn't a family, just a collection of forgotten and useless individuals. Why would I want to meet parents who hadn't wanted me enough to get their act together? All except Aidan, but I couldn't really remember him; he was probably part of another family and must have forgotten all about me.

That's what I used to feel. But now Dad had let me down, and my family was smashed to bits. Aidan needn't be a ghost any more. He could be my brother again.

'Cass?'

I nearly jumped out of my skin. 'What? Oh, Ben! What is it? It's late.'

Ben was all bundled up in his dressing gown, eyes blinking behind his glasses, hair rumpled up. He looked like a small, distressed owl.

'I can't sleep.'

'What's the matter?'

He sat down on my bed, stared at his slippers. 'No one likes me.'

'They're stupid. Ignore them.'

'But they've all got people to laugh with and even if I try and laugh at them, no one laughs with me.'

Over the years, Ben's been to loads of doctors and educational psychologists and special educational needs teachers and so on, and no one has ever really said what it is that makes him different. He's not autistic and he's not dyslexic and he's not dyspraxic and he doesn't have classic Asperger's, although one psychiatrist said there might be similarities. There's nothing anyone seems to be able to do, anyway, to help him catch on to the trick of making friends, which is all he wants in the world.

'Are they being mean to you?' I pretended to consider my options. 'Shall I come and meet you after school? Have a word with the bullies? I could scare them for you.'

Ben screwed up his face. 'I'm not sure that would work,' he said, so polite and thoughtful that I felt terrible for teasing him.

'No, I don't think it would,' I agreed. 'Be fun, though.' Horrible brats. How difficult would it be for them to be nice to him? And how happy would that make him? If I went to Bonny's, I'd probably spend my whole time wading in to defend him. What were the teachers doing there? Why didn't they sort it out?

'They don't hurt me physically,' he said, carefully – Ben's learned over the years to be very precise when explaining to school and family how bad things are. 'But they say things about Dad and they laugh.'

'Oh, Ben, poor you.' I hugged his scrawny little body. 'Isn't there anything you can do? Can you tell a teacher?'

Ben shook his head. 'I tried that already. Not doing it again.'

At primary school, Mum and Dad were in and out of the head teacher's office every time Ben came home crying. Every member of his class had been in trouble for bullying him by the time he was ten. Moving school, he had been determined to change his strategy. It was gutting that it hadn't worked.

'Ben, you've got to tell someone. They can't get away with being horrible to you.'

He shook his head. 'I'll tell Mum I've got a tummy ache tomorrow. Maybe they'll forget to be nasty to me by Monday.'

'Maybe,' I said. To be honest, Ben might as well stay at home. He'd watch his wildlife programmes and read his books, and probably get himself a better education than he would in a day at Bonny's.

'What are you reading?' I asked, and watched his face brighten as he told me about his latest Michael Morpurgo book, about a boy and his wolf, the adventures they have, their search for a home. Ben wanted a dog, but Mum and Dad worried about his allergies, which were many and various and gave him asthma and eczema. But maybe a dog would actually help him? One of those anti-allergy dogs. There was no point talking to Mum about it though. She wasn't fit to consider a cockerpoo. She couldn't even look after herself properly. Maybe in a few months.

We talked about books and animals, until Ben started yawning and I told him it was time to go back to bed.

He wouldn't have to act a tummy ache tomorrow: staying up until 1 a.m. was probably enough to bring on one of his migraines.

'Cass,' he said to me, rubbing his eyes. 'Cass, will we actually have to see this Annabel person?'

'Don't worry about her,' I told him. 'Go to bed.'

'We won't, will we?'

'I'm not sure,' I lied. 'Go to bed.'

'OK.'

He left, but I was still wide awake. I lay in the dark worrying about him. School was bad enough, but how would Ben cope with meeting Dad's new partner? What about when their baby was born? How could I talk to Mum about this when she was such a wreck?

That's when I remembered the boy on the bus. He was actually offering to help me with Ben. He'd noticed that things weren't going well.

I got up again, padded across the room to find my school blazer. I found the crumpled card in my pocket. Fluorescent green writing on black. Will Hughes. Private Investigator.

Private Investigator? What?

7: CASS

Dad moved out officially on a school day. We came home that afternoon and there were big gaps among the pictures on the walls: the long, thin rectangle which was his group photo from college; the three small gaps in a row, original cartoons from the *Daily Telegraph* poking gentle fun at him; the bigger one to the left, his framed front page from the election.

I didn't think he'd be framing the front page of *The Sun on Sunday:* MONTY'S FLING WITH SEXY INTERN.

'Perhaps we should redecorate,' said Mum. 'It looks awful. I can't bear to look in the wardrobe, there's so much empty shelf space.'

'I could move some stuff in there,' I suggested. 'Everything's crammed into my cupboard.' Actually, I had more than enough space, but I could easily rearrange my clothes to make her feel better.

'Oh, thank you, darling Cass. And maybe you could take over his study, too? It'll give you space to spread your books out.'

'I'm OK in my room.' In my room I could pretend that Dad was still living with us. 'Why don't you use it?'

'What would I use it for? Please, darling.'

'Oh, all right.'

'It won't be for long, anyway. We'll have to put the house on the market.'

'We have to sell the house? Why? We still need somewhere to live!'

'Well, we can't afford to buy your dad out of his share, and he'll need a constituency house, anyway. In fact, he was talking about buying me out – giving me a lump sum to buy a new house, and then he can have this one.'

'What? He'd move Annabel in here? That's ... that's obscene!'

'You'd still have your bedroom ... and so would Ben ... It would mean less disruption.'

I felt like she'd punched me in the stomach. 'I can't believe this! I can't believe you'd let him get away with it!'

'If it's that or show lots of strangers around our house ... I mean, there's no good solution here, Cass, is there?'

I wanted to scream and shout, but I didn't want to shout at her, so I marched up to my bedroom and lay on my bed and breathed in and out.

My phone rang. Dad.

'How's it going, sweetheart?'

I growled through my teeth.

'How do you think?'

'I know it's not easy. I'm sorry, darling Cass.'

'You're going to chuck us out of our house, and move Annabel in ... How can you live with yourself?'

50

'That's just an idea. We'll probably end up selling. Cass, this will all be easier when you have met Annabel, and we've all moved on. It's horrible at the moment, but people do get through the pain. I know it's not easy, sweetheart. I miss you and Ben terribly. How about we all go bowling on Sunday?'

'What, with Annabel?'

'No, just the three of us.'

'I'm busy,' I told him. 'I've got an essay to write.'

'We can talk about it when I see you. You know I love helping you with your homework.'

'You can't just pretend nothing's happened.'

'I'm not. Give me a chance, Cass.'

I knew why he wanted to go bowling: I couldn't lose my temper in a public place. But in some ways that made it safer for me. I really didn't want to lose complete control. I was scared of what I'd unleash.

'OK,' I said. 'For Ben's sake.'

Sunday came and Mum dropped us off at the bowling alley. Dad was waiting by the counter where you change your shoes, talking into his iPhone. A new one, I suppose. We waited patiently while he went on and on about inspection regimes for children in care. Occasionally he waggled his eyebrows at us, the sort of thing I used to find funny a million years ago.

'Cass! Ben!'

I sidestepped his hug.

'I've missed you!' he said, ruffling Ben's hair.

Ben hugged him back. 'I miss you, Dad.'

I wanted to point out that Ben needn't be missing Dad at

all if he'd just refused to leave us, however pregnant Annabel was. Or if he'd just resisted the temptation to sleep with his intern. Instead, I snorted and did up my bowling shoes super-tight.

'Come on, kids,' he said. 'Let's see if you can beat us, Ben.'

I searched for the right size ball, weighed it in my hands, visualised chucking it at Dad's head, knocking him out, smashing his nose. Oh, how the newspapers would love that: DAUGHTER BOWLS MP OVER IN FREAK ATTACK.

'When were you planning to tell us, then? When the baby was born?' I asked.

'Come on, Ben, your turn first,' said Dad, laughing in a completely fake way. I hated him. I despised him.

Ben stepped up to take his turn. Dad took the opportunity to mutter to me: 'Look, being hostile isn't going to help Ben. We've got to support him through this. I accept I haven't handled it well, but I didn't mean to hurt anyone—'

'Yay!' I shouted. 'Ben! Great strike!'

He's only short and his arms and legs are spindly, but this is his sport. He's so proud every time he bowls a strike that I get tears in my eyes watching his capering little celebration dance. Ben doesn't get to be proud often enough.

I took my turn. Dad took his. Then the muttering started again: 'I never meant things to work out like this. I didn't even know she was pregnant until a few weeks ago. It's not easy for me, either.'

'Oh, my heart bleeds.' It was great to get angry. I felt better than I had for weeks.

'How's your mother?'

Neither of us noticed that Ben scored eight and is back with us. 'Mummy's lonely and sad,' he says. 'And she won't even go to the Women's Institute.'

Dad winced. 'She's bound to be … it's a big change for everyone … Your go, Cass.'

I'd never bowled with such power before. My ball sent the pins flying.

'Strike!' shouted Ben. 'Well done, Cass! You're usually rubbish!'

I was usually rubbish on purpose. I couldn't help myself today. It was too satisfying to have the chance to smash something.

'Mum's better off without you,' I said, 'she's enjoying herself. She doesn't have to do all that constituency crap any more. Annabel can do it.'

I was only semi-lying. Mum was completely miserable, but I'd watched her for years, being smiley and gracious, listening to people's problems and views with a patient smile. Perhaps it would be good for her to stop being a supportive partner for once, to be an independent woman, to be free. She'd be a good role model. Finally.

Dad looked relieved to be taking his turn. The ball rolled down the lane, heading for the centre pin, crashing, smashing … two lonely pins were left standing, one either side of the mass destruction. Pregnant Annabel – she was like a bowling ball, I realised: even Dad got crushed by her.

Ben's turn. Dad said, 'You're going to have to meet Annabel. You're going to have to accept her. You'll have another brother or sister before too long.'

Ben scored a nine, turned to us, disappointed.

Dad clapped. 'Well done, Ben! Nine's good! Nine's great!

You can't get a strike every time!' Ben aimed for the single pin and Dad resumed his campaign to persuade me that everything was going to be OK. 'You're going to have to meet her. She's part of my life now. And then there's the—'

'Woo! Another strike! Well done, Ben!'

So we went on. A conversation in bits and pieces whenever Ben was playing.

'I just think for Ben's sake, we ought to prepare him, make Annabel part of his life ...'

'For *Ben*'s sake?' My voice was shaking. 'If you'd been thinking about Ben in the first place—'

'Great strike, Ben!' I knew that voice. I spun around.

Will Hughes, in a neon pink T-shirt and emerald-green jeans, was applauding Ben's strike from three lanes away. Dad and I hastily joined in.

'Great stuff, old man,' said Dad, patting Ben on the back. 'Well done! You're on fire!'

'You weren't watching,' said Ben.

'We certainly were. Didn't respond right away because we were awestruck, weren't we, Cass? Struck dumb with admiration. Come on, give me some pointers on where I'm going wrong.'

I looked over to where Will was playing. He was with three girls and two boys, all completely normally dressed, no one I knew. They were laughing and joking, messing around. I wished I were with a group like that, and not this pathetic little family outing.

Will caught my eye and gave me a smile. I thought he was about to come over, but then Dad and Ben called me to take my turn. And when I'd scored my seven, he was sending his shot rolling down the lane. And scoring a strike, I noticed. One of the girls (pretty, blonde, short) gave him a hug.

Was he with that girl? What did I care? I turned my attention to Ben, chatting to him, cheering his efforts, ignoring Dad's attempts to bring up the subject of Annabel again.

Unfortunately, when the game was finished – Ben won, of course – Dad bribed him with cash for the slot machines. Ben loves them. I had no choice but to stand around with Dad while he droned on and on again.

'She's a nice person, Cass, a lovely, kind person. She didn't mean to hurt anyone. All the fault is mine, you can't blame her. You need to meet her, darling Cass, you have to accept her. Her and the baby. After all, it will be your brother or sister.'

He'd said it again. That was the last straw.

'No, it won't,' I hissed. 'It's nothing to me. It's no relation.'

'Cass, you're my daughter and this baby is mine, too. I know you don't like what's happened, but you just have to accept it—'

'Hi, Cass!'

I had never been so grateful to see anyone in my life. Even though it was the annoying Will Hughes, so-called private investigator.

'Hi, Will!'

Dad looked grumpy and said, 'I don't think I've had the pleasure—'

I would have prolonged the awkward moment, but Will leapt forward, stuck his hand out and said, 'I'm Will Hughes. I'm Ben's peer buddy at school.'

'Jolly good, jolly good,' said Dad, clearly overjoyed to be

seen shaking the hand of an ethnic minority youth in the heart of his constituency. The only disappointment for him was that there was no photographer to capture the moment.

I wondered why I'd never realised before what a big, fat hypocrite he was. All those years thinking he was a hero, and now realising what a fool I'd been.

Will turned his attention to me. 'Hey, Cass,' he said. 'How's it going?'

'Fine, thanks.'

'Think about my suggestion at all?'

I glanced at Dad, who was clearly curious.

'I'll be in touch,' I said.

'Great! Brilliant! I'll just go and say hi to Ben.'

'Seems like a nice lad,' said Dad, in much too loud a voice. I cringed, hoping that Will hadn't heard. 'Friend of yours, Cass?'

'Didn't you hear? He's Ben's peer buddy.'

'He seemed keen on you, though. Anything going on that I should know about?'

I didn't even bother answering that.

'I see, I see,' said Dad, who didn't see anything because there was nothing to see. Well, nothing related to Will, anyway. 'Shall we get a pizza?' he suggested, as Ben finished his game. Ben loves pizza, but I'd had enough.

'I've got an essay to write,' I told him. 'I'm going to get the bus. Ben, you can have a pizza if you want. I'm sure Dad can drop you back at home.'

'Cass—' said Dad, but I was already heading for the bus stop.

*

CASS

I enjoyed the peace and quiet of the journey home. I cleared my mind of Mum and Dad and Ben, of Will and his friends, so happy, so relaxed. I thought about me and Aidan, how weird it was to be in touch with him, but how right. He could tell me so much about myself. He could fill in the gaps, tell me who I really was. I'd thought this life was real, solid, secure, but now I saw it was not.

I couldn't wait to meet him. But I wasn't stupid enough to think I could just go waltzing off by myself. I needed an ally. And I had an idea who that could be.

8: CASS

Will Hughes suggested meeting at the outdoor swimming pool, even though it was October and getting chilly. 'Not to swim, unless you want to,' he said. 'But the café there is one of my favourite places.'

'Oh, right,' I said. I hadn't been there for years. It was old and faded and crumbling – most people I knew were members of the big health club on the outskirts of town. I was surprised the lido hadn't been closed down years ago.

We arranged to meet at 2 p.m., and I made sure to get there a little bit late, so he'd be waiting for me. But at 2.15 there was no sign of him. I wondered if I'd been the target of some elaborate joke.

The lido dated from the same era as the art deco cinema. It must have been stylish and fun in the 1920s, but now the paint on the changing room doors was peeling, and the tiles at the side of the pool were overgrown with moss and grass. Amazingly, there were people swimming. They must be crazy. I was freezing, and I had my winter coat on.

The café was just some tables and chairs around a little kiosk. I ordered a hot chocolate, sat down, and pulled out my phone in case Will had texted me to cancel.

'Hey! Cass!'

The shout came from the pool. Will was bobbing in the water, waving at me.

'Oh! I didn't know you were there.' I felt instantly stupid.

'I lost track of time. Sorry! I'll be with you in a minute.' He grimaced. 'Getting out is the worst bit.'

I dipped my head down to my cup as he pulled himself out of the water. His hair sparkled with droplets of water, and his body – well, I wasn't really in the habit of ogling boys. I just got an impression of long limbs, a little scattering of chest hair, before he wrapped himself in a towel and disappeared into a cubicle.

Five minutes later he dropped into the chair next to me. Will Hughes's out-of-school post-swimming outfit turned out to be a fire-engine-red hoody, chocolate-brown tracksuit trousers and a long-sleeved top that was striped orange and black. I mentally christened him Tigger.

'You should have come for a swim. I wasn't sure if you'd want to, because I don't know you, but it's so awesome this time of year.' He took a sip of coffee. Will's beverage of choice was a double shot cappuccino, which would have kept me awake for about a week.

'Isn't it freezing?'

'Only when you come out. The water is incredibly warm, and once you've dried off, then you can sit here and drink your coffee and pretend you're back in 1930.'

I spluttered into my polystyrene cup. 'Why would you want to do that?'

'Don't you ever do that? Try and do time travel? You just have to find the right place. I spent a whole summer holiday once trying to transport myself back to Victorian times. There are loads of places in London which feel almost right – the problem is when you spot a bus stop or a Starbucks or something out of the corner of your eye ...'

I had to laugh. He grinned back. 'That's better. You were looking disapproving before.'

'Was I? I didn't mean to.'

'You've just got one of those faces, then.'

'What? What about my face?'

'When you get to be a headmistress, you'll terrify all the kids without even trying.'

'Oh!' I couldn't believe my ears. A virtual stranger was telling me that I was ugly enough to scare small children.

'I don't mean to be offensive,' he said. 'I just mean you've got the kind of demeanour that commands respect. You might not want to be a headmistress. You could be prime minister, maybe. Or a High Court judge.'

'I don't seem to command much respect from you.' I was cringing inwardly. Naturally he thought I wanted to be a politician, just because of my dad. Some girls at school used to think it was funny to call me Maggie Thatcher. I knew better than to react, and they soon got bored with it but, still, it wasn't exactly the image I wanted to project.

Who was I kidding? I had no idea what image I wanted to project.

'Oh, you'll have to get used to me,' he said, easily. 'I never mean any harm.'

'Good.'

'Blimey,' he said. 'You *are* offended. I'm sorry. Let's start again.'

'Look, I came to talk about Ben. He needs help at school.'

'Poor kid,' he said. 'The problem is that he takes things far too seriously.' His dark brown eyes met mine. 'A bit like his sister.'

I gasped, and then laughed. What else could I do?

'They're being mean to him. The boys in his year, and some of the older ones as well. It hasn't helped, all the stuff with my dad. It's just another thing to tease him about.'

'No point trying to stop them,' he said. 'I think I'll find a few girls in his year who might take him on – keep an eye on him in the playground, that kind of thing. They're a bit more civilised than the boys. That is, they're constantly bitching about each other, but they'll be nice to Ben if I point out the benefits.'

'What benefits?'

'My approval.' He said it in such a self-satisfied tone that I started laughing again. 'What?'

'It's just, you! You're so arrogant! You think they're all in love with you, don't you?'

'It cannot be denied,' he said. 'The whole of Year Seven is in love with me. Boys and girls. And quite a few of Year Eight, as well.'

I'd never heard anyone so big-headed.

'No point looking like that. It's true. Ask Ben.'

I had asked Ben about Will. His little face lit up and his eyes shone and he said, 'He's just the nicest person in the world! And have you seen what he wears!'

Of course I couldn't tell Will that – it would just feed his

61

gigantic ego. So I said, 'Maybe I will,' and tried to keep a straight face.

It didn't work. He crowed, 'I see you have already!' then threw back his head and laughed.

'Maybe your charm only works on naïve eleven year olds.'

'Oh, no, it works very well on naïve sixth formers as well,' he said, putting his hand over mine so suddenly that I blushed and squeaked as I quickly moved it away.

'Look, we're here to talk about Ben,' I said, quite cross, and he nodded and said, 'Yes, ma'am.'

'Can you really keep an eye on him?' I asked. 'Because he is upset about what's going on at home, but he's always been a bit like this. All his life. He's not had an easy time.'

'Must have been difficult.'

'Yes, it's horrible for him.'

'Not so easy for you, either.'

'Oh, well, I can cope.' I said, slamming my cup down on the table.

Will raised his eyebrows. 'Glad to hear it.'

'What's all this about being a private investigator?' I wanted to change the subject. 'You're not really one, are you? It's just a joke?'

'Well, not really a joke. It's my business. I thought it would be more fun than a Saturday job at Waitrose.'

'Do you get any business?'

'Lost cats. Lost dogs. Cheating boyfriends. I trailed one guy all the way to Leicester Square, took pictures of him meeting some girl.'

'Really?'

'His girlfriend was extremely grateful.'

'I bet she was.'

'Of course, she needed some counselling to help her cope with the emotional implications of our investigation. But I provide that as well.' His grin was in danger of becoming a smirk. I raised my eyebrows.

'This job is nothing like that.'

I didn't want to tell Mum about Aidan. She was too fragile, too upset. She couldn't cope. But I really, really wanted to meet him. I was just waiting for him to send me the photo and any other proof of identity he could come up with.

'I'm sure I can satisfy your every need,' said Will. I decided to ignore the innuendo. He was annoying, but I could also see that Will Hughes would be an excellent bodyguard. Something about him - his height maybe, or his bouncy air of confidence – made me feel safe.

'What do you charge?' I asked, cautiously.

'Depends on the job,' Will said. 'And the client. For you, I'd have a special rate.'

'Why?'

'Because you're Ben's sister, obviously, and he's my job anyway. We are talking about Ben, aren't we? Or do you have a boyfriend for me to trail?'

Annoyingly, I blushed again. I sidestepped the boyfriend question. 'I might need a kind of bodyguard. Just someone to come along with me to a meeting. Not actually there at the meeting, but just to be there, in the background. Just in case it goes wrong.'

I knew Will was desperate to know more. He leaned forward on the table. 'You intrigue me, Miss Montgomery.'

'It'd mean going up to London. Camden.'

'What's the meeting about?'

'It's private,' I said. 'Look, if you're not interested I'll ask my friend, Grace. I'm sure she'd come with me.'

'Grace Lilley? As your bodyguard for a top-secret meeting? That sounds like a fantastic plan.'

I couldn't help laughing. It was absolutely true that if I asked Grace to come along then the entire town would know about Aidan within twenty-four hours.

'How do you know Grace?'

'Cass, just because you don't choose to socialise, it doesn't mean that the rest of us plebs have to ignore each other.'

I wasn't sure if he was accusing me of being snooty or teasing me for being shy. So I got to the point. 'Are you up for it?'

His huge hand thrust forward over the table. 'I'll do it for the special rate of twenty quid. Let's shake on it, Cass Montgomery.'

9: AIDAN

I swing my legs out of bed, shivering in the cold. I'd like to switch on the central heating, but we've decided to keep it for emergencies. Clive doesn't charge us much rent, but the heating bills are a killer.

'Aw, Aidan, love, why're you getting up so early?' mumbles Holly, and Finn makes himself comfortable on my side of the bed.

It's so tempting to lie back down next to her. All I want to do is be with her, so warm and inviting and safe. But Finn is there and he's a bit smelly and besides, I'm on a mission.

'I'm going to see Rich,' I tell her. 'Just check he's OK. You know. Now he's out of hospital, he might be a bit lonely in that bedsit.'

'Can you be back by midday? I wanted to go down the market today, to get some stuff for Finn's birthday. Mum said she'd watch him, but she's only free for a few hours.'

'I'll be back as soon as I can, I promise. Truly, Holly, I do have to see him. I don't know how long I'll be. Enfield, you know. It's a long way.'

Holly snuggles up to Finn. 'I just thought you'd want to come shopping. You know, get him some little presents and stuff. He's so excited.'

'But I'm busy,' I say, before I can stop myself, and then, immediately, 'Sorry. Sorry, Finn. Sorry, Holly. Look, I'll do my best.'

She sighs and says, 'Never mind. We've got a few weeks. Maybe I'll take advantage of Mum babysitting and go and have a swim, eh? You make sure Rich is OK.'

'I don't deserve you,' I say, and I bend down and kiss her. I'm so tempted to get back into bed. But I need to get on.

Holly knows that I won't be back by midday. I'm just incapable. Once I leave the flat, time doesn't seem to exist any more. I'm back in my old life, mooching around here and there, catching buses just to see where they go, talking to random people.

Sometimes I get into situations, and it takes ages to get back.

That's why Holly is so hot on arrangements and timetables and me getting to work on time. Sometimes I find Holly's nagging annoying and sometimes it makes me angry, but mostly I understand why she's doing it. I can't just carry on the way I used to, now I'm with her. I've got responsibilities. Mostly I remember that.

Anyway, I'm feeling bad now, because I don't like lying to Holly. But I have to see my mum, and if Holly knew that, she'd have felt sad and left out, and I hate that. So it's better not to tell her.

My mum's been working in a hairdresser's in Southgate, and I think she's still there. I've visited her there a few times, and she would have told me if she was planning to leave. At least, I think she would.

But when I get to the salon there's a sign on the door saying 'Under New Management', which might mean the staff has changed as well.

'Can I help you?' asks the bored girl on the reception desk, and I grin at her and say, 'Can I just have a quick word with Janette? It won't take long.'

Phew, she doesn't say, 'Who's Janette?' I'm expecting her to call Mum over, but she gives me a long look up and down instead and stops chewing her gum just long enough to jerk her head towards the line of mirrors. 'She's there, at the end.'

Mum is cutting some woman's hair, scissors flying, talking about a wedding in *Hello!* 'That dress is too young for her,' I hear her saying. 'I wouldn't bet on it lasting.'

'Hey, Mum,' I say.

'Aidan!' she says, blades still for a moment. 'Why don't you ever warn me? You can see I'm busy.'

'Sorry.' Of course I didn't warn her. What if she said no? Anyway, I haven't even got her number.

'You'll have to wait,' she snaps, pointing with her scissors at the sofa in reception. 'Ellie-Mae will get you a coffee if you ask nicely.'

I back away.

'He's gorgeous,' says Mum's client, who must be sixty.

'That's my son,' says Mum. 'He's nothing but trouble. Ought to be his middle name.'

'Lovely looking boy. I like the mixed-race ones.'

'You should've seen his dad,' says Mum.'A soldier. Died in Kosovo. A hero. Course, the British army never gave me a penny because we weren't married.'

I back off more quickly. I can't stand it when she starts her stories. My dad, as far as I can work out, was a soldier. She never got anything from the military or anyone else, because when he died he was married with four other kids.

He wasn't much of a hero, as far as I'm concerned.

Mum's still complaining about me to the client. I can hear her right across the room.'Yes, he looks like a lovely boy, but you can't judge a book by its cover.'

I sit on the sofa and look at the pictures in the magazines and wipe my clammy hands on my jeans. I only see my mum every now and again, and each time I've forgotten what it's like.

'Coffee? Tea? Hobnobs?'

Ellie-Mae is the gum-chewing girl at reception. She tells me she's the daughter of the new manager. His name is Brian and he's got a chain of hair and beauty places in Essex, Hertfordshire and North London.

'Impressive,'I say, and she says,'You should come for model night. Free cut, and your picture taken by a professional.'

Holly would love that. She's always going on about how expensive it is to get your hair done properly. But that'd mean Holly meeting Mum, which would be a terrible idea.

'Here you are.' Mum's finished with her client and she's standing in front of me.'I've got five minutes before my next one. What do you want?'

'Can we go outside or something?'

'I'm taking a fag break, Ellie-Mae,'says Mum, and we go out

into the high street. She fishes in her bag for her packet of Silk Cut and offers it to me. I'm meant to be giving up – Holly's really strict about never smoking in the flat – but I take one.

'How are you?' she asks.

'I'm fine. Good. I'm working and I'm living in a nice place and I'm going to learn to drive.'

'That's good,' she says. 'Make sure you don't cock it all up, as usual.'

I've found Cass! That's what I want to tell her. I imagine the look of joy and surprise on her face, the love and pride. I imagine her flinging her arms around me. *Aidan, I'm so happy! You've found my little girl!*

But I can't tell her. I haven't even met Cass yet. Maybe she won't want Mum to know.

Since that first time, we've swapped messages a few times. I'm slow because writing's not my thing, but I can do it, just about. Cass wants to see a photo from when we were small before she'll meet me. She's sensible. She thinks about things. She's completely different to me.

'Mum, I just wondered, have you got any pictures? From when I was a kid?'

'What for?'

'Just, you know. To remind me of the good times.'

She snorts. 'I'd have thought you'd want to forget.' Then she rummages around in her handbag, opens her purse. 'How about that?'

Cass, red-haired and smiling. Me, dark and scowling. Gran's scratchy brown sofa. I can almost smell it, the unique mix of cigarette smoke and stale cat food.

'Wow, Mum. You keep it on you?'

Mum thaws, just a little bit. A tiny smile. 'I want to remember the good times, too,' she says, so sad all of a sudden that it reminds me just how bad those times were. She crushes her cigarette under her kitten heel. 'Look at the two of you. My beautiful children.'

'Can I have a copy?'

'I suppose so. You can get it photocopied at the newsagent. I want it straight back, mind you.'

'Thanks, Mum.'

She reaches up and pecks my cheek. I breathe in her smell, cigarettes, musky perfume, hair products.

'I'm glad to see you, Aidan. I hope the good times last.'

'Thanks, Mum.' This is as good as it gets with her. It's pretty special.

Back in the salon a man is waiting for her. 'What's going on? Janette?'

He must be her new boss. He's all spray tan and sideburns.

Mum steps backwards. 'Brian! Sorry! This is my son, Aidan.'

Brian shakes my hand, bares his dazzling white teeth. 'Nice to meet you, Aidan. I'm sure you'll understand that Janette's got clients to see, and Saturday is our busiest day. Let's try and keep family visits to break times, eh, Jan? And fag breaks out the back, not in the high street. Doesn't look good, seeing the staff puffing away, right outside.'

'I didn't know my son was coming,' says my mum, 'and he's going now, aren't you, Aidan? It's OK. He doesn't come and see me often, do you, Aidan?'

I smile at Brian, grin at Mum. 'I'll just get it photocopied,' I tell her, 'and drop it back to you.'

Brian follows her as she clip-clops over to her next client,

70

and Ellie-Mae asks me if I want her to copy the picture. She does it on their photocopier in the tiny back office, and she leans right in towards me as she's doing it. Her arm accidentally-on-purpose brushes against mine as she hands me the photo, and somehow I can see more of her bra and cleavage than I could before.

I don't have to do anything, though. A photocopy isn't much of a favour. Anyway, her dad might walk in on us.

'Shall I take your number? So I can tell you about the next model night?' asks Ellie-Mae, and I smile at her again and say, 'Tell you what, why don't you get it from my mum,' although I'm not sure that Mum's ever saved my number.

Then I go and wait for the bus to Enfield and it takes ages to get there, and it's past two already, and Holly's rung and left voicemails, but I don't reply because I know I'll feel bad to lie. In the end, I text her a smiley face and a love heart, and I hope that'll keep her happy. She texts back a confused face; I send her a kiss.

I knock at Rich's door, steeling myself for what I might find if I have to use my spare key. I'm relieved to hear him open the door.

Rich is looking a hell of a lot healthier than the last time I saw him. His hair is newly dyed – a bright, showy red – and his eyes are focused on me, and he's smiling. I tell him he's looking good. I know the new look means he's trying to put it all behind him.

'How's it going, mate?' I ask him.

'Oh, you know. Not too bad. My social worker came round, helped me clean up a bit.'

The bedsit looks a hell of a lot better than the last time I saw it. Someone's sprayed air freshener to get rid of the smell of vomit.

'That's good.'

'They're going to look at my meds again. See if they can find a better anti-depressant.'

'Excellent.'

'They might find me a counsellor.'

Rich has had counselling before; he's been on happy pills for years. It helps a bit, I suppose, but it would help him more if he could find someone like Holly. Someone who felt like home. Every bloke he meets he thinks is The One, but no one ever thinks that about him.

'Rich, something's got to change. You can't keep doing this.'

He shrugged. 'I don't want to live like this. Nothing ever changes.'

'Come on. Let's get out of here.'

We walk to the pub. We drink some beer. Then we argue a bit about where to go next. Nando's? Into town?

And then I find myself just blurting it out: 'Rich,' I say, 'I've found Cass. I've talked to her on Facebook. I've really found her.'

I couldn't have found a better person to tell. Rich knows, he really understands, how much I missed Cass. How losing her was like punching a massive hole in the middle of my life. He laughs, he cries, he hugs me. 'That's the best news ever!' he says. 'Let's celebrate!'

I forget about Mum. I forget about Holly. It's like the old times with Rich. We drink a lot, we laugh a lot. He's all right, is Rich.

By the time I get on the bus, it's already late.

AIDAN

And in the dark and in my joy it's hard to remember where I'm meant to be getting off. I'm at King's Cross before I realise it. The night crackles with possibilities. I want to dance. I want to meet new people. I need a drink.

My phone is heavy with messages. It stays deep in my pocket.

10: CASS

The picture that Aidan sent me was almost exactly the same as the one in my Life Book. For a minute I felt as though someone had crept into my room and taken the book away from me.

This must be Aidan, I thought. Who else would have the picture?

But the quality was awful – it looked like a copy of a copy. Maybe the picture was on my social work records? Maybe some old foster family had a copy? A photo can't really prove anything, can it?

He sent me a picture of him all grown up. I stared at it for ages, trying to match up the curly-haired boy from then with the stubbly guy from now. Dark hair, check. Sweet smile, check. Big, dark eyes – well, they weren't as big in his adult face, but they were still staring right out of the photo as though he could look into me. He was wearing a check shirt and a white T-shirt and jeans. He was drinking beer out of a can, raising it in a toast to the camera.

He looked OK. If I had seen him in the street, I'd have thought he was good looking.

I used to worry about that sometimes. Growing up and meeting a guy and falling in love and then finding out we were related. Not just Aidan, but a cousin or something. I used to think I'd have to go somewhere far, far away if I were ever going to find someone to marry. But since Dad had left that didn't worry me any more, mainly because I doubted I'd ever trust anyone enough to marry them.

I had a history essay to write, and three books to read for English literature. But I was not doing any of it. I was on Facebook, just flicking from picture to picture, from my wall to chat, waiting to see if Aidan messaged, waiting to hear when we could meet ...

A message! But it was just Will Hughes, bugging me.

Hi Cass,

Do you think your Mystery Meeting will be during half-term? Because I've got a lot on at the moment and I want to make sure I'm free.

Will xxx

Grrr. I was seriously regretting involving Will in this. Not only was he arrogant and irritating, he also never stopped asking me about the arrangements for a meeting that might never happen if Aidan didn't get a move on and suggest something. If Aidan was Aidan. Back to the picture. Did this man ... boy ... man ... look like the brother I couldn't really remember?

I'd actually cracked and asked Grace how she knew Will. What a stupid mistake. Her eyes nearly exploded and she did a totally fake double take.

'Will Hughes? Oh my God! Why are you asking if I know him?'

'No reason. Ben mentioned him.'

'Oh my God, it *was* him, wasn't it? Shouting to you on the bus? What's going on?'

'Absolutely nothing. He's Ben's peer buddy or something. I just wondered what he was like.'

'He's a legend. Have you seen his clothes? And he's so tall and gorgeous.'

'He's not all that special,' I said, completely accurately. 'He's just an attention-seeker. The clothes are ridiculous.'

'They'd be ridiculous on anyone else, but on Will – he looks great! And he's so clever and so funny. He'd be perfect for you! Why didn't I think of it before?'

'We've got nothing in common,' I said, before I realised that I'd inadvertently and totally accidentally made it sound as though I was actually taking seriously her mad idea that there could be anything between me and Will.

'You'd complement each other! You'd be the serious one! So, has he asked you out?'

'Grace, you're crazy. There's nothing going on between me and Will.' I paused. 'I bet he's got a girlfriend, anyway.'

'As far as I know he's not seeing anyone. He broke up with Ruby over the summer. I can find out, of course.'

'Look, I'm not interested. I just wondered if you knew him. Ben thinks a lot of him and I wondered if he was a nice person.'

'He's amazing! He's, like, incredibly nice! He's got this way of looking in your eyes and asking how you are, like he really, really cares. And he's so cool! He plays the sax and he's in a band and his sister's been on *Holby City*.'

Luckily, the bell rang just then and I was able to escape to my economics class. We had a test for which I'd totally forgotten to study. I chewed my pen and tried to cobble together some answers, and cursed Will Hughes for the bad mark I was going to get.

Back to Facebook. I replied to Will:

- *It might be at half-term. I suggested Monday, waiting for confirmation. Don't worry if you can't spare time in your busy schedule because I'm sure I'll be fine on my own.*

He wrote straight back:

- *No way are you going without me! As your security consultant, I specifically forbid it.*

OK, fine.

- *I'll let you know then.*

- *Yes, ma'am, at your service xx*

I opened the history essay document and tried to concentrate. Russian history. 'Compare nineteenth-century Tsarist rule with communist rule under Lenin.' I knew about this. I really did. I just had to focus.

My phone rang. Will Hughes.

'What do you want?' I probably sounded rude, but surely texting was a perfectly adequate way of communicating?

'Have I offended you?' His voice was amused rather than contrite.

'No, of course not. I'm just working on a history essay.'

'You'll have to get used to me. People usually stop finding me annoying after a while.'

'You surprise me.'

'I knew you had a sense of humour buried away under your Ice Queen exterior. I like it.'

He was *incredibly* annoying. But the thought of finding someone else to come with me to see Aidan – someone who didn't know my parents, someone who wouldn't gossip, was too exhausting.

'Sorry, I haven't got time for this. I have an essay to write.'

'So have I. Tsars versus communists, who were the biggest bastards to the Russian people. Discuss.'

'That's what I'm doing. Although not exactly that title.'

'I like to adapt the titles. Liven things up a bit. Make the teacher smile.'

'Good luck with that.'

'We should get together to study sometime. I hear you're the cleverest girl at your school.'

'I just work hard.'

I'm not really clever at all. I'm just very conscientious and I do lots of work and I listen to what the teachers say. When I got my GCSE grades, I was actually shocked. I knew I was in line for 10 A*s but, seeing them written down, I felt as if I'd pulled off a successful con trick.

Sometimes I feel like I've pulled off the same trick just to be accepted as a Montgomery. When I'm with all the relatives and everyone's so effortlessly clever and confident and knowledgeable ... what am I doing there amongst them?

Would I feel different with Aidan?

'I got 8 A*s and 3 As,' said Will. 'Best in my school. Not sure if I'll make it to Oxford, though.'

'You want to go to Oxford?'

'No need to sound so surprised. They do let black people in.'

'Are you calling me racist?'

'Of course not. Just joking. Don't be so touchy.'

'I'm not touchy!'

'That's a shame.' Will's laugh was more of a chuckle. I ground my teeth.

'Are you trying to annoy me?'

'Am I succeeding? Anyway, Lenin's much more annoying.'

'That's true, and I'd better get on with writing about him. I'll let you know when I have a date for the meeting.'

I went back to my essay. But I couldn't stop thinking about Will and how irritating he was.

Mum stuck her head round the door. 'How's it going?'

'OK. Lenin. Not very inspiring.'

'Do you like having more space?'

I was working in Dad's old study, trying to forget it used to be his. 'I like the space. Not the reason.'

'Make the most of it.' Mum sighed. 'Keep this to yourself, but I talked to the estate agent today.'

'Mum, no! Why is Dad doing this?'

'This is what happens. We're not the first family to go through this.'

'But you put so much work into this house!'

Mum and Dad bought our house about a year before they adopted me. It was an old farmhouse, and it needed completely modernising. Dad wasn't an MP then: he worked for a bank in the City of London, while Mum worked at home as a freelance editor and supervised the builders. She found the furniture at auctions and antique shops. She picked the wall colours. She co-ordinated the architect, the plumbers, the builders, the electrician. She did less and less editing and more and more home-building. She was making the house ready for me. That's how the story went.

'It was a full-time job,' she told me once. 'To make up for the emptiness I was feeling about not being able to have kids.'

When I came, Mum gave up the editing altogether. The social workers advised her to dedicate herself to me 100 per cent in the first year. Essential bonding time, apparently. Then Dad got elected and she got pregnant with Ben.

'It was like a miracle! After all those years of trying! I'm sure it was down to you, Cass. I had my wonderful daughter and somehow that kick-started my system.'

Dad bought the flat in London just after he was elected, because of the late-night sittings at the House of Commons. It worked out well financially to have a second home, and he didn't want to spend his life catching the last train or driving for hours late at night. We stayed there sometimes, but it never felt like home. This house was full of antiques, family history: the portrait of Dad's ancestor who fought at the Battle of Waterloo; the dining table that belonged to Mum's great-grandparents. The London flat was bland, beige, modern.

Even so, I hated the idea of Annabel being there. I suppose selling this house was better than letting her invade and colonise it.

'I'll keep everything tidy,' I told Mum, and she kissed my forehead.

'Thanks, darling.'

Back to the computer. Facebook again. Two messages.

One from Will:

- *Lenin said: Give us the child for eight years and it will be a Bolshevik for ever. Agree?*

And one from Aidan.

- *monday 2pm? camden markit? let me no?*

11: CASS

Camden is one of those places that teenagers are meant to like – full of noise and people, shops and stalls, clothes and music, and cheap stuff to make you feel like you're very individual and different.

I didn't like it. It was too crowded and dirty, too smelly and unpredictable. It made me feel small and nervous. I could easily get lost somewhere like this. I wondered why Aidan chose to live here.

I was actually grateful to have Will with me.

'I can't believe you won't tell me what this is all about,' he complained. 'I mean, what could it be? Are you a spy?'

'No. I am not a spy.'

'You could be, with your government connections.'

'I promise you, I am not a spy.'

'Is it an internet date?'

'No, it is not an internet date. Will, I'm not going to tell you, all right?'

'How far in the background do you want me to stay?'

'About five miles. Seriously, I don't want him to know you're there.'

'Oh, it's a he, is it? And not an internet date? Are we talking secret lover?'

'No!'

'You'll tell me eventually,' he said, and I vowed silently that I would never tell Will Hughes anything about Aidan. Ever.

Half an hour to go. I was calm, in control, absolutely fine – on the surface, anyway. Underneath, I felt sick, scared, and like I could quite easily forget how to breathe. Will being there helped, because there was no way I was going to let him see how nervous I was.

We arrived at the café Aidan had suggested. My plan was to find two tables – one for Will right at the back, and one for me at the front.

Disaster. The whole place was completely packed with tourists.

'Oh no!' I moaned. 'What can we do?'

'You'll have to head him off out here,' said Will. 'I'll be behind you. Completely invisible. Don't worry.'

'I suppose so ...'

Quite unexpectedly, he grabbed my hand, squeezed it. 'Cass. I don't know what this is all about, but I won't let anything bad happen to you.'

I took my hand back, hoping I wasn't blushing. 'Thanks.'

I'd tied my hair back as usual that morning, and dressed in jeans and a pale blue T-shirt and a grey cardigan. Then I looked at myself in the mirror. Somehow, my normal ponytail made me look severe, off-putting; somehow my ordinary clothes seemed drab and boring. So I'd let my hair loose and I'd found a bright blue shirt that Grace had bought me for my birthday and I'd never worn before.

I wanted to look different for Aidan. I wanted to look more grown up than usual. I even took more care over my make-up than usual – well, I put on mascara, which I only do for special occasions.

Even Mum had noticed when I left the house. 'You look lovely, Cass. Going anywhere special?'

I had my story all planned out. 'I'm meeting some friends and we're going up to London. There's an exhibition at the Imperial War Museum. Our history teacher recommended it.'

'Is Grace going? Megan?'

'No, she's away all week. Pony-trekking in Andalucía. And Megan doesn't do history. It's just people. No one you know.'

'Oh, well, have a good time. When will you be back?'

Mum always wants to know where I am and who I am with. Normally, I hardly notice that she's asked. That Monday I was lying and lying. 'I'm not sure. We might see a film or something.'

'Oh, well, ring me if you're going to be late. I'll come and get you from the station if you need me to.'

'It's OK. I've got taxi money.'

Will looked at his watch. 'Five minutes to *rendezvous*. I'm off.'

'Where will you be?' Suddenly, I didn't want him to go.

'In the shadows, round the corners … don't worry. I can blend into the crowd.'

Off he went. Six foot two – so he claims – and his hair adds another two inches at least. A dark indigo hoody and green skinny jeans.

I'd asked him if he had the right clothes for surveillance when we met at the station. 'What do you mean?' he replied. 'This is completely neutral for Camden! I go there all the time!'

Will was completely unblendable ... What was I doing ...?

'Cass?'

I whirled around. That must be him. Aidan. Dark hair, a slight frown on his face. He looked as confused and nervous as I felt.

'Aidan?' I had thought I'd remember right away. But seeing his picture had confused me. What if I only felt as though I knew him because of the photograph he'd sent?

Then he smiled. His eyes crinkled at the sides, and I could see his teeth – a gap between his front two, just like mine before I spent two years in a brace.

I knew him! I remembered him!

'I thought you'd be inside the café,' said Aidan. 'I was right at the back. Then I came out looking for you.'

'I'm sorry! I was going to come in but it looked so busy. I didn't know if I'd find you.'

I was burbling, because I'd never actually talked to anyone who looked like Aidan. He had three piercings in each ear – a line of studs in the lobe – and a ring in his left eyebrow. The tattoo on his neck wasn't the only one: where his lumberjack shirt was unbuttoned at the top, I could see blue ink and a tangle of dark hair.

I didn't know what to do. I stuck my hands behind me and said – too posh, too formal – 'It's very nice to meet you.'

'Don't I get a hug?' he asked. 'It's been a long time.'

'Oh! OK!' We had the briefest of hugs. I could feel my whole body go tense and my shoulders hunch up to my ears.

He released me. 'It's so good to see you,' he said.

'Where shall we go?'

'Maybe the park? I know it's cold, but it'd be good to get away from all the people. We get loads of tourists around here.' He pointed the way and we started walking.

Momentary panic. Was he just some internet nutter? I glanced over my shoulder to try and see if Will was following us. No sign of him. Oh, Jesus, I was breaking every rule of personal safety that my parents had drummed into me: walking somewhere with someone I didn't know; someone who was older than any of the boys I'd ever socialised with; someone who was more of a man than a boy, in fact.

But I *did* know him. He was Aidan. He was my brother. I was almost certain I remembered him.

We walked away from the crowds, past huge houses with pillars at the front. We crossed a road. 'Here we go,' said Aidan, and we were in a park. Regent's Park. Mum and Dad had brought us here before, to have a picnic and watch a cricket match. Press versus parliamentarians. I wondered if the journalist who broke the story about Dad and Annabel had been playing. Did he even know what damage he'd done? Did he care? Or was it just a game for him, the journalistic equivalent of hitting a six?

'There's a café at the top of the hill,' said Aidan, and we kept on walking.

The hill wasn't much more than a gentle slope, and the café had tables inside and out.

I asked for a cappuccino, he ordered two. The bill came to £5.80. Aidan dug into his pocket for change, spent ages counting it in his hand.

'I can get this,' I said, hastily. He couldn't earn much, working in some salvage yard.

'I can get my sister a coffee,' he said, handing the change over the counter.

'Oh. Sorry.' I hoped I hadn't offended him.

We went and sat outside. You could see right across the park. No sign of Will anywhere.

'So,' said Aidan. 'Here we are.'

'I can't believe it.'

'It was so easy. Thank God you're on Facebook.'

'I shouldn't be, really. After all the stuff with the papers, Dad's press person said I ought to make my profile more private.'

'You've not got much there. No party pictures.'

'That's what I thought. And I don't like being told what to do by Party workers.'

He frowned, just slightly.

'I mean, people who work for the Conservative Party ... you know ...'

'Oh, right,' he said politely, stirring his coffee. I didn't know if he understood me or he didn't, and whether he thought I was an idiot or the most patronising person on the planet.

'Um, so, how's your job?' I asked.

'Yeah, it's good. I got a half-day off today. Clive was pissed off with me, but I told him I had to see my social worker.'

'Who's Clive?'

'He's my boss. He's OK. 100 per cent straight.'

'Oh. OK.'

'People kind of assume he isn't because of the shop. You know. But it's all kosher.'

86

I wasn't sure if he was talking about his boss's religion or his sexuality or what, so I just nodded and smiled and said, 'Oh, that's good.' I felt like a member of the royal family, visiting some scheme for young offenders.

He leaned forward. 'Are they good to you? Your parents?'

How could I answer that question? It felt as though I didn't really have parents any more – just two individuals. 'Well, you know, it's been a bit difficult lately. They've just split up.'

'So ... you're not happy?'

'Yes, well, I thought I had the perfect family and everything was fine. So you can imagine what we're going through.'

He smiled. 'I never had much of a perfect family. Not until now, anyway.'

I ran my hands through my hair. 'Oh, I'm sorry. I didn't mean ...'

'Don't worry about me. Everything's good for me at the moment. Especially finding you.'

I'm embarrassed. 'That's really nice of you to say so.'

'Tell me what it's like, growing up in a perfect family.'

I had no idea what to say. 'I mean, we live in a nice house and I go to a good school and we have holidays in lovely places. All the middle-class trimmings.'

He laughed. 'Pony riding? Ballet? That kind of thing?'

'Everything.'

'My girlfriend grew up a bit like that. She didn't like it. Too much pressure. Everyone pushing her to go to university.'

'There is that, yes. I always feel ... well ...'

'Go on.'

'Like I have to do the best I can. To thank them ... sort of.'

'For rescuing you?'

'That sounds awful. I don't mean it like that.'

'No, I get it.'

'Aidan? Do you think it was better for me to be adopted?'

He shrugged. 'I don't know. It was hard, that's for sure.'

I'm not certain if he meant it was hard to lose me, or hard to be left behind. Either could be true.

'I don't know much about our background,' I say, tentatively. 'They gave me a Life Book with photos and things but it didn't have many details.'

'I had one of those. It must have got lost along the way.'

'Aidan, why didn't you get adopted, too? Mum – I mean *my* mum – said that's what she thought had happened to you.'

He looked away, staring over at a football game between two teams of little boys. I glanced over my shoulder to see if I could spot Will, but there was no sign of him.

'That's what she said? She never talked to you about me?' Aidan was still looking into the distance.

'They said the social workers thought you needed a family of your own, to give you lots of attention.'

'Oh, right. Well, I think that was their plan. But no one wanted me.' It sounded bleak, but he made a funny face as he said it, so we laughed together. 'The older you get, the more difficult it is. You were lucky. One more year and you'd have been like me. Unadoptable.'

'Oh, Aidan, that sounds awful.'

He shrugged. 'I had some brilliant foster parents. There was one couple – Betty and Jim – Auntie Betty and Uncle Jim, I called them. They lived out near Epping Forest.'

'Did you stay with them for long?' I'm thinking of my Life Book, how I stayed with one couple for six weeks, another for nine months. Was that what Aidan's whole life was like? No wonder he'd lost his Life Book.

'I stayed with Betty and Jim for four years. From when I was eight, to just after my twelfth birthday. They were talking about adopting me, too.'

What went wrong? That's what I want to ask, but I can't think of a tactful way to phrase it. So, instead, I ask if he still sees them at all and he shakes his head and says no, he hasn't seen Betty and Jim since he moved out. 'I didn't have a mobile.'

Not having a mobile seemed to me to be a pretty lame reason to lose touch with people who might have adopted you. What about landlines? What about letters? But Aidan was looking into the distance again, and something told me that it might be better not to ask any more. After all, these people changed their minds about adopting him. I couldn't begin to imagine how much that must have hurt.

'That's a shame.'

He switched on that smile again. 'That's how it goes. But, anyway, tell me about you. You're at school? You like it?'

'I like some things about it. History. Netball. English.'

'English was my worst subject. They hated me, the English teachers. I couldn't do it at all.'

'Do what?'

'Anything they asked me to do. I didn't get on with school. Dropped out when I was 14 or so.'

'At least you thought about it. I never think about whether I actually want to be going to school or not, I just do what- ever's expected of me. I'm meant to be applying to Oxford next year, and I'm not even sure it's what I want to do ... But I'll end up doing it ...'

Aidan whistled. 'Oxford University?'

'If I get in. I probably won't.'

I was lying. I was almost guaranteed a place at Oxford. As long as I got the grades, I'd get in. But how to explain that to Aidan? He couldn't even spell.

'You'll get in,' he said. 'Why wouldn't you?'

'You have to be really good.'

'I bet you are.'

As we talked, I was trying all the time to match his face with the boy in the photos. Straining after tiny flashes of memory.

I remembered Mum plaiting my hair. I remembered her tying pale blue ribbons into it. I remembered her telling me that I'm going to see Aidan, to say goodbye.

'Do you remember the last time we saw each other?' I asked him.

He paused, scratched his head, looked away into the distance. 'Do you?'

'No. I can't remember anything much.'

He shook his head. 'I don't think so,' he said. 'It's all muddled up in my memory.'

12: AIDAN

It's one of the most difficult conversations I've ever had, and I've had some shockers in my time.

She hasn't got a clue. No idea what foster care is like. No idea about children's homes. She knows nothing about Mac or Mum, or why she was adopted. She knows nothing about me. It's like the social workers waved a wand and sent her to frigging fairyland.

She's probably never met anyone who doesn't live in a big house, goes on holiday to swanky hotels, or gets top marks at school.

That makes me sound bitter and jealous and full of hate, but it couldn't be less true. I think she's great. It's extraordinary just looking at her. She has shiny red hair, like those elegant dogs with long floppy ears. There are a few freckles on her nose, which is straight, a smaller version of my big beak. She looks nothing like me – of course, why should she, we have different dads for a start – but the way she holds her head, the curve of her jaw, her neat little ears . . .

It's like looking in a strange, mixed-up mirror. She's a little bit of me and Mum and Gran – and him, of course, he's there, too. You wouldn't think it was possible, but it is.

Mac. The monster who hurt everyone he came across. I'm looking at Mac in my sister's pretty face and it chills me inside, it's actually scaring me, just that twist of her mouth, the way her eyebrows arch.

'Aidan?' Her voice is nothing like mine or Mum's or – thank God – Mac's. Her voice is posh and confident and completely her own.

We've been chitchatting about this and that, her school, my job, her parents. I don't say much about Holly because I haven't told her anything about Cass, so it feels disloyal to talk about her.

Obviously, I should have told Holly this morning, but I sort of felt a bit awkward about the whole thing, plus she might not approve of this. She might think it was against the rules, because it is, and although Holly doesn't like rules much, she might go for this one, she might agree that you shouldn't see your family before you're eighteen and only with your hand held by social workers and counsellors, because Holly believes in all that stuff a lot more than I do.

I don't think the rule is fair, because the new family have had Cass for 99 per cent of her entire life, and I only want a few hours or whatever.

Anyway, Cass just looked at her watch and I have to go and pick up Finn soon, so maybe we're going to avoid the most difficult questions of all.

'So, do you see much of her? Our mum?'

OK, we're not going to avoid them all.

'She's ... well, she's got her life together now. She's got a husband and two kids – two more kids, I mean – and she's a hairdresser.'

Cass raises an eyebrow just slightly. Is she too posh to have a mother who cuts hair for a living? What about a brother who unpacks boxes of salvaged sleeping bags or stacks bricks in a yard?

'Two more kids? We have more brothers? Sisters?'

Oh, shit.

'One of each. The boy's about eight, the girl's younger.'

'Wow! What are their names? Have you got a photo?'

'Louis, the boy's called. Louis. I think the girl is Scarlett. I'm not part of their life.'

She's shocked.

'But why not? I thought you were in touch with her?'

'Yes, but she, kind of, she keeps things separate. Them and me. I just see her now and again. She's not really like a mum to me.'

'What is she then?'

'She's ... I don't know ... someone I used to know. I see her, you know, sometimes.'

I'm sweating. This is going wrong.

'Oh! That's sad. I'm sorry, Aidan. I'm probably saying all the wrong things.'

'No, don't worry about me. My life is good! I have a great place to live – a beautiful flat. I have a girlfriend, a job. It's really something. It makes a big difference.'

'But you've had a hard time in the past.'

What does she expect? Not everyone's life is all holidays and riding lessons.

'Well, everyone has, you know, challenges. I'm fine now. It's all behind me.'

'Are you sure? I mean you're only, what, eighteen?'

'You grow up really quick in care. They chuck you out when you're sixteen, and you have to cope on your own.'

'Really? I can't imagine that.'

'They put me in a bedsit. All on my own. I thought I was going to go crazy.'

'I wouldn't cope for a week!'

She would, actually. She's clever and she's pretty, so she'd probably get a job easily. She knows lots of people with money, so she'd be able to get loans, sleep on their sofas. She's got connections. I've got them too, but only through Holly. Good connections through Holly. I've got some bad connections of my own.

'I was lucky. I met my girlfriend and she offered me a room. I was her lodger at first, but then we got together. Except we have to keep it a bit quiet because you know ... it might affect our benefits ...'

Just a moment too late I remember that her dad's a government minister. The sort that thinks that anyone on benefits is a scrounger.

'You won't tell, will you?'

'Of course not.' She seems offended. 'So, can you tell me anything else about our mum? And my dad?'

'He went away a long time ago,' I say. 'No idea what happened. I can't remember much about him. Mum's OK most of the time. A bit touchy. She seems happy with her bloke.'

'Do you think she'd want to meet me? Not now, but maybe one day?'

I know she would. I'm not sure I'm ready, though.

'Maybe. She's unpredictable.'

'She must be if she doesn't want to let you know her other kids. Maybe she'd feel the same about me.'

'Maybe,' I lie. 'Maybe.' I'm sure Mum would love to introduce Cass to Louis and Scarlett. She'd be their new big sister.

My phone beeps at me. Time to pick up Finn. I'm proud that I've remembered.

'I'm sorry,' I say. 'I've got to be somewhere.'

'Aidan, has this been OK? Shall we ... can we ...'

'Yes! Of course! We'll do it again!' I mean it. It's just that her questions have opened up all kinds of memories, and she's hardly started. She doesn't even know the questions to ask.

'I'd like to meet your girlfriend.'

'She'd like that, too.'

I'll have to tell her about meeting you first, though.

We're making our way back through the market, standing there, saying goodbye, trying to get over the awkwardness, when it happens. A shout of excitement, and then something grabs me round the knees.

'Aidy!' shouts Finn. 'Aidy! Aidy!' He rubs his runny nose on my jeans. 'I sawed you!'

What the hell? I look around for Holly. Why is Finn running around Camden Market on his own?

'Finn! Where's Mum? Why aren't you at Poppy's?'

'Granny!' he shouts. 'Go park!'

That's all I need, the Wicked Witch of Primrose Hill.

I hoist him up into my arms. 'Finn,' I say, 'meet Auntie Cass.'

13: CASS

'Daddy, Addy!' the little boy shouted. 'Addy!'

I shouldn't have been so shocked, I suppose. I knew people did have children young; in fact, Dad was always talking about teenage mums and how to discourage them. Janette, our mum, she'd been really young when she had Aidan and then me. Of course it was natural that he'd have done the same thing.

Anyway, Aidan might only have been eighteen but he seemed a whole lot older than the boys I was used to seeing on the bus and in Starbucks. Boys like Will, for instance.

What I was surprised about was that he hadn't mentioned having a little boy all the time we'd been together, and he hadn't said anything in his messages, either. He'd talked about the flat where he lived, and a bit about his girlfriend, Holly. Nothing at all about being a dad. And this wasn't a tiny baby. Aiden must have started really young.

An older woman pushing a buggy came rushing up to us.

'Finn!' she said. 'You mustn't go running off like that! Naughty boy!'

Finn screwed his face into Aidan's neck, but Aidan put him back into the buggy, which made Finn cry and kick his legs. 'He could've been hurt or lost or anything,' he told the woman.

'Don't blame me!' she snapped back. 'The buckle doesn't do up properly. Tell Holly I'll buy her a new buggy. Finn, you're a naughty boy to run off. Say sorry to Granny.'

Granny! I thought for a minute that I was going to faint. My knees wobbled and I felt hot and cold and clammy. But then I looked at her again. She was blonde and smart and she wore nice clothes – a grey wool coat and a soft blue scarf – but she was easily sixty. She was far too old to be my birth mother.

'No!' Finn kicked and arched his back to break free of the buggy's straps. The buckle sprung open, and Aidan held Finn down in the seat and forced the clasp back together again. I could see it wouldn't last long. Aidan stayed bent over the buggy, trying to work out how to mend it.

Granny didn't give up. 'Say sorry!' she insisted.

'Sorry, *borry!*' screamed Finn, clearly intending the 'borry' to cancel out the 'sorry', lashing out with his fists and catching Aidan in the eye. Aidan swore, and the woman made a tutting noise.

Strangely enough, Finn fell silent. His legs gave up kicking. His thumb went into his mouth and he gazed thoughtfully from Aidan to his granny. He and Aidan looked so alike, with their dark curls and light brown skin, their dark eyes and worried frowns, I felt almost jealous. Aidan was my brother, but we couldn't have looked more different.

'Umm,' said Aidan. 'Sorry, Juliet. Sorry, Cass. Sorry, er, Finn. It just slipped out.'

'I'm sorry, Aidan,' said Finn's granny. 'Of course he shouldn't have been out of the buggy. He just wriggled out … nearly gave me a heart attack.'

'Good thing I caught him,' said Aidan.

'I don't think he'd have run off if he hadn't seen you.'

Her voice didn't quite fit the way she looked. Cockney upgrade, my dad would call it. Nouveau riche, I found myself thinking, and hated my parents for making me a snob.

'I didn't know you had Finn. I thought he was at the child minder,' Aidan mumbled. 'Holly asked me to pick him up. I was just on my way.'

'I waited there for you. But you were half an hour late, and Poppy needed to get on with other things. You must learn to be more reliable.'

Aidan didn't bother to answer. He hung his head, like a sulky child.

I was feeling incredibly awkward, just standing there. Surely he should have introduced me? She must have been wondering who I was. I held out my hand. 'I'm Cass,' I said. 'Cass Montgomery.'

Juliet frowned and took my hand with as much enthusiasm as if I had offered her a dead rat. 'Hello, Cass,' she said, and then to Aidan, 'Holly says he's been a bit unsettled at the child minder's, poor little Finn. She said she'd been trying you, your phone was switched off, and she wasn't sure you'd remember you were meant to do the pick up.'

Aidan puffed out his cheeks, jiggled from foot to foot. 'He's

OK there,' he said. 'He likes it. Poppy's got loads more toys and stuff than we do. And I was on my way.'

'We're going to have a little walk in the park before meeting Mummy for tea, aren't we, Finn?'

Finn nodded and removed his thumb. 'Duck!' he said.

Aidan winced, but Juliet said firmly, 'Yes, darling, we're going to feed the ducks.'

'I didn't realise you had Finn,' I said to Aidan, and then I wished I hadn't, because Juliet's thin eyebrows went up and her mouth tightened into a smirk.

'Yeah, I should've … there wasn't really … it's complicated,' he said, staring at his feet.

'I'd better go,' I told him. 'It's been great. Really great. I'll give you a call.'

'I'll walk with you to the tube,' he said. 'Bye, Finn. I'll see you later.'

But Finn gave out a huge shriek, and screamed, 'No! No! Addy come ducks! Addy come tea!' so I patted Aidan's arm and said, 'Don't worry. You go and have a nice time with Finn.'

'Cass,' he said, glaring at Juliet, 'Cass – be in touch, OK? It was so good to see you.'

I smiled, although I suddenly felt like crying. I wanted to hug him, kiss him, something, but with Juliet watching and Finn kicking, I didn't feel that would be appropriate. I didn't know what to do. So I stuck out my hand and Aidan stared at it, and then grabbed it and we shook hands. Which was totally wrong, but the best I could do.

I nodded politely to Juliet, who was still maintaining absolute permafrost towards me. 'Goodbye,' I said. And then

I was backing away and walking blindly through the crowds, in the vague direction of the tube station.

As I walked away, I heard Juliet say, 'Well! A new friend, Aidan?' but I couldn't hear Aidan's response.

Will caught up with me just before I got to the tube station and just after I'd given up hope of finding him. He emerged out of the crowd and grabbed my arm. I thought he was a mugger, and hugged my handbag to my chest, letting out a tiny, embryonic scream.

'It's me, you idiot!' he said.

'Oh! You didn't have to grab me like that!'

'You were about to rush into the tube station! What were you thinking – perhaps I'll bump into Will on the Northern Line?'

'I'm sorry. It's just, I thought, I was ages and I thought you must have gone hours ago.'

Will rolled his eyes. 'No faith at all! I've been hiding in corners spying on you. A bit difficult, mind you, in Regent's Park where there *are* no corners, but I found suitable trees.'

It was sunny but cold, and I felt bad to think of Will hanging around for more than an hour just so I could feel safe talking to my own brother. How stupid I was, thinking that I needed a bodyguard.

'You must be freezing, I'm sorry.'

'I am freezing. And starving. Shall we get something to eat?'

He didn't wait for an answer, but opened the door to a Turkish café and ushered me in. The place was completely empty.

Will headed for a table in the corner. I hesitated. I didn't really want to have a meal with someone I hardly knew, when

I could have been analysing my meeting with Aidan, but I couldn't think of an excuse. Will looked at the menu. The café was warm and quiet, it smelled of cumin and lamb stew, and the owner brought us cups of mint tea without asking.

'Mezze ... are you OK if I order ... anything you hate? Vegetarian? No ... OK ...'

The waiter brought us hummus and pitta bread. Will took a bite and chewed.

'So,' he said, mouth half-full. 'The tall, dark stranger. The half-hearted hug. The heart to heart. The little boy. The older woman – she really doesn't like him, does she?'

'I have no idea,' I said, frostily. The waiter put down six more little plates of food.

'Yum!' said Will. 'I love Turkish food, don't you? Here, try this one. You're going to have to tell me, you know. Do you want me to die of curiosity?'

'Yes.'

He clutched his chest, made a choking noise and slid under the table. I ignored him and helped myself to a kebab. I did like Turkish food, I discovered. After a moment he was back in his chair.

'You are made of ice. What if I'd really had a heart attack? I thought you'd at least try and give me the kiss of life.'

'You picked the wrong person.'

'I was sure you'd know how to do it. You must have been a Girl Guide at some point. You're just the type.'

Stung, I retorted, 'What type is that?'

'Do you really want to know?'

'Probably not, but I'm going to hear anyway.'

'You're a joiner. You like being involved. Orchestra, choir, debating society ... That's why you were definitely a Girl Guide. Am I right?'

'I don't like being involved. But I was a Girl Guide. Well done, Sherlock. That's how I know a real heart attack from a completely fake one.'

'And that's why I'm desperate to know what the story is! Girl Guides do not run around London with guys who look like that! Earrings! Metalwork in his eyebrow! A tattoo on his neck! Hasn't shaved for a day at least! Who is he? Is he an ex-boyfriend?'

'No!'

Will drummed his fingers on the table. 'Now you're the annoying one.'

'Sorry.'

'Who will you tell?'

'What?'

'Are you going to tell Grace? Because that's incredibly unfair, what with me coming all this way and lurking so excellently that I bet you never saw me all afternoon.'

'I didn't see you, that's true. You are a superb lurker. Surprising in one so attention-seeking. And I'm not going to tell Grace anything. She's great, but she's got a big mouth, as you know.'

'I haven't got a big mouth. I'm incredibly discreet. You can totally trust me. Besides, this is a professional relationship. You can add a confidentiality clause.'

'To what?'

'To our contract, which I will draw up this week for us both to sign.'

'Oh, well, I'll wait until my lawyer's checked it out.'

'But you will tell me then?'

I didn't answer. He leaned forward. 'I mean it – you can trust me. If you need someone to talk to, give me a try. I'm here, that's all. Underneath all my messing around, I'm actually a nice person.'

'Well, thanks,' I said. 'I'll remember that.'

'What are you up to for the rest of half-term?' he asked. 'I thought I'd go to Oxford one day. Check it out for next year. Maybe at the weekend. Do you fancy coming to have a look?'

'I'm busy next weekend.'

'Oh. OK. No problem. I've got a few other friends who are thinking of applying. I just thought you might like to come, that's all.'

Why was I like this? Why was it so hard to just relax and say yes to someone who was trying to be friendly?

'Ben and I have got to go and see our dad next weekend. We've got to start, you know, weekend access. I'm a bit worried about Ben. It's going to be confusing for him.'

'So you feel you've got to be all strong and selfless for him?'

God, Will Hughes was annoying! I was trying to talk about Ben; he was completely missing the point.

'There's not really an alternative.'

Will traced a pattern in the leftover hummus.

'How's everyone going to cope when you leave home?'

I'd been deliberately avoiding thinking about that.

'Oh, well, it's not for ages yet. Anyway, I might take a gap year.'

'I think you should come and look at Oxford,' he said, decisively. 'Spend a day thinking about your future. You don't need to come with me if you hate the idea so much, but it'd be good for you to get away from all this family stuff. And if you did decide to come with me, it'll be fun, I promise. If you can bear the idea of spending a day with someone as irritating as me.'

There were so many things I could have said to this. About how my family and my future were no business of his. About how I knew Oxford really well, because my granny and aunt lived there. About how I had a load of homework to get finished. About how he had no idea what I'd find fun.

But I was kind of exhausted by meeting Aidan and I fell into his trap. 'It's not *you* … I don't *hate* the idea … it's just that next weekend is no good.'

'Oh, well, that's easy, then. How about Thursday?'

He was grinning at me, very smug and pleased with himself, and I was panicking because I didn't know if this was a date or a friendly gesture or a wind-up or what.

And then I thought about my mum. My birth mum, Janette, teenage mum. And Aidan, not even nineteen yet, with a son … If I'd grown up with them, I'd know how to handle situations like this. I'd be confident about boys and dates and sex and all sorts of stuff. Grace was right. I was a frigid freak, sweet sixteen and never been kissed, and somehow that seemed much more awkward and difficult and wrong than it ever had before. It wasn't that I was interested in Will Hughes, or that anything was going to happen. He was definitely a flirt, though, and a day with him would be good practise for when I found someone more suitable.

'Thursday?' I said. 'I think that's OK. As long as I've finished all my half-term homework, then I could probably do Thursday.'

14: AIDAN

Don't ask me why Holly's mum hates me so much.

Maybe it's because I'm not posh like her, or perhaps because I didn't finish school, or maybe it's something to do with Holly being a few years older. Juliet was OK when I was just the lodger. But she came round one morning to surprise Holly, drop off some toys for Finn's first birthday, and she let herself in with her key, and I was in the wrong bed. With Holly. She's never got over it.

Clive says it's because she wants to see Holly married to someone who's older and richer, with a proper job. 'She's got big ideas, my ex sister-in-law. Never stopped nagging Bernie. No wonder he buggered off to Marbella and hooked up with that tart, Monica. Not your fault, Aidan, but you're not what she had in mind for Holly. And she's never going to let you forget it.'

Juliet winds me up all the way to the park. 'So, not working this afternoon, Aidan?' and, 'Was that a new friend, Aidan?

She's a very pretty girl. Can't be more than about seventeen?' then, 'Do you think Finn's got a cold? They do pick up germs at the child minder's, don't they?'

This one offered me an escape. I crouched down, took a good look at Finn. 'Maybe you're right,' I say, 'he's looking a bit under the weather. Tell you what, I'll take him home. You go and have a cup of tea with Holly, and tell her I'll see her at the flat.'

'Oh!' I've nutmegged her and she doesn't like it. 'Are you sure? But he's looking forward to feeding the ducks! And I promised him a toasted tea cake.'

'Can't be too careful,' I say, grasping the buggy and wheeling it round. Finn's asleep, luckily, so we don't have to say any goodbyes.

On the way home, I call Rich and tell him about Cass, how great she was, how we knew each other right away. 'I owe you a favour,' I tell him. 'If I hadn't seen that newspaper in the hospital that day ...'

Finn only wakes up when we're five minutes from home. He spots a pigeon. 'Duck!' he says, loud and clear. 'Finn go feed ducks!'

We're at our flat door. I undo Finn's straps, tell him to go up the stairs. He doesn't want to. 'Ducks!' he yells. 'Ducks!'

So I have to carry him up three flights of stairs. He's getting heavy, and he's kicking me in the chest. I'm still talking to Rich on the phone, but only half listening to what he's saying.

'Go park!' screams Finn. 'Go park with Granny!'

'Is that Finn?' asks Rich. 'Jesus, Aidan, you've got the patience of a saint.'

'Call you later,' I say, although I know he's got more to tell me about his counsellor, and the new guy he's met, and the college course he's thinking of signing up for.

'Aidy!' shouts Finn, as I open the front door and put him down. My back is aching – I'm not as fit as I should be.

Sod's law, the first thing Finn sees are his toy ducks, which ought to be in the bathroom. 'Ducks!' he cries, and then the penny drops that there's not going to be any duck-feeding or special tea with Granny, or treats for Finn today.

His face goes red and then white. His eyes screw into little slits and squeeze trickling tears. The volume of his crying goes up and up and he kicks his legs at me, at the furniture, at the telly ...

'Not the telly!' I yell at him and I pull him away, because although I don't really think he could reach up to smash it, he needs to know now that telly-kicking's a bad idea because if he goes on like this, he's going to cost us a fortune by the time he turns three.

So he attacks my shins instead, and I'm hopping around saying all the words that a toddler's not meant to hear.

And I just don't need this right now. I don't. I don't want Finn bringing me down.

'Stop it! Shut up!' I'm screaming at him now. He's still crying, raging, kicking out at me.

Holly and I have talked about this. She's really hot on parenting stuff, reads all the books and magazines. I can hear her voice in my head: 'Pick him up. Take him into his room and put him in the cot. Shut the door. Walk away. Calm down.'

My mouth is clamped shut so I don't shout at him as I take him into his room. Finn's room used to be my room. But when I moved into Holly's bed, Finn's cot got moved in here. He doesn't remember, but I still feel a bit guilty. And I feel bad that he's still in a cot when he's too big for it really, but we've been waiting to see if Clive gets some children's beds in the shop.

He's screaming and yelling and struggling. 'I hate you, Aidy! I hate you!'

My whole body tenses.

'I don't want you! Go away!'

'Bedtime,' I tell him.

'No! No bedtime!' He's wriggling and gasping like a fish.

'Yes!' I shout. 'Bedtime!'

He lurches backwards, and I lose my grip on him. Just for a moment. But it's enough for him to bang his head on the side of the cot. His screams get even louder. I bet Clive can hear them downstairs. What if he thinks I've hurt Finn on purpose?

His scream is higher, more piercing, unbearable.

'Finn! I didn't mean to hurt you! Finn!'

'Bad Aidy! Bad!'

I'm confused. I ought to walk away, get calm. But what if I've really hurt him? My stomach clenches. I'd never hurt Finn, never. I know how it feels.

'Finn, let me see your head.'

Finn flails like an old boxer who can't land his punches any more. 'No! Want Mummy! No Aidy!'

I stumble out of the room, shut the door, slide to the floor. My heart is racing, my breathing shallow. Finn's still scream-ing. He hates me. He doesn't want me. I stuff my fingers in my ears.

'Do you remember the last time we saw each other?'

I lied to her. I do remember. It was one of those places where they have supervised visits. Toys that smell of bleach.

Bright red sofas and shiny floors. I hadn't seen her for six months: I'd been living with some foster parents. I can't even remember their names.

Cass looked different to how I'd ever seen her before. She was wearing clothes that I'd never seen. Her face was thinner. Her hair was tied into pigtails with pale blue bows.

She wasn't my sister any more. She belonged to them. She was their little girl.

The social worker had explained it all beforehand: 'It's not Cass's fault, Aidan,' she had told me. 'It's just the way it worked out.'

All I remember is that as soon as I saw Cass I was so full of hatred that I thought my head would explode. 'You look stupid,' I told her. 'I hate your hair like that.'

'Aidan!' said the social worker. 'Don't talk like that to Cass! Come on, let's see what's in the toy box.'

Cass just stared at me. She held onto the social worker's hand.

'Look, here's a jigsaw! Shall we do the jigsaw?'

Cass and her social worker started doing the jigsaw. I hid behind the sofa, watched her from there.

She was the same and she was different. She didn't know who I was. She'd forgotten me. She didn't care about me or Mum at all.

'Come on, Aidan,' my foster mum said. 'Come and join in.'

They got me to come to the table. I looked down at the jigsaw. It was a picture of a house: a little white cottage with roses climbing up its walls. A blue sky, a shining sun, a cat on the doorstep. They'd done about half of it.

I picked up a piece, tried to shove it into place.

'That's wrong,' Cass told me. 'It doesn't go there.'

'It does,' I insisted, pushing it so hard that half the pieces sprang into the air.

'You broke it!'

I shoved her then, hard, in the chest. 'Go away!' I told her.

Then she cried and the social worker took her away and they tried to talk to me, but I knocked the table over and scattered all the jigsaw pieces and then I kicked my foster mum and I was in trouble again.

That was the last time I saw Cass. I don't think she remembers it at all. I've carried it around, all those years, how angry I was, how mean and scary, and she had no idea.

I don't know whether to laugh or cry. Crying seems most likely, so I go into the living room where it's harder to hear Finn. A big fat tear rolls down my cheek. I need a drink. I need to go to the pub. But they won't let Finn in there. I take deep breaths and whimper pathetically into my fists. I'm not even sure why I'm crying. Only a few hours ago I was the happiest I've ever been, just at the idea of seeing Cass again. But seeing her again hurt more than I'd thought it would, and now Finn hates me, and doesn't want me.

I need a drink. I need to make myself numb.

Mac used to drink whisky. Whisky didn't numb him. It made him meaner. He reigned by fear, did Mac. He'd shut me in my room with no supper. He'd whack Mum round the head for answering back. He loved Cass, though. That was the joke. He hated the rest of the world, but he loved his daughter.

Mac played with your head. He'd make out everything was your fault. He'd make me confess to every crime, beg him for punishment. I hate him worse than anyone else who ever hurt me, because he was the first person who put it into my head that I don't deserve much. He opened the door to anyone who ever wanted to do bad things to me, and there were plenty of them, just waiting.

Finn's stopped crying now, and he's calling for me, so I stagger into his bedroom and pick him up, and carry him back into the living room. He traces the tears on my face and says, 'Poor Aidy,' and that makes me cry some more, which scares him I think, because he goes completely quiet.

I switch on the telly and pick our favourite DVD and we watch David Attenborough in silence. It's the one about the penguin chicks: the parents go away and leave the chicks, and they all huddle together in a big group, but the parent knows the chick and the chick knows its parent by the way they whistle and call. The parent makes the chick wait for its food, makes it cry for it. Eventually the mum or dad penguin coughs it up.

We fall asleep together on the sofa. I only wake up when Holly bangs the front door shut.

'Hello, gorgeous,' I say, lifting my head from Finn's warm curls.

'Is he all right? Mum said you thought he had a cold.'

'He's fine. He knocked his head on the cot, but it was only a bump.'

'Oh, Finn, sweetie, let me have a look.' She lifts him out of my arms. It's cold without him. 'There's a bruise. I'll be glad when he has a proper bed. Maybe we should just buy one.'

'They're expensive.'

'Mum would help out.'

She's avoiding my eye as she cuddles Finn to her. What

have I done wrong now? It wasn't my fault he was running around the market – or was it? Was I meant to have mended the buggy?

'When were you going to tell me?' Her voice is calm and even, and I know she's hiding something. She's angry or upset. I wish she'd show it.

'Tell you what?'

'That you've found her, Aidan. You've found Cass.'

15: AIDAN

I'd been planning to tell Holly about Cass, eventually. When I'd got my head around it, and I'd met Cass and I'd made sure that there wasn't any reason to keep her and Holly separate. You never know. But of course Holly's mum had to turn up at the wrong time, nose into my life, give everything away.

'Why didn't you tell me before?' She's trying not to look hurt but I know Holly better than that. 'How long have you been in touch with her? Is this where you were the other day?'

'What day?'

'You know ... when you didn't come home all night and I thought you were dead.'

Whoa! She never said that at the time. I thought she'd swallowed my story about Rich being in a state, needing me to stay over.

'I didn't ... Rich ...'

'Oh, come on, Aidan. I called Rich at midnight. He said he'd seen you onto the night bus.'

'You never said ...'

'What would have been the point? I didn't want to fight with you. So, were you meeting Cass?'

I'd gone to a club, was the truth, and I'd drunk a lot and I'd woken up in some girl's bedroom and sneaked out without asking any questions. I don't know if anything happened and I'm leaving it that way.

'No – today was the first time we'd met. I've been in touch online.' I can't help boasting a bit. 'I messaged her and she messaged me and we had a whole chat. In writing. A long one.'

'And you won't even send me a text.' Holly looks exhausted. She sits down next to me on the sofa, stroking Finn's head, rocking him, checking his forehead.

'It's not just a bruise,' she says. 'Look, it's swollen.'

I take a look. I'm sure it wasn't like that before.

'He just knocked himself when he went into the cot. He was wriggling around, you know how he does ...'

'How long has he been sleeping? Was he sick? He might have concussion!'

'He's fine! He was yelling and screaming, going off on one.'

'Why? What was the matter?'

She's talking about a little kid. There doesn't need to be anything actually wrong. Finn's always making a huge fuss about nothing. When I think about what was happening when I was his age, well, I don't think he's got much to complain about.

'He was upset about not feeding the ducks.'

'I was upset about that! I'd arranged it all, called Mum, got her to pick him up so I could meet them ...'

'You never told me! I was on my way to pick him up!' This comes out much more sulky than I expected.

'Take a look at your phone sometime.'

I pull it out, switch it on. Four missed calls. Five texts.

'Honestly, Aidan.'

'I didn't know you were going to change everything. Mostly you're cross because I don't pick him up.'

'You need to keep it switched on! I need to be able to get hold of you!'

He's your kid, not mine. I'm doing you a favour.

Of course I don't say this. And, after all, where was my dad when I was Finn's age? You have to take what you've got when it comes to parents. And Finn's got me right now.

I lean my head back against the sofa. 'Holly, meeting Cass was huge for me. I was going to tell you about it afterwards. I wasn't sure how it would go, whether she'd even turn up.'

Holly's forehead is all pinched together, like her mother's. 'But she did. Was she nice?'

'She is nice. She's very nice. She's clever. She might go to Oxford University.'

'That's good,' says Holly. She's looking at the bruise on Finn's forehead again. I remember too late that she's a bit weird about the whole university thing. She went to Cardiff for one term to study psychology before she decided it didn't suit her.

'She's incredibly posh. Posher than your mum, even.' I'm thinking of how Cass stuck out her hand and introduced herself to Juliet.

'Aidan, how did Cass find you? Was it through your social worker?'

'He doesn't know about it. Cass and me, we just found each other. Through Facebook. It was easy.'

'She found you through that profile I set up for you?'

'Yes ... sort of ...'

Finn's waking up. He looks at Holly and back to me. I hold my breath. If Finn decides that I'm to blame for the bump on his head then it could be disastrous.

He doesn't. He flaps his hand at the telly. 'Where penguins, Aidy? Where?'

'We were watching David Attenborough,' I explain to Holly and she's so happy to see that Finn's OK, that there's no concussion, no brain damage, that she kisses him on the head and goes to make us a cup of tea.

I think everything's going to be all right. But then Holly starts again.

'You never even look at Facebook.'

'I know, I know, but ...'

'So how did you even know she'd contacted you?'

'Well, it was me, I looked for her. I worked out her name.'

I told her the whole story. She doesn't say how clever I was, all that reading and writing, finding Cass from a picture. No, she gets jealous. 'So Rich knew – you told Rich before me?'

'Only because he knew about Cass, from when we were in the children's home.'

'But I knew about Cass. You told me about her.'

'I know, but Rich, he understands what it's like ...' I trail off.

'I'm meant to be your partner, Aidan. You should tell me first. I understand too. Rich has met your mum, hasn't he?'

'Yes, but ages ago.'

Mum came to visit me in the children's home, three or four

times. No, three times. After the first time, I made sure Rich came with me. It was easier. Mum talked to him and he talked to Mum and admired the baby and they got on OK, and I sat in the corner of the room not looking at them. Especially not the baby.

'So, what was she like, Cass?'

'Yeah, she was nice.'

'You said that before. Can I meet her?'

'Well, you know … If she wants to meet me again, I can talk to her about it. She's only sixteen, Holly.' Cass seemed younger than sixteen in some ways, and older in others. She spoke like a teacher or something, but she had no idea about quite basic stuff.

'And what about your mum?'

'What about her?'

'Is Cass going to meet her?'

'I dunno.'

'Can I meet your mum?'

Holly's asked this so often that it's boring.

'This is about Cass, not Mum. It's different. I'm not even thinking about Mum right now.'

Thinking about Mum tends to spoil my day, so I'd rather not.

Holly pouts. 'I don't understand why you won't introduce me.'

I swear, Holly's obsessed with my mum.

'She's not part of my life, Holly. It's easier that way.'

'Do you think she wouldn't approve of me?'

'What, like your mum doesn't approve of me?'

'She doesn't mean it. She just thinks you're a bit young.'

'Yeah, well, one disapproving mother is enough.' I mean it as a joke, but she doesn't take it like that.

'There's nothing actually wrong with our age gap. If it was the other way around, if you were older than me, no one would care.'

I'm not actually sure about that because when Denise at the children's home was seeing an older bloke, we did all think it was a bit dodgy. The gap was bigger though, about fifteen years, and Denise was only fourteen.

'It's nothing to do with you. Why would my mum disapprove of you? It's not about you, Holly.'

That came out all wrong. I try again. 'Look, it's complicated. Don't bring my mum into it. It'll be great when you meet Cass.'

'But you hardly know her. Do you really think you've got that much in common?'

She doesn't say it, but the words 'a girl who's going to Oxford University' are floating in the air.

'That's different. Cass and me, we went through a lot together. I suppose it was the best thing for her, being adopted. I mean, obviously it was, as she wouldn't be going to Oxford University if she'd stayed in care or with Mum or whatever.'

'You don't know that. She might be one of those people who's just naturally brilliant, whatever her circumstances.'

So, Holly thinks I'm just naturally thick. 'She might, but the thing is that because she was adopted we never got to see each other. We lost each other. And now ... now ...'

'So you're not actually officially meant to see each other?'

Just for a minute I think it's a threat. That Holly's going to call the social worker, or the police or Cass's parents; that she's going to stop us meeting again. Without even knowing it, my hands ball into fists.

'I don't know.'

'It's so unfair! They really treated you badly. They didn't find anyone to adopt you, and they banned you from seeing your sister!'

I let myself breathe again. My hands relax.

'They did find someone – Jim and Betty! They said they wanted to ... but Mum contested it ...'

'I know, that was awful, but you were eleven then. Why didn't they find someone before? Like they did for Cass?'

She asks these questions without thinking how much it might hurt to tell the truth. That no one wanted to take me on. That I was unadoptable. I'm not even certain that I've got it right about Jim and Betty, or whether it's a story that I made up to make myself feel better... If they'd wanted me that much, wouldn't they have taken me back when Mum and Keith chucked me out? I asked the social worker I had then and she said it wasn't possible, but I never understood why. Maybe Betty and Jim were glad to be rid of me, too. They just put on a good show of hiding it.

Anyway, after I did what I did, maybe they didn't want me any more.

I shrug. 'There aren't enough people out there. I mean, who wants to take on some screwed up kid?'

Finn's DVD is coming to an end.

'I'll make supper,' says Holly. 'Can you put Finn in the bath?' Her hand strokes Finn's bump again. 'Take care, monster. Don't wriggle too much. You don't want to hurt yourself again.'

'It wasn't my fault,' I say, quickly.

Holly looks at me, startled. 'I never said it was.' A beat of silence. Then she asks, 'Spaghetti, OK?' and I say, 'Time for Finn's bath,' and life goes on. Normal, ordinary family life.

How long can it last?

16: CASS

Will stood behind me, hands over my eyes. I could feel his breath on the back of my neck, his fingers soft on my skin.

I was completely distracted from what he was saying.

'Just turn a little bit to the left ... and then wait ... go away, tourists ... OK ... now!' He took his hands away. I was looking over one of the quads at Trinity College, all honey-gold buildings and velvety grass.

'Imagine you're wearing a silk dress. A corset thingy underneath. OK, and so it's 1850. Just try and put yourself there.'

Just for a moment I do it. I hear the rustle of the dress. I imagine another Cass, a Victorian girl, hair in a bun, petticoats swishing.

'I wouldn't even be here. I don't think they took women students until later on.'

He laughed. 'You got it, though, didn't you? You time travelled. I could tell.'

'How could you tell?'

'There was something about the way you were standing. You changed your posture.' He imitated me, dropping his shoulders, lifting his head. 'You looked like a swan.'

'More like an ugly duckling!'

'Are you fishing for compliments? You're looking very good today.'

I blushed – I hated how he teased me. 'Of course I'm not. Fishing for compliments, I mean.'

'You always wear such boring clothes,' he said, mournfully. 'It's such a waste. With all that hair. Why did you tie it back again?'

'It's neater.'

'Neater!' said Will, in such a disgusted voice that I had to laugh. He reached out for my hand. 'Come!'

We walked across the quad, pushed at a door.

'We can go in!' Will was as thrilled as a little boy. I was just grateful he'd picked this particular college: one I didn't know all that well, one where there was no danger of . . .

'Cass!'

Oh, no. No, no, no. Just what I'd worried about.

'Darling! Why didn't you tell me you were coming?'

She was walking down the corridor of the wrong college.

'Auntie Kate! I didn't think . . . this isn't your college—'

'I've just been meeting a colleague. We are allowed to cross each other's thresholds, you do realise?'

'Oh, yes, well, obviously.'

'How lovely to see you, darling.' My aunt planted a cool, crisp kiss on my cheek. 'Aren't you going to introduce me?'

'Oh, yes, sorry, this is my . . . my friend, Will. Will Hughes. Will, this is my aunt. Kate Fielding. She's . . . she works here . . .'

CASS

'What a shame I didn't know you were coming,' said Aunt Kate, looking at Will and raising her eyebrows slightly, just so that only someone who knew her really well would notice.

'We only decided yesterday,' Will said, shaking her hand. 'We thought we'd come and look around. Get a feel for the place, you know, before we apply next year.'

Aunt Kate looked faintly amused. 'Well, I'd have thought Cass had a good feel for the place already,' she said.

'I'm just showing Will around,' I said, squirming inside.

This was naturally the cue for her to start quizzing Will about what he planned to study – 'History! Excellent!' – and start advising him about college applications and interview technique.

Will was all enthusiasm. 'Wow, that's great, thank you so much.'

'I'd take you both to lunch, but I have a faculty meeting. How long are you staying?'

'Not long,' I said. 'Next time, I promise I'll give you more warning.'

'Do, Cass darling. We're all so concerned about you. How is Ben coping? Your mother seems to be bearing up.'

'Ben's fine,' I told her.

'I'm his peer buddy at school,' Will offered. 'I've been introducing him to some kids, helping him make friends, that kind of thing.'

'Excellent,' said Aunt Kate. 'I'd love to hear more about it, but I'm afraid I have to get going. Do give my love to everyone. Tell Susie I'll give her a call. Good luck with the applications, Will.'

'Bye,' I said, and off she went.

Will stared after her. 'Did she just give me the brush off? Or am I being super sensitive?'

'No, she's always like that.' I was so used to Kate's briskness that I hardly noticed it. 'All my mum's family are like that. Not my mum so much, but Granny and Kate and Mum's other sister.'

'Blimey,' said Will. 'And she's what – a professor?'

'She's not a professor. She's a Fellow in History at Corpus Christi. That's not quite as senior as a professor.'

'Yes, I do actually know that. What's her specialism?'

'France in the eighteenth century. The enlightenment. Maybe you've heard of it?'

I thought he'd call me out on my sarcasm, but he ignored it.

'Wow,' he said. 'Just wow. Well, no wonder you're applying here.'

'What's that meant to mean?'

'Well, you know. You virtually live here already ...'

'I'm not applying to Corpus Christi. I'm not looking for special favours.'

'No, but it's got to help ...'

'Well, I thought I'd get in on my own merit,' I said, stung. 'I don't want to get in because of my family. But I'm happy to ask for inside information on your behalf if you want me to.'

'Yes, do,' he said. 'We ordinary people need as much help as we can get. Actually, Corpus Christi was on my list.'

I turned and walked towards the door, went out into the quad, headed for the gate. Will followed me.

'Oh, Cass, don't go off in a strop. I'm very impressed, that's all. And kind of daunted. The nearest I've got to a Fellow at Corpus Christi is my cousin, Derek, who's the head teacher of a school in Croydon.'

'Yeah, well, it's not so amazing having family here. It means that everyone expects ... they just take it for granted ...'

There were tears in my eyes. I turned away so he couldn't see.

'Well, it'll be nice for you to have family around. I don't know anyone in Oxford, supposing I get in. I'll be all alone in a strange city. I just hope you'll be here too, to keep me company. Show me the ropes.'

'It'll be just as strange for me as it is for you.'

'Oh, come on, Cass! Don't be so touchy! You'll fit right in at Oxford. It's in your genes.'

That did it. 'Look, if I get to Oxford I'll probably be the first one in my family to go to university. My biological family, anyway. I'm adopted. My birth mum's a hairdresser. I'm just as ordinary as you are.'

Will stared at me. For about five minutes. It was so unlike him to be quiet for so long that I began to feel self-conscious and worry that I'd accidentally said something really insulting.

'What? What's the matter?'

He grabbed my hand. 'Come on.'

'What! Get off!'

He took no notice, but increased his speed. I ran with him, through the gate, back out onto the street, along the pavement, into a café. 'Sit!' he ordered.

'You're incredibly bossy!'

'I thought girls liked it when men are masterful.'

'You're not a man and no, we don't.'

'Well, tough. And who qualified you to judge who's a man or not?'

I was nearly certain I was blushing again. 'You're at school. Wait until you've left to call yourself a man.'

He deepened his voice. 'I can see I'm going to have to prove my manhood to you, Miss Montgomery.'

'No thanks!'

'Oh, well, at least I've got you out of your strop. Although you are magnificent when you're angry.'

'Where do you get your lines from? Old movies? Mills and Boon?'

'Old movies!' A waitress appeared by our table. 'I'll have a tuna melt and a cappuccino, thanks.'

I hadn't even looked at the menu. 'Oh, I'll have the same.'

Will smiled. 'Good. I thought you might walk out on me there.'

'I'm hungry.'

'So practical. I can just imagine you at Guide camp, counting out the sausages, working out how many baked beans everyone should have ...'

'I could always get a sandwich on the train ...'

'No, don't. I want to talk to you. I didn't mean to upset you.'

'I'm fine. I'm not upset.'

'Good, because I think I've worked it out.'

'Worked what out?'

'That's who it was. That guy in Camden. He must be your brother – am I right? Your real brother.'

17: CASS

'Not "real",' I said, flustered. 'Ben's just as real—'

'Your birth brother. Am I right? I'm right!'

'Half-brother, actually.' There was no point in lying. 'You're right.'

'Oh!' He was bouncing with excitement. 'I love it when I work things out! Sherlock Holmes, you are so *rinsed*!'

'"So rinsed"?'

'I'm reviving it. Vintage slang.'

I wanted to hate him but I couldn't. And it was good to tell someone about Aidan. I'd been bursting to talk about him.

'Tell!' he ordered.

'Why should I tell?'

'Because I was so clever and guessed. I deserve a reward. Or shall I pick something different?'

'No,' I said, hurriedly, 'I'll tell you about it ... I've been keeping it to myself because I don't want my parents to know. I would talk to Grace or Megan or someone, but they all gossip so much and all their mothers know mine ...'

'No danger of that with me,' he said. 'Do tell me, though. I've been dying of curiosity.'

'I hadn't seen him since I was four. That's when I was adopted. He's two years older than me. We weren't in touch at all. Then he contacted me, out of the blue, a few weeks ago.'

'You haven't seen him for twelve years? But you knew him right away, didn't you? The way you two looked at each other ...'

'I can't explain it. I knew him.'

'Well,' he said. 'Well. This is something else. What's he like? Does he have a name?'

'Aidan. Aidan Jones. He's nice. He's really keen to include me in his life. He works in a shop, selling second-hand stuff. He's got a girlfriend, he lives with her, and he's got a little boy. You saw him, right at the end.'

'He started early.'

'Yeah, well, I suppose some people do.'

'Did Aidan get adopted as well?'

'No, he was in foster care most of the time, I think. Maybe a children's home as well.'

'How old is he?'

'He's nineteen in a few months.'

'You're going to meet him again?'

'I hope so. We talked about meeting his girlfriend.'

'Maybe I could come with you? To lurk? You don't have to pay me this time.'

'Oh, God, I'm so sorry! I never paid you.' I pull out my purse. 'I've actually only got twenty pounds on me.'

'Whenever you want to pay,' he said. 'I'm not bothered.'

'I'll get lunch.'

'No, my treat. After all, you're showing me around.'

I felt bad that I hadn't told him how well I knew Oxford. I'd meant to. But when we were on the train and he started telling me about the research he'd done, showing me places on his map that I'd known for ever, well, I just didn't have the heart.

And now I was here and it was strange being in Oxford without my family. In fact, it was making me wonder why I'd always been so sure that Oxford was my goal. Was it because I couldn't imagine doing anything that wasn't connected with my family? What would it feel like to plan a future based on exactly what I wanted?

I had no idea at all where I would even start.

'I love Oxford,' I told him. 'We could go punting this afternoon, if you want. It's a bit late in the year, but it'll be quiet, and the sun's shining.'

'Would it be good for time travelling?'

'Very good. It could be any time.'

'Cass, I didn't mean to upset you before. I was just teasing. I'm sorry.'

'It's OK.'

'I had no idea you were adopted. How about Ben?'

'No, my mum got pregnant after I was adopted. Apparently it happens quite often. People try for ages for a baby, nothing happens and then they fall pregnant as soon as they adopt.'

'Do you have any memories of before you were adopted?'

'Not really. I have some photos and things. That's how I knew about Aidan.'

'Four years, though. That's a long time without memories.'

'How many memories have you got from before you were four?'

'Loads! When I was two and a half my oldest sister took me shopping and lost me. I remember asking a lady if she knew where Layla had gone. When I was three I fell off a climbing frame and broke my wrist. When I was three and a half, I got a toy car with mobile controls for Christmas. When I started nursery school, a boy asked if my skin colour would wash off.'

'No!'

'Yes! Quite confusing for both of us.'

'That's awful.'

'Not really. He was just a kid. That's what happens when you live in a town where you look different from 80 per cent of people.'

'Try being ginger,' I told him. 'When I was six, I emptied a pot of black paint on my hair. I thought I could dye it.'

'Now, that is tragic. You must stop hiding it away. You've got to embrace the ginger.'

'It's not really ginger any more,' I said, defensively.

'Ginger rocks. Ginger is cool. Ginger is the new black.'

'It's got a lot darker.'

'Dark ginger,' he said. 'Burnt ginger. Raw ginger. Stem ginger. Crystallised ginger.'

I was so sure that he was going to say something about chocolate-covered ginger that I completely lost the ability to think of anything witty. I was sure I must be blushing. Luckily our food arrived, and I was able to look at my sandwich and avoid his gaze.

'Oh, shut up.'

'"Oh, shut up" is not worthy of you. Especially as a leading light of the interschool debating competition team. Not that I'm bitter or anything.'

'I only summed up. The others did the hard bits.'

'We went out in the second round.'

'That wasn't your fault, though.'

'A compliment? From the County interschool debating champion team captain?' He pretended to faint. I chewed my sandwich and ignored him.

'So, where next? Any more secret relatives you forgot to mention? Head librarian at the Bodleian? Professor of Mathematics at Christ Church?'

'Actually, my grandfather was a professor,' I told him, in the interests of full disclosure. 'Of English literature. My mum studied Old and Medieval English. She gave it all up to be an MP's wife, and mother. Now, of course, she's been made redundant.'

'She's still your mother.'

'Yeah, true. She's going to have to work out what else to do with her time, though. At the moment, she's looking at smaller houses and seeing her solicitor.'

'That can't take up all her time.'

'Having her hair done and going to Pilates.'

'Do you think she'll get a job?'

'Maybe. I don't know. She's got to work out a financial settlement with Dad, sell the house and all that.'

'It's rough for you and Ben.'

'It's OK. I'm fine. Ben's getting there.'

'You are so tough,' he said. 'The iron lady.'

I made a face at him.

He bounced up from his seat. 'We're wasting our time. I've

always wanted to go punting. I looked it up. This is the last week you can do it. Come on! It'll be fun.'

The route to the river took us through the covered market, and he stopped by one of the stalls. 'Just what I was looking for.' He picked through a heap of scarves.

'Oh, come on,' I said. 'You're already wearing orange and purple. You can't possibly add a pink scarf.'

'Come here,' he said. He held up the scarf. It was a deep, dark pink, the colour of beetroot soup. 'Perfect.'

Before I could stop him, he unwound my grey, woolly scarf and tossed it into a rubbish bin.

'What are you doing?'

He wound the pink scarf around my neck. 'So much better. Never wear that dishcloth colour again.'

'That was my favourite scarf! This is going to clash with my hair.'

Will paid the stallholder five pounds.

'The clash is the point. Take a look.'

There was a full-length mirror propped up against the stall. I looked. Will, tall and dark and laughing; me, pale and stressed and only brightened up a little bit by the scarf.

'Take the ponytail thing off,' he said, bossing me around again.

I let my hair loose. Watched as the girl in the mirror instantly looked more relaxed, and even a bit older.

I was nearly certain that this proved Will thought we were on a date. Do you buy a present for a random girl? Do you have days out with random girls? I didn't think so. I wished I could be sure. I was not completely hating the idea, to tell the truth, but I needed clarity.

'Better, eh?' he said. 'Right. Show me what punting's all about.'

Punting is not all that easy, and I was secretly hoping that Will would find it impossible, so I'd have to take over. It's a matter of shifting your weight to lever the pole most efficiently. Dad taught me a few years ago. But Will seemed to get the hang of it really quickly, and insisted that he did all the work. 'You relax,' he said. 'I want to practise.'

Sitting in the punt, moving through the water, it was easy to travel in time. I was a medieval princess. I was a Victorian lady. I was someone who didn't have to take exams, worry about university, try and be perfect all the time.

'I wish we could actually time travel,' I said. 'We could time travel instead of doing our A levels. Just skip the next few years.'

'A levels are a lot of work, aren't they? That's why you have to make time to do other things. Oof! This is hard!'

'Let me take over,' I said, but he mopped his brow theatrically and said, 'I can cope.'

'I still haven't finished my essay. I really shouldn't have come out today.'

'You're not back at school until Monday.'

'I know, but I've got to go away at the weekend.' I should have finished the essay easily, to be honest: I'd had two full days. But between thinking back to my meeting with Aidan and worrying about this day with Will, let alone the weekend with Dad and Annabel . . . I couldn't concentrate.

'Why do you want to apply to Oxford?' I asked him. 'Why not somewhere else?'

'Because it's there,' he said. 'Or, rather, because it's here. Because I can. And because I failed the exam to get into the sodding grammar school and my parents have paid a small fortune to send me to Bonny's, and I'd like to show the grammar school that they were wrong about me and my parents that they were right. Also, I like history and there's a lot of it here.'

'That's a much better reason than mine.' Will seemed so sure of himself. Next to him I was a marionette. Wooden and controlled and hollow.

'What did I say? You look sad.'

That was the thing about Will. Most of the time he was bouncy and annoying and I couldn't tell if he was serious or winding me up. And then he'd stun me by being so kind and nice that all I wanted was to carry on talking to him forever.

'I'm not sad.'

He sighed. 'No, you're fine. I know you are. You're always fine.' The punt lurched as he shoved the pole deep into the river.

We made our way to the station as the sun set, moving closer together as the light faded, his arm bumped against mine.

'Hey,' he said. 'What's that down there?'

'What?'

He led the way down a little alleyway.

'What are you doing? The station is that way.'

'We've got fifteen minutes,' he said, 'and I want to ask you something first.'

'Why can't you ask me on the train?'

'I don't think you'd say yes. You don't like people looking at you.'

'Why would they be looking at me?'

'Because I'd like to kiss you. But I wanted to warn you first, or you'll do that thing you do whenever I touch you.'

My mouth went dry. 'What? What thing?'

'The blushing and screaming thing.'

'I don't scream!'

'Squeaking, then. The blushing and squeaking thing.'

'Oh! You are so annoying!'

'I know, but can I kiss you anyway?'

'I don't know, I'm not sure, I don't think ... why do you want to? What does it mean? Does it mean we're going out?'

'What do you want it to mean?' He was getting closer.

'I don't know what I want it to mean. I won't know unless you do it. Look, OK, kiss me, but just on an experimental basis. It doesn't commit us to anything.'

'Purely experimental. Do you want me to write down any scientific data? Time of day, location, length of experiment, anything like that?'

'No, you don't need to do that.'

'You realise that just one experimental kiss won't be enough? We'll have to do some under different conditions to compare?'

'Only if I think I want to,' I said, totally aware that I'd shown myself up as a completely inexperienced idiot. 'Go on then.'

'"Go on then"? How romantic.'

He slid his arm around my shoulders, leant down and brushed his lips against mine.

'That wasn't much of a—' I said.

And then he kissed me. For about two minutes. His hand stroking the side of my face. His lips moving against mine.

Our first experimental kiss.

I decided right away that it wouldn't be the last.

18: AIDAN

Holly's tired, so I'm giving her a lie in and taking Finn to work with me.

Finn loves the shop. There are toys and cardboard boxes and corners for hide and seek. It's like an adventure playground for him. We've got cheese rolls for a snack and orange juice in cartons.

Clive doesn't really like me babysitting Finn in the shop, but he doesn't often come in Saturday, and there's nothing much to do except unpack some bedding and tidy up the storeroom. Finn and I play Hide in the Box, which he loves, and then we build piles of boxes and topple them down. I find a load of old bubble wrap and we stamp on it to make the bubbles pop. And then we – less successfully – sweep the floor until he starts grizzling and rubbing his eyes and I put him in the buggy and wheel him around the shop a bit and he's crying but it's because he's tired, and soon he falls asleep.

AIDAN

When he was a baby – when Holly was just my landlady – I used to babysit for her a lot. I didn't like it much, to be honest, because I couldn't bear him crying – it made me a nervous wreck because I didn't know what was wrong with him. But then Holly taught me the difference between hungry cries and tired cries and angry cries and it was much easier to cope with. I could be with him without panicking most of the time.

With Finn asleep, there's actually nothing for me to do, so I put my feet up on the desk and prepare for a little snooze myself. But then the door opens.

A customer. Except that I recognise him.

'Well, if it isn't Aidan Jones.'

I tense right away. Glance over to Finn. Can I nudge the buggy out of sight in time?

'Hey, Neil,' I say. 'Long time, no see.'

'You being funny?' Neil's acquired some new tattoos since I last saw him: a spider on his hand and some letters on his knuckles. It's probably good that I can't read them.

'No, just saying.' It's a bit much if Neil's going to start being all sensitive about spending time inside. He shouldn't have got involved if he wasn't prepared to serve his sentence. But then logic was never Neil's thing.

'How's the girlfriend?'

I'm confused. I'm absolutely certain that Neil's never met Holly. We've been together for just over a year, and Neil went down for eighteen months, if I remember right. Armed robbery.

'What girlfriend?'

'That little runt. What was his name?'

'Rich,' I mutter. 'C'mon, Neil.'

Neil laughs. 'Just joking, Aidan. I heard you had a lady, though. Nice one.' He jerks his head towards Finn. 'He's your boy?'

'No.'

'Ah. Like that, is it? Well, well. And she knows the whole story, does she? Knows all about you? Well, what it is to be loved.'

There are lots of things I could have said, like, How would you know? Like, What do you mean? But I don't. I might not be able to read and write very well, but I do know a bit about how you talk to someone like Neil.

He's looking round the shop, picking things up, examining them. A stand for earrings. A plaster angel. A big cut-glass vase.

'Funny sort of shop, this. What's the idea?'

'It's salvage stock. Stuff that was in floods and fires. It's all good stuff but the insurance has written it off.'

'I see,' he says. 'Bits and bobs that no one wants. Damaged goods, eh, Aidan? Damaged goods. I bet you feel right at home.'

I haven't seen Neil for years. I'd forgotten how much I hated him. I'd forgotten how he used to run that home, the things he did, the way he got other kids to fight his battles.

There's stuff I'd never forget, though. How he punishes people. How he enjoys hurting people. What he did to Rich. What he did to me.

Every time he moves near to Finn I want to shout at him, tell him to get out. I don't. I know better. I'm still scared. But if he – or anyone – ever does to Finn what was done to me, then they're dead.

'Nice kid,' he says. 'Nice face. Pity if anything happened to it.' He's still holding the big vase, and he pretends to drop it, catching it as it slips out of his hand.

'Nothing's going to happen to his face.' I try and keep my voice steady. I can't show him that I'm so scared that I could easily hurl.

'It's hell looking after kids, isn't it? Got to watch them every minute. It's so easy for them to have an accident. Run out into the road, stick their fingers in the power socket, get their hands on a knife.'

We stock knife blocks, but we keep them locked away in a glass cabinet. I'm trying very hard not to look at them.

'Your girl must trust you a lot if she's leaving you watching the baby. It'd be terrible if something happened to him. Left him with a scar or something worse.'

Bang! Neil drops the vase onto the wooden floor and Finn wakes with a shock. He starts screaming and I try to get to him, but Neil's in the way.

'Hang on a minute, Aidan. I want to ask you something.'

Finn screams for me. I'm rooted to the spot.

'What?' I bark at Neil. 'What is it?'

'I want you to do me a favour.'

'What favour?'

'Well,' he says. 'I've got something that needs keeping safe. And somewhere like this ... it's just what I've been looking for.'

'No,' I say, and then I see that he's picked up a piece of glass from the floor.

He's looking from Finn to me, and back again.

'I mean, yes. Anything you want, Neil. Just tell me what I can do.'

19: CASS

When I first saw Annabel, sitting on the edge of the sofa – our sofa – in Dad's flat – our flat – she looked so glossy and perfect that I knew she'd be easy to hate.

She had a degree in Politics, Philosophy and Economics from Oxford University and a post-graduate something or other in International Relations from Cambridge. Dad gave us the history in the car after he'd picked us up from the station, but the *Daily Mail* had told us everything weeks ago.

Her skin was flawless ivory, her hair shiny chestnut, she wore over-sized glasses with black frames – all the better to show off her big, brown eyes – and a stylish blue dress that clung to her chest and flowed over her body, so that you could tell she was pregnant, but not in a flaunting-her-belly kind of way. She was twenty-three. Only six years older than me.

Her glossiness reminded me that my hair was frizzy (the

weather suited the occasion – all wind and drizzle), my unmade-up face was pale and freckly, and my jeans and sweatshirt made me look like a thirteen-year-old tomboy.

I'd been thinking of slightly changing my style, but I hadn't had a chance to go shopping. I was wearing my dark pink scarf though. It smelled ever so slightly of Will.

'Come in, come in,' said Dad, right behind us. 'Come and sit down. This is Annabel, obviously. Annabel, this is Cass and this is Ben.'

Annabel made a brave effort to make eye contact. I stared at the wall behind her head. I might have to be there physically, but I could remove myself mentally. I tried to focus on key dates in twentieth-century European history, but found my mind wandering to Will, and how we'd kissed in Oxford, and then sat on the train and kissed some more, and then it'd been quite awkward on the tube and the train home because I was nervous someone might see us, even though I didn't recognise anyone, and he'd kept on leaning right over to me and teasing me when I pulled away.

'What are you laughing at, Cass?' asked Dad now, and I quickly rearranged my face and said, 'Nothing.'

Will and I had met up the day after Oxford – I felt it was important to set down some rules about experimental kissing, just in case it got out of hand. We went to the park, which was nice and quiet, thanks to the weather.

'Look, I just want to make it clear that I'm not in the market for a relationship,' I told him.

'Oh, you made that clear enough. We're experimenting, yes? I don't suppose I could come under your umbrella? I'm getting soaked.'

141

'OK,' I said, a bit annoyed because once he was holding the umbrella there was no choice but to walk really close together, which made us look like a couple when, of course, we weren't. Also, he was better at stopping the wind turning it inside-out than I was, moving it skilfully to avoid the gusts of wind that were battering us.

'Have you got any ground rules? Or shall we see where our experiments take us?'

'No coupley stuff, no talking about boyfriends and girl-friends, no being seen together in public, no Facebook statuses or cuddling in Starbucks, or on the bus ... you know ...'

Will laughed at me. 'That wasn't really what I meant—'

What else could he mean?

'I mean ... oh, look, the bomb shelter ...'

There's a brick bomb shelter from World War II at the edge of the park that smells of wee and is littered with broken bottles. Really the council ought to clean it up – in other cir-cumstances, I'd have taken a picture on my phone for Mum to mention to the local councillors. Anyway, once we were in the bomb shelter, we experimented with kissing again. Longer kissing this time, with additional neck stroking and a small amount of hip grinding.

After about half an hour, the rain stopped and Will said, 'Actually, I was thinking more of guidelines about this ... you know ...'

'I don't have any guidelines about this. That's why we're experimenting.'

'Oh.' Will blinked a few times. 'You are quite unlike anyone I've ever kissed before.'

I was going to reply to this but then I spotted the deputy

head walking her standard poodle, retrieved my umbrella and insisted that we took separate routes home.

The loathsome Annabel was talking to me. Reluctantly I stopped thinking about Will's kisses and focused on her impossibly perfect face.

'This is horrible, isn't it? I'm sure you completely despise me. What can I say? I understand totally if you don't want anything to do with me.'

Oh God, she was pretending to be nice. Just when I was successfully managing to forget all about her.

'I don't think Ben or Cass feel like that,' said Dad, in his fakest politician's voice.

'I can't answer for Ben,' I said, making absolutely sure that I was not smiling or moving or doing anything at all to make the situation less awkward than it was, 'but you've got it just about right as far as I'm concerned.'

Ben had a *Star Wars* action figure in his hand – Yoda – and he stared intently at the little guy's pointed ears and baldy head.

Way to go, Ben, I thought. Let's look as crazy as possible. And then I felt horrible and disloyal and mean. No wonder Dad had abandoned us. Ben was strange and I wasn't a nice person.

'I'm so sorry,' said Annabel.

'Don't be silly, Annabel,' said Dad. 'You've got nothing to apologise for.'

'Yes, she has,' I said. 'She's broken up your marriage. She's hurt all of us. At least she's got the guts to admit it.'

Annabel tried to give me a sympathetic smile. I kept my face stony.

'Oliver, darling,' she said. 'Why don't you go and pick up some stuff from the deli? We'll be fine.'

Dad huffed a bit, but agreed. We watched him go in silence.

'That's better,' said Annabel. 'No good having him here. He feels so guilty that he'll just get upset.'

'He should get upset.'

'He is. He truly is. Give him a chance to make it up to you. He loves you both so much.'

'He should have thought of that before.'

'I know. But what's done is done. And we will be friends eventually. At least we've got the scary first meeting over with. It only gets better from now on. I promise you.'

'Don't bother promising anything,' I snarled, 'because this is not going to happen often. Eh, Ben?'

'What do you mean it gets better?' asked Ben, talking to Yoda.

Annabel wasn't in the slightest bit fazed. 'Well, I've been in your position myself, you see. Daddy's been married twice – but with plenty of girlfriends in the meantime, and Mummy's on her third. I know all about meeting the new partner. Ghastly business.'

'If you know what it's like, then why did you do it to us?'

'I fell in love,' she said.

How convenient it was to have a catch-all excuse. I promised myself I would never lose control over my emotions in a selfish way that hurt other people.

'I know how much you must resent me. But it all works out in the end, truly. I've got loads of lovely half- and step-siblings now. And step-parents, and, actually ex-step-parents – in fact, one of Daddy's ex-girlfriends is my best mate, and I honestly wouldn't want it any other way. I feel as though my family's got bigger and bigger.'

That's all right for you, I thought, furiously. You are never going to be my best mate. And I don't need you to provide a bigger family. I have Mum and Ben, and now I have Aidan and pretty soon I'm going to meet Holly and Finn and maybe my mum and Scarlett and Louis and perhaps she'll tell me more about my real dad. My family is growing and growing.

'Are you really all friends?' asked Ben.

'All of us,' she said, firmly. 'I'd like to be your friend, too.'

'Can I be friends with all your sisters and brothers?' Ben asked, and I wanted to hit him. Just because you haven't got any friends, Ben, you don't have to like her! You can do better than that!

If Ben was going to like her, then I'd have to hate her all the more.

Dad came back with a bag full of deli treats – stuff he knew we liked: crackers and tapenade and olives. He and I sat in silence. I was remembering family holidays, eating olives in Spain, rosemary flatbread in Tuscany. I don't know what he was thinking about.

Annabel talked to Ben. I have to admit she was good at it. She knew a lot about *Star Wars*, and she liked *Dr Who*. She'd probably been reading up, watching DVDs, studying for meeting her lover's children as though she was taking an exam. Pathetic.

My exam preparation wasn't going so well. The history essay had been my perfect excuse for getting out of coming to London for the weekend. I'd told Dad about it on the phone that morning: 'I don't think I can spare the time,' I'd said. 'They've really put the pressure on and I'm a bit behind.'

'That's not like you, Cass,' boomed Dad. 'Well, you'd better bring it along. I mean, I'm sure Ben would prefer it if you were there.'

I might have known he could manipulate me into doing what he wanted. He is a politician, after all.

'Did you get that essay finished?' he asked me now. I told him I hadn't and he started telling me what to write.

'I can do it,' I snapped.

Annabel and Ben went into the kitchen so she could show him how the new coffee machine worked. I wondered how much Dad had spent on it.

'Can you try and be nice?' Dad was frowning at me.

'I've got a headache. I'm a bit stressed.'

'Mum says you've been out all the time this holiday. Are you sure you're spending enough time studying? This is a crucial year if you want to get into Oxford.'

'It's my business, how I spend my time. And why were you speaking to Mum, anyway?'

'We're still your parents. We're determined to carry on doing our best in that role. Together.'

'Oh, well, good luck with that.'

'Don't be cheeky. Cass, this isn't like you.'

'A lot has changed,' I said. 'Haven't you noticed?'

'Cass, you're going to have to accept this, whether you like it or not.'

'I don't like it,' I said. 'Look, I'm not up to this right now. I'm going out. I'll see you later.'

'Cass – no, Cass, wait—'

I stuck my head round the kitchen door. I didn't want to, but I couldn't just abandon Ben.

'I'm going out,' I told him. 'See you later.'

'Look, Cass, I can froth milk!' he told me.

'Excellent,' I told him, trying not to show him my disappointment that he could be bought off so easily.

'See you later, Cass,' said Annabel, and I nodded in her direction. I'd have preferred to ignore her, but I had no intention of acting like a stroppy teen. Dignity and disdain, that was the aim.

I walked down the stairs and out of the apartment block. Down the street, across the road, into the tube station. I dug around in my bag, found my Oyster card. I was down the escalator before I knew where I was going.

Camden Town.

My other family.

Aidan.

20: AIDAN

The doorbell jangles again as Neil's inspecting the store room, deciding where he wants to stash whatever it is he wants to hide. It can't be good. I'm betting weapons, but it could be drugs, or even money. Or stolen goods. As the whole yard looks like a fence's paradise anyway, we do have occasional visits from the police who want to see all the paperwork. Could I use that to put Neil off?

I look up to see who's come in. A group of customers would be good. Something that might scare Neil away. A policeman would be best.

'Aidan!'

It's her! It's Cass! What the hell?

Neil mustn't realise. If he knows I've got a sister then she could be in danger.

Finn's nearly back to sleep again, grumbling in his buggy. So I jerk my head towards him and put my finger over my mouth. 'Shhh.'

She whispers. 'Oh, sorry! I just thought . . . I was in London and I thought ... I asked one of the stallholders and he told me how to find the shop. He knew all about it.'

'Well, hello!' Neil appears from behind a pile of boxes. 'I don't think we've met. Friend of yours, Aidan?'

I mutter something, and Neil grins at Cass and says, 'The boy's got no manners. Must've been dragged up. I'm Neil. Me and Aidan go way back. I don't think we've met.'

Cass has been too bloody well brought up for her own good. She sticks out her hand. 'I'm Cass,' she says.

'Cass, great to meet you. You do look familiar. Are you from round here?'

'No, I don't live in London.'

Shut up, don't talk to him, don't give anything away ...

'Come far, have you?'

'No, not far.'

'So how do you two know each other?' says Neil. 'I'm sure I remember you from somewhere ... hmm ... not the children's home.'

'Were you two together in a children's home?' Cass's eyes are wide. She's probably thinking that a children's home is a bit like an orphanage in the olden days: all of us sitting with our bowls of gruel, wondering who'll dare to ask for more. Or maybe she thinks it was like some boarding school, with midnight feasts and practical jokes.

Well, it wasn't like either of those things.

'Oh, yes, we knew each other very well, didn't we, Aidan? Shared a lot. All them memories, eh?'

I have a very clear memory of Neil breaking my finger because I wouldn't deal drugs for him at my school . Quite soon after that, I stopped going to school altogether. Safer.

'Yeah, yeah, loads of memories. All them parties, eh?' I smile weakly. 'You want to buy anything, Neil, or were you just going?'

'I've seen exactly what I'm looking for,' says Neil, looking Cass up and down.

Her face turns pink.

'Bye, then, Aidan and Cass. And the lad, of course. I'll be back soon, Aidan. Later today, maybe.'

'My boss'll be back soon,' I say.

'No worries. We'll keep an eye out. Cass, good to meet you.'

Jesus. Jesus! Now he's going to be trying to find out who Cass is. What if he uses her to get at me? At least she didn't tell him her surname.

At the door, Neil turns and comes back. 'I think I've got it!' he says to Cass. 'How I know you! What did you say your surname was?'

'You never met her, Neil. She doesn't live round here,' I say.

'No, I'm sure of it. Some big party. I'm right, aren't I?'

'No,' says Cass. Good for her. She sees through him.

'You're an actress? On telly? I know I've seen you.'

Cass hates this. Her cheeks are pink and she's looking away. I hate Neil more than I ever did before.

'Leave her alone. You don't know her,' I say.

'It's killing me!' says Neil. 'Hey, didn't your mum have red hair, Aidan? I remember her visits. Blimey, the fuss you made about having to see her. Understandable, I suppose. In the circumstances.'

'Bye, Neil,' I say, as firmly as I dare.

'See you around, Aidan.'

The door slams behind him. Finn wakes up again and

screams. I lift him up, cuddle him close. 'It's OK, Finn, everything's OK.'

'You're really good with him.' I think Cass means Neil and I'm confused, but she doesn't. She's talking about Finn.

'Oh, well, you know. I've been like a dad to him. Holly and me, we've been together for more than a year now. Holly doesn't have any contact with Finn's real dad.'

'I thought he was yours.' Cass seems to have forgotten Neil the minute he walked through the door. I wish I could. 'He looks like you,' she adds, although it's not really true. It's our skin colour that's the same, and our dark hair. Finn's hair is a lot frizzier than mine, and his face is round and cute like Holly's. But, judged by colour, Finn and I are more alike than Holly and Finn, or me and Cass. Blood isn't everything.

'Why are you here?' I ask. 'I mean, it's great to see you, but kind of unexpected.'

'I was at my dad's, to meet his new girlfriend, and I just felt suffocated. I needed to escape. So I came to see if I could find you.'

I look at my phone. 'It's almost time for lunch. Let's shut up early, eh? I need to deliver Finn to Holly, anyway.'

'Oh, can I meet her? I'd love that.'

I'm suddenly shy. What if it all goes horribly wrong?

'She'd like that, too.' It's true. I'll have to hope for the best.

I lock up the shop, put up the 'Closed' sign, bump Finn's buggy down the front step. Clive doesn't like it when I close up during the day ('Just bring some sodding sandwiches,' he said last time, when I explained that I needed to go for lunch at 1 p.m.,' and besides, no one gets a three-hour lunch break.

I should sack you, really I should') but he'll have to lump it. I'll tell him Holly was ill, that I had to check up on her.

Cass follows us up the stairs, making faces at Finn so he laughs all the way. I'm kind of excited about showing her the flat. I bet she'll be surprised when she sees how nice it is. I don't know anyone else who lives in a flat like this. She's got to be impressed.

'My boss is Holly's uncle. He's converted the flat and he lets us live here. He'll sell it eventually, but until then we take care of it for him.'

'So one day you'll have to move out?'

'Yeah, but not for ages, probably. Holly's a single mum, and she works part-time at a GP's surgery and she's not got much money. Clive wanted her to have somewhere nice to bring up Finn '

'He sounds nice.'

'Holly's lucky. She's got a big family and they all help out.' I open the door. 'Holly! We've got a visitor!'

Holly's not looking her best. She's still in her dressing gown and she's got no make-up on and she hasn't brushed her hair so it's all over the place. She's pale and her forehead is all pinched up again.

'Aidan! Why didn't you warn me?'

Cass steps forward. 'I'm so sorry, it's all my fault. I just turned up out of the blue. Aidan didn't know. I'm Cass. You must be Holly.'

'It's lovely to meet you.' Holly's putting on a brave face. 'I've just got up. I'll go and get dressed. Aidan, why don't you get Cass a drink? Oh, Finn darling, are you hungry?'

Finn's bellowing for food. I pick him up, steer Cass towards the living room.

'Here we go!'

She steps in and stumbles over one of Finn's toys. 'Sit down!' I say. 'I'll just tidy up a bit.' Obviously, if I'd known she was coming, I'd have done this already. I sweep all the toys into the toy box, ignoring Finn's shouts of fury, pick up the plates and mugs on the floor where we'd left them last night, and straighten the rug. 'I'll just get Finn some food,' I say, scooping him up. 'We've got a kitchen as well as this room. And two bedrooms!'

Holly hasn't cleaned up the kitchen, either. She made spaghetti last night and there are splashes of tomato sauce all over the worktop. I plonk Finn in the high chair and give him a pitta bread, wipe the tops, do the washing up.

Cass stays on the sofa where I left her. She's talking on her phone. I can hear her voice but not what she's saying.

Holly comes into the kitchen. She's looking a lot better. A pretty top – pink flowers, a bit see-through – and jeans. A bit of a muffin-top spilling over the top of her jeans, which makes me want to touch her right there. I don't though.

'I'm sorry!' she hisses. 'I didn't know you were going to come home! I thought you were working all day!'

'I couldn't keep Finn at the shop all day! You know that.'

She yawned. 'I'm just so tired, Aidan.'

'Are you all right?' Sometimes Holly loses energy and stays in bed a lot. She's trying all sorts of things to fight it. Yoga is one, and vitamins, and she's been thinking about taking up tai chi. Her mum is always nagging her to go back onto anti-depressants, but Holly kind of reacts badly to being told what to do by her mum. You'd have thought Juliet would have realised by now but, no, she keeps on with her, 'Just consider seeing the doctor', and, 'Perhaps a counsellor would help, sweetie.'

Holly puts it down to glandular fever, says she had it when she was seventeen and never got over it 100 per cent. She was seventeen when her dad ran off to Marbella, so that was a pretty bad year. And then the next year she had a go at university, but that didn't work out, and then she had a few bad relationships. And then she got pregnant, but the dad wasn't interested. And the next boyfriend ... well ... Holly's not had it 100 per cent easy, which actually helps us get along.

Cass comes into the kitchen. Holly smiles and gives her a hug. 'I can't believe you and Aidan have found each other! It's so exciting!'

'I can't believe it, either,' says Cass. 'That was my dad on the phone. He's really angry with me.'

'Why's he angry with you, sweetie?'

'I'm meant to be staying with him, meeting his new girlfriend. I just walked out.'

Holly shook her head. 'It's the worst! When my parents split up, Dad wanted us to meet the new girl right away. She was only young, a year older than my oldest sister. I can't stand her—'

'It's a shame, because otherwise we could go and stay with them and it'd be a free holiday in Spain. Finn would love it.' I've pointed it out before, and I get the same response as usual.

Holly shakes her head and says, 'Not a good idea, Aidan.'

'It might be better than you think,' I say.

'I hadn't even thought about holidays,' says Cass. She pulls a face. 'He won't want us tagging along. Not with Annabel and a new baby.'

'Make sure he doesn't use you as a free babysitter,' I tell her.

Holly starts clattering around with the kettle. 'Cup of tea?' She sounds pissed off. I'm not sure why.

Cass is looking at us curiously. I wish she hadn't seen Holly without make-up. She's lovely whatever, but without it you can totally see that she's a bit older than me. I feel like Cass is judging us. I don't want her disapproving, like Holly's mum.

Holly makes tea and cheese sandwiches and we go and sit in the living room. I can see bits of dust dancing in the sunshine. Finn and I start putting together his train set and Cass and Holly sit on the sofa. And then Holly starts with the questions.

'How do your parents feel about you meeting Aidan again? I've seen that programme on ITV – you know, the one where they reunite birth parents and children – and I sometimes wonder what the adoptive parents think. They keep them off screen mostly. Don't even talk about them a lot.'

'I haven't actually told them,' says Cass. 'I suppose I will, eventually. It's so stupid. You're meant to wait until you're eighteen and do it all with a social worker holding your hand. Well, I don't need that. Meeting Aidan is one of the best things I've ever done.'

'I suppose it'll be your mum, next,' says Holly. 'I tell you what, why don't we do it here? I can make a little party, you can invite your mum, Aidan, and we can get all the meetings over together.'

I drive Finn's train over the bridge and let it roll into a line of trucks. Finn squeals with laughter.

'I don't think so,' I say.

'Maybe it would be easier,' Cass says, 'if there are other people around. And she might want to bring her kids.'

Holly's mouth drops open – if she was in a cartoon, her entire lower jaw would have dropped to the floor with a huge crash. 'Her kids? She's got other kids? Aidan! You never told me!'

I concentrate on threading train track under Finn's bridge. It's a really cool train set. Naturally Juliet bought it for him. 'I've only met them once or twice. I don't think she'll want to bring them.'

'Well, just her then. Just her and us and Finn and Cass. Do you have a boyfriend, Cass? Anyone you'd like to bring?'

'No,' says Cass. Then, 'Well, sort of. Maybe. Probably not.'

'We'd better do it soon. Before the Christmas rush gets started.'

'I'm at school,' says Cass. 'It would have to be a weekend.'

'Oh, that's no problem.' Holly's all excited. 'It'll be wonderful to reunite a family!'

'It might be,' I say, cautiously. 'Mum might not want to, though. She's a bit funny.'

'What mother won't want to see her daughter? You're so lovely too, she'll be thrilled.'

Cass is looking so pretty today. She's got a pinky purple scarf wound round her neck which ought to look bad with her hair, and somehow doesn't. Her hair is wild and curly. She's glowing, a golden girl. She doesn't need any slap to look good.

'You're really kind,' she says to Holly.

'It's nothing. Anything for you and Aidan. Tell you what, why don't I open a bottle of wine? We should toast the occasion.'

They talk about Holly's job at the GP's surgery, how people can be really aggressive and nasty when they can't see a doctor right away, and how Cass wants to study history.

'How did you and Aidan meet?' Cass asks.

'Hasn't he told you?'

I freeze. What's she going to say?

'He was working in the shop. He was very shy, weren't you, Aidan? Wouldn't talk to me. I had to make all the running.'

'I wasn't shy. Just, things were different, then.'

'I had no idea that you were only sixteen. He looked a lot older, Cass. Do you think I'm awful, a cradle-snatcher?'

'Of course not,' said Cass. 'You can't be much older, anyway.'

'I'm twenty-one.'

Cass hardly blinks. I do, though, because actually Holly will be twenty-three in two months' time.

'He told me about himself. No family. Coming out of care. Sixteen years old, living in a bedsit ... Can you imagine? Anyway, I offered him a room in the flat.'

This version of events is kind of irritating, because it leaves out a lot. Holly's obviously got her reasons though, so I stay quiet and concentrate on the train track. 'Look, Finnster, let's line the engines up here. Then they can have a race.'

'That was nice of you,' says Cass. 'Where were you living before, Aidan?'

'In a bedsit. But the ceiling fell in.'

I'd got back after a night out and found my room covered in soggy plaster and my bed soaking wet. Someone had left a tap on upstairs in a room that'd been empty for a few weeks.

It was too late to call the landlord or a social worker or anyone. I didn't think they'd let me back into the children's home – I'd been gone for six months by then. The room stank and everything was wet and I couldn't stay there. The pubs were closed and, anyway, I was under age. The other people in the building – well, I wouldn't want to draw their attention at night when I had nowhere to sleep. The caretaker knocked off at seven. I was all alone.

I'd sat there for a bit looking through the handbook the council gave me when I left care, looking for a page which told you who to call in a night-time emergency. There were pages about claiming benefits and what to do when you got into trouble with the police. Details of religious holidays. A list of words you might not know the meaning of. Words like correspondence, solicitor and subsistence. Pathway plan, amenity, eligible, accountable. Entitlements, eligibility and fundamental. Martyrdom. Words to tie you up in knots and keep you prisoner. Useless words. Scary words.

My head was spinning and the words were dancing. The choice was the street or the shop. I picked the shop.

Clive had given me keys a few weeks before to open up in the mornings, and so it was easy to let myself in. I knew we had a stack of sleeping bags, and I hadn't even needed to switch the light on to find them. I climbed up the stairs to the upper floor and curled up on one of the beds. I even set two alarm clocks – we had about twenty. I'd be up and out by eight, all ready to come back again for Clive at nine. I wasn't due to be opening up the next day, and I didn't want him to get suspicious.

The bed was a hundred times more comfortable than the one in the bedsit, and I felt cosy and comfortable, lying there among all Clive's treasures. I was yawning and sleepy and wondering if I could do this every night, and never have to go back to the bedsit. There aren't many places that are improved by a whacking great hole in the ceiling, but my room was one of them.

Then I heard them. The baby crying. Shouting. A huge thump, a crash.

And Holly's scream.

21: AIDAN

I ran down the stairs, stumbled through the shop, opened Clive's desk drawer and found his bunch of keys. Then I let myself out at the front, opened the door to the flat and ran up the three flights of stairs to its front door. I was panting by the time I got to the top, but I kept going.

They didn't hear me at first because Finn was crying so hard. They were in the front room, screaming at each other: Holly and her boyfriend. Some loser called Don. I'd seen him a few times, carrying Finn, pushing the buggy. A big, muscley bloke. I'd disliked him on sight for no real reason.

Now, I had a reason. He had his hands on Holly's shoulders and he was shaking her, and there was blood trickling from her snubby little nose.

'Get your stinking hands off her!' I shouted, running across the room and grabbing Don's arm. He let go of her and swiped at me. I hit him, hard in the jaw. He staggered backwards.

'Christ! Where did you come from?'

'Call the police!' I told Holly, but she went running to pick up Finn, and stood rocking him, crying, shivering.

'You've got no right coming in here!' Don told me. 'I'm calling the police!'

'You were beating her up!'

'She's not going to say anything.'

I kicked him in the shin and he doubled over.

'You get out of here, now.'

Holly was shushing Finn, rocking and shushing, and I saw her nose and the blue shadow of an old bruise on her jaw and I remembered my mum. All those years ago. Shushing us and rocking us and telling us that everything would be all right. And it wasn't all right. It was never all right.

'You're never going to hit her again,' I told Don. 'You're going to pack your bags and get out.'

'You can't throw me out!' He was taller and bigger than me, but I was more used to fighting, and I wasn't drunk.

'You want to bet?'

Don spat abuse at her, ugly names, names I'd heard from Mac's mouth when I wasn't much bigger than Finn. Holly held Finn tighter, kept her head down.

I hit Don again, straight in the mouth, enjoying shutting him up. He flailed around, trying and failing to land a punch on me. He roared like a toothless lion.

'Don't call her names. OK, don't pack a bag. Get going.'

Now the blood was coming from Don's mouth. 'I'm going! You can have her! She's good for nothing, anyway!'

He stomped out of the room. We heard the flat door slam, and then the distant sound of the front door as well.

Finn was still wailing, but Holly's tears had stopped. Finn's cries turned to whimpers, and then stopped altogether. The only noise I could hear was a faint buzz of traffic and calling sirens, the sound of London at night. I waited, suddenly embarrassed. How could I explain where I'd come from?

'Thank you,' said Holly. 'I'm sorry you had to see that.' She rocked Finn in her arms. It made my heart ache watching them.

'What were you doing here?' She was puzzled. 'The shop can't be open, can it?'

'I was sleeping there,' I told her. 'Don't tell Clive ... please ...'

'I won't.' She blinked a few times, trying so hard not to cry. 'I'm so embarrassed. Don, he's just, he was drunk, that's all. I made him cross. It wasn't really his fault.'

'Don't take him back,' I told her. 'For you, for the baby's sake, don't do it.'

'I love him. How can I just finish it?'

'What's to love about that?'

'You don't understand. I'm all alone.' She glanced down at Finn. 'It scares me, Aidan, having to do this all on my own.'

'He's not the dad, is he?' I'd guessed that because Don was big and white, and Holly was little and white, and Finn was small and definitely half-black. Plus Clive had filled me in on how worried the family was because Holly seemed to go from one bad bet to another.

'No, but it's not so easy to find someone when you're ... when ...' She couldn't talk any more. She held her fists to her mouth.

'Call a locksmith in the morning. Pack up Don's things – he

162

can get them from the shop if he's got the balls to come back, which I doubt.'

'What if he comes back before I get the locks changed?'

'I'll stay here on your sofa,' I told her, even though I knew that meant Clive would find out that I'd slept in the shop. My sleeping bag and the alarm clocks would give me away. I'd have to hope that he understood it was a crisis.

So that was the first night I spent in the flat. Lying awake, listening for Don. Worrying about Clive. Remembering Mum and Mac and Cass and me. And full up with love for Holly. Nothing to do with sex – I just wanted to care for her, protect her, make sure that her smile never left her face.

Clive was pissed off with me, but when I told him what had happened, he changed track right away. 'Thank God you were there,' he told me. 'I knew he was bad news. I'll call the locksmith right away. Call my solicitor too, get a restraining order on him. Holly's so soft she'll end up taking him back if we don't act now. You can sleep in the shop for now. Call your social worker, get him to sort out the bedsit.'

Two days later, Holly asked me to come up to the flat. She opened a bottle of wine. We sat on the sofa, side by side.

'I never really thanked you.'

'That's OK.'

'I was just so shocked. You came out of nowhere.'

'Sorry. I heard the noise and I had to do something.'

'You could have phoned the police.'

'I'm sorry. I didn't mean anything wrong. I was worried about you and Finn.'

'I know. I mean, lots of people wouldn't have got involved like you did. I appreciate it.'

'I'll be downstairs,' I told Holly. 'For a few weeks, at least. So if Don comes back, just call me.'

She sighed. 'He was great when he was sober.'

I didn't say anything. I'd heard it all before.

'Aidan, I was talking to Uncle Clive. I've got a spare room and you've got nowhere to stay. Why don't you move in? As my lodger? Got to be better than a bedsit.'

'Really?' I couldn't believe it. The flat was beautiful. She was nice, and kind, and smiling. This was the best thing that had ever happened to me. 'Are you sure? Really sure?'

'I'm totally sure,' she'd said.

It was kind of awkward at first. I spent most of my time in my room, because I wasn't sure she wanted me to be in the kitchen or the living room. Then she started asking if I wanted to watch stuff on telly with her. Offering to share her supper – 'I've made a curry and there's loads of it' – and asking if I could watch Finn for her. We got used to each other.

After two months, I ended up in her bed. I was sixteen, nearly seventeen, and she was twenty. Best thing that ever happened to me.

I can understand why she doesn't tell Cass any of this. It's personal. But it also kind of pisses me off that I don't get the credit for being a hero.

'My uncle's really pleased with Aidan. He's done a great job in the shop.'

OK, now Holly is talking about me like I'm about eight and she's my mum. I'm more than irritated. 'Look, Finn, the train's going round and round and then ... *smash*!' Finn thinks this is hilarious. He loves accidents.

AIDAN

'Aidan needs to pass his driving test, though – the theory exam is holding him up. You find it difficult, don't you, love? I'm sure he's dyslexic.'

'I'm not dyslexic.' I try and make a joke of it. 'I'm just thick.'

'I'm almost certain you are dyslexic. I wish you could get properly tested.'

I shrug. 'It's too late.'

'My mum knows some people,' says Cass. 'My little brother, Ben, he's had loads of tests.'

I don't really see what good that is to me.

'Crash it again, Aidy, crash it again!' says Finn.

So I do.

22: CASS

I loved seeing Aidan. I loved meeting Holly. It couldn't have been more different from everything I'd ever known.

Their flat was so small – one tiny bedroom and then Finn's room, which was barely more than a cupboard – and nothing matched, not the furniture or even the plates. It all seemed to come from the shop where Aidan worked. Second-hand junk. And it was really messy – they obviously don't do much tidying up. It felt young and free and unstuffy.

They opened a bottle of wine mid-afternoon. Mum and Dad always wait until 6 p.m., which they call wine o'clock. I had a few sips of wine, but not much. I was in enough trouble with Dad as it was.

I got a bit of a shock at first when I realised that Holly was loads older than Aidan – maybe ten years, I thought, although she looked younger when she put on some make-up and tight jeans. Actually, she's nearly the same age as Annabel. How strange is that?

They were always touching. She put her hand on his shoulder, or he stroked her leg, or they sneaked a kiss when they thought no one was looking. It was cute. It made me wish I had a real boyfriend, someone who loved me, not just an experimental kisser. I'd have to move on from Will pretty quickly, I thought. But only after my A levels, and only if I could find the right person. I could go on one of those volunteer schemes in my gap year and meet someone in Costa Rica who was into helping the environment.

I was lucky really, that Will seemed fine about keeping everything private and experimental and non-involved. Let's face it, he was probably relieved that no one had to know he had anything to do with me, given that I wasn't like the sort of girl he usually went for. Just the idea of people gossiping about us made me cringe. If people knew, they'd try and define us – not that there was 'an us' – they'd talk about me, judge me. The pressure would be too much. I didn't mind experimenting with kisses. I knew I would never want to fall in love.

Did that make me abnormal and cold? Quite probably. Being with Aidan and Holly made me sad, in a way. Being brought up in care obviously hadn't closed Aidan off to love and partnership; in fact, he was living as part of a family before he was out of his teens. It must just be me that was somehow unloving. I couldn't blame it on genes or upbringing.

I got back to Dad's flat, and managed to be polite to everyone, and he didn't tell me off for running away because (I assumed) he was so grateful that I'd come back. They were taking Ben out for a pizza, but I stayed at home, using my essay as an excuse.

I didn't write the essay. I poured myself a glass of wine from a bottle I found in the fridge, lay on the sofa, closed my eyes and imagined being grown up and independent and free. And sexually experienced. I imagined that as well. I tried to imagine a fantasy boyfriend for when I was Holly or Annabel's age. I wouldn't go out with some older man or younger boy. He'd be my age, handsome and rich. He'd have a starred first from Harvard or Cambridge in economics or possibly philosophy.

He'd be extremely serious and never make stupid jokes. He'd very possibly be American or Canadian. I'd be working in a museum or an archive or something and he'd take me out to smart restaurants and then back to his stylish flat. He'd think I was wonderful ... respect my intellect ... He'd never make demands on me, but he'd be effortlessly charming and impressive. If we got married, we'd have a very traditional white wedding, and my dress would be ivory raw silk with a fishtail ... *urgh*. I was like a six year old, imagining her dream wedding. No, we'd get married in a registrar's office and I'd wear a suit. No, we wouldn't get married at all, I'd live in London and he'd live in New York and we'd Skype a lot.

My phone rang. Will.

'Hey, just wondered how it was going with the Big Bad Girlfriend.'

'Oh, it's OK. I'm here on my own. They've taken Ben out for a pizza, but I'm meant to be doing my essay.'

'Meant to be? I thought you were definitely writing it today. Are you bunking off?'

'I just can't be bothered. Who cares anyway? It's all happened, and everyone's had their say.'

'Hmm,' he said. 'If you say so. So what's she like?'

'Much older than him, but really nice. She wants to invite my mum round.'

'I thought he'd run off with a younger woman?'

'Oh! You mean Dad! I went to see Aidan today.'

'You went without your bodyguard?' Will made tutting noises.

'I went to see him in his shop – actually, there was someone a bit dodgy there – and then I saw his flat. And I met Holly. Finn's not his baby, she had another boyfriend then.'

'So she's an older woman? OK, figures. And what's Annabel like?'

'Perfect. Fake. She's charmed Ben.'

'But she won't charm you, eh?'

'Never.'

'No, because you take a whole load of charming.'

'That is true.'

'Have I charmed you yet?'

'No, you're going to have to work a lot harder.'

'I'll write your essay for you,' he said, 'if it'll win me any points.'

'I don't approve of cheating,' I said, thinking how great it would be if I could just magically create an essay out of thin air.

'Well, hurry up and finish it,' he said, 'and then we can continue with our very interesting experiments.'

'It's so long though, and such hard work.'

'I thought you were quite enjoying it so far. Enough to continue, anyway.'

'Not the experiments, the essay.'

'I have offered to take it off your hands. Think about it. Then we could go to the cinema tomorrow night. Experiment in the back row.'

'No,' I said. 'No cheating and no public experimentation. This is a secret project. I told you that on the train.'

'But that's so unscientific! You might find that experimenting in public is the key factor that makes up your mind.'

'Makes up my mind about what?'

'Well, I don't know. You were the one going on about working out what it all meant and the need for scientific analysis of the situation. I'm quite happy to be a little more spontaneous.'

Spontaneity seemed a bit dangerous to me. We'd so nearly been spotted on the train, and in the park.

'We could just forget the whole thing,' I said.

For a second I had him. There was an uncharacteristic pause.

'OK, if that's what you really want.'

'I just don't want to be gossiped about.'

'That's it? The sum total of your concerns?'

It suddenly occurred to me that perhaps Will was slightly insulted that I wasn't parading him in front of the crowds in Starbucks. That he thought I was ashamed of him. That my natural cautiousness was coming over as ... no, it couldn't be ... racism?

'I just think we might find it easier to get to know each other better without loads of attention. I know that you live and breathe by your social life, but I'm not like that.'

'I understand. You've been in the spotlight a lot recently, with your dad and all that.'

This was a much better excuse than the truth. But I couldn't tell Will that I both wanted him and didn't want him at the same time.

'And we hardly know each other.' I told him, as briskly as possible. 'We might get fed up with each other after a week or so, and then it's better if no one else knows.'

'You say the sweetest things.'

I laughed. And laughed some more.

'Miss Montgomery, have you been drinking? You sound remarkably cheerful for someone who is having a miserable weekend meeting her father's hateful new girlfriend.'

'Only a glass of wine,' I confessed.

He sighed. 'What a shame I'm not there. This would be a perfect experimental opportunity. We haven't even *begun* with artificial stimulants.'

'Shh,' I said, trying to stop giggling. 'I think they're back. I'll ring you tomorrow.'

I rushed to the kitchen, rinsed the wine glass as they trooped through the front door. Ben was yawning, Annabel chatting and making him laugh. I kept my face unamused and unfriendly.

Dad asked how I'd got on with the essay. 'Fine!' I said, leaping up to collect my books together before he could demand to read it. 'I've nearly finished! I'm really tired. I think I'll go to bed.'

Dad's flat has two bedrooms, and Ben and I are used to sharing when we're here. Annabel tactfully disappeared to the kitchen to make tea, so we wouldn't have to see her going into the room that had always been Mum and Dad's. I tried very hard to forget that she'd be using Mum's en suite bathroom, sleeping in Mum's bed with Mum's husband.

'She's nice,' said Ben. 'I like her. She understands all about how I feel.'

'Ben, she caused how you feel.'

'No, she understands about school. She said she never had any friends, either. Everyone thought she was a geek.'

Annabel was a big, fat liar in my opinion. Except she's obviously never been fat in her life. Even her baby bump is slender and toned.

'She's going to be my friend. And she's going to introduce me to her little brother and her sister, and her big brother and her half-sister, and they're all going to be my friends.'

All his life I'd loved Ben, felt every hurt he suffered. I never minded that he was the 'real' son, the biological one. I stood up for him, tried to help him ... and he'd let me down. Betrayed me. Allowed himself to be manipulated by the offer of some extra friends.

Well, two can play at that game.

'Ben,' I said. 'Can you keep a secret?'

'What secret?'

'You have to promise.'

'I promise.'

'I'm going to introduce you to more friends, too. A friend called Aidan and another friend called Holly. And a little boy called Finn. And maybe one day some children called Louis and Scarlett.'

'Who's Aidan? Who's Scarlett?'

'Aidan is my brother, just like you're my brother,' I began.

'How can he be?'

'You know how I was adopted? I came from a different family? Aidan comes from the same one.'

It took him a while but he got there. 'But why don't I know him? If he's your brother, too?'

'You will meet him, and his girlfriend Holly and her baby, Finn. You mustn't tell, Ben. Mum and Dad don't know.'

'Who are the others? Louis and Scarlett? How old are they?'

'A bit younger, I think.' Ben does tend to go around with people younger than him. 'They're also from the same mum. I haven't met them yet.'

He sat up in bed, squeezing his knees. 'How come we don't know them now?'

'That's how adoption works. You join a new family and you leave the old one behind. You don't have contact any more.'

That's not true, actually. Mum explained it to me once. She said there are all sorts of levels of adoptions, and some people have open adoptions where they exchange letters and meet up with the birth parents occasionally. That wasn't deemed appropriate in my case; mainly, I think, because Dad was an MP.

Ben yawned. 'I want to meet them,' he said. 'I want more friends.'

'You will, Ben, one day,' I promised. I loved him so much. He'd been my brother all his life, and Annabel had only just met him. If Ben was getting any more family, it was going to come from me.

23: CASS

'Will Hughes!' said Grace at school on Monday morning. 'Will Hughes! *Will Hughes!*'

'What about him?' I tried to look unconcerned, but inside I was furious. Will had obviously been talking.

Grace was as smug as a little girl with a secret. 'You! And Will! On the train! Together!'

'Who's gossiping about me?'

'You were spotted,' said Grace. She tapped her nose. 'I've promised to protect my source.'

'Well, anyone who spotted us can tell you that there was nothing going on. Will is a friend, that's all. He's Ben's peer buddy at Bonny's. I happened to bump into him on the way back from London.' I was pretty certain that this was the train she was talking about, not the one from Oxford to London.

Grace's face made it obvious she didn't believe me.

'Ben's not happy at Bonny's. He's Will's special project.'

174

'Cass, Will Hughes is a legend. Please tell me you're going to go for it this time.'

'I don't know what you mean.'

'Duh! Any boy who's ever plucked up the courage to approach you gets crushed and sneered at, and treated like dirt.'

'I do not treat anyone like dirt!'

'Declan? When he dared to ask you to the Year Eleven prom at Holy Virgin High School?'

'Oh, honestly. Declan! I mean, why did he even bother?'

'Simon Potter? Darius Mainwaring?'

'Who?'

'Will Hughes is in a different league!'

We'd reached our history class. I winked at Grace. 'Talk later,' I said.

History is my favourite subject and Mrs Harper is a good teacher, but my mind wandered as she went on and on about people fighting in faraway places a long time ago. In fact, I started to wonder if history was really what I wanted to study at university. What was the point, after all? Reaching back into the past to theorise about what could have, should have, might have happened. Maybe I should study something more relevant to today? Maybe I should think harder about what I actually wanted to do when I left uni. At the moment, I had a list of things I didn't want to do: no teaching, no politics, and vague clichéd ideas about museums or theatres.

Would it be easier to be someone like Aidan, who just left school and found a job and then got on with it? Or someone like Holly, who dropped out and got pregnant and got a job? Actually, that sounded really dreary. I'd have to grit my teeth and concentrate.

What if I hadn't been adopted? What if I'd stayed with Aidan and his mum, my real mum? What if we'd been a real family and I'd grown up in north London somewhere. Would I be a hairdresser?

'Cass!' said Mrs Harper. 'I asked you a question!'

I had absolutely no idea what she was talking about. I blushed, apologised. 'I don't know, I'm sorry, Mrs Harper.'

She looked disappointed. 'Well, perhaps Grace can tell us something about the cult of personality as it applies to Stalin.'

Grace could and did.

When the lesson was finished and we went our separate ways (English for me, biology for her), Grace nudged me and said, 'Day-dreaming about Will? See you at lunchtime.'

But at lunch I had a prefect's meeting and she was rushing off to play hockey and we didn't get another chance to talk until the end of the day, when we got on to the bus.

'So!' she started, but I glared at her and said, 'Let's go for a coffee if you insist on interrogating me.'

'Oh, I think you'll want to interrogate *me*,' she said.

No Will on the bus, I was relieved to see, and no sign of him in Starbucks either, although there was a big group of Bonny's sixth formers. I found us two seats in a relatively quiet corner; Grace queued up to buy us lattes. I kept my head down, checked my phone.

'Well! Fancy seeing you here. I didn't think you deigned to mix with the rabble.'

I might have known it. Will was towering over me, coffee in hand, on his way – I hoped – to the huge group of Bonny's kids in the corner.

'I don't. I mean, I don't usually come here, but I'm having a quick coffee with Grace.'

'You got your essay finished, then? Shame you couldn't come to the movies.'

He'd kept his voice soft enough that no one would over-hear, but I still frowned at him. 'Shame,' he said again, 'it was good. Oh, well, see you around.'

I wondered if Will had other girlfriends to take to the cinema. After all, there was nothing to stop him: we hadn't made any promises to each other – quite the opposite, really.

Grace sat down. 'He was talking to you!'

'About Ben, actually.'

'Oh, yes. Very likely. Cass, you have to tell me everything.'

'Nothing to tell. No, really, nothing. He's just an acquain-tance. He's looking out for Ben in the playground. You know my brother has a difficult time making friends.'

'Well, make the most of it. Will just broke up with Ruby, remember. He won't be on the market for long.'

Ruby was in our year, but we'd never been in the same form or had the same friends. She was blonde and girly – not the sort to be a prefect, or get involved in debating or anything like that. I couldn't imagine what she'd put on her UCAS personal statement.

'So he's on the rebound?'

'So you *are* interested? Oh God, Cass, you're smiling!'

I rearranged my face. 'I'm allowed to smile.'

'I've never seen you smile like that.'

'Oh, come on. Can you see us together?'

'You need to scrub up more, Cass. If you'd make a bit more effort with your clothes and make-up ... you're really pretty when you can be bothered.'

I was actually wearing mascara that day, which proved her wrong.

'That's not what I mean,' I snapped. 'He's completely weird, him with his stupid Dora bag and tweed jackets. He looks ridiculous. Why on earth would I be interested in him?'

'Aw, Cass, he's lovely. Everyone at Bonny's is in love with him.'

'It's a cult of personality. Like Stalin.'

I glanced over to the Bonny's kids. Stalin was right at the centre, telling some long story that involved silly voices and big, sweeping gestures. The group was full of girls, laughing, staring, admiring. One was the blonde girl I'd seen him with at the bowling alley. Just his type.

'You'd better get on with it, if you are interested,' said Grace. 'Looks like he's got a long line of admirers.'

'I'm so not interested,' I told her, and we talked about other stuff. Her pony, and her plans to study management at Exeter or Bristol, and her campaign to go out with some boy called Leon.

Grace tried – she really tried – to be the caring friend, asking me how the weekend had been. 'What's she like, Annabel?'

I wrinkled my nose. 'She's super-fake. Trying to be all friendly. I don't want anything to do with her.'

'But you'll have to, eventually, won't you? I mean, when she has the baby ... and aren't they going to get married? When the divorce comes through?'

'Where'd you read that? The *Daily Mail*?'

Grace flinched. 'I'm sorry, Cass. It's just – I worry about you. I'm your friend and I care, and you don't tell me anything.'

'There's nothing to tell,' I said. 'I just want to get on with my life. I'm not someone who likes agonising over all the gory details.'

'Sorry,' she said, but I could tell by her pursed lips and tiny frown that she thought I was odd. I suppose she expected floods of tears.

'It's just the way I deal with things,' I told her, and we quickly moved on to the politics of the netball team, and which university open days we were going to.

And, all the time, Will was sitting with his friends, talking and laughing and entertaining everyone. My skin prickled with irritation. I hated myself for trying to hear what they were saying.

Ten minutes later, Grace went to the loo, and I found my phone. Without thinking too much about it, I texted Will: 'I'm going home in ten. If you get the same bus we could get off a stop early.'

I watched him pause midstream, reach for his phone. Take it out and read the text. Nod his head, give a little smile, glance in my direction.

I ignored him. I didn't even look at the blonde girl at his side. I was in control. I was the Ice Queen.

24: CASS

You'd have thought that people would be used to my dad. After all, most of the people I was at school with had started alongside me in the junior section when we were only five.

But he still turned heads. Every school concert; every parent-teacher evening. Of course, people were even more interested now he'd left us. This was the first time my parents had been seen out together since Dad had left home. Thankfully everyone was too civilized to film us on their phones.

Mum and I had tried to work out a system so they didn't have to spend much time together: maybe if Dad came to history and philosophy, and Mum to economics and English. But he said that'd be more noticeable than if we just pretended everything was OK. 'We'll manage fine,' he told us, all breezy and confident and virtually smelling of Annabel. 'Big smiles all round. Won't be the end of the world.'

'I wish you hadn't come,' I hissed at him as we stood in the queue for my English teacher.

'Of course I came. I care about your education. We may not be together, but we're still your parents, Cass. We'll do everything we can for you.'

'What you can do is stay away!' I whispered. 'Can't you see how difficult it is for Mum?'

Mum wasn't standing with us. She'd spotted her friend, Anthea, and was chatting to her. Mum was wearing lipstick and she'd had her hair done. The heartbreak diet and the Pilates meant that on the surface she looked great. But I knew, and Dad should know, that it was all a façade.

'Cass, this is not the time or the place,' said Dad, keeping his politician's smile in place. 'Now, what was all that from the economics teacher about a failed test?'

'I didn't have time to study, OK? I've been a bit busy recently, propping up the people you left behind.'

'Cass—'

Mum was back with us. 'Everything all right?' she asked.

'Fine,' I said.

'Fine,' said Dad. 'Look, they're about to leave.'

I thought it would be a relief to sit down and talk to the English teacher, Miss Graham. I was totally mistaken.

'Cass, what's happened?' she asked. 'I kept back your latest essay because I couldn't believe you'd written it. I'm used to you getting As and A*s, but this barely scrapes a D.'

I'd totally forgotten about that essay. I'd cobbled it together at the last minute in a study period – the study period I'd set aside for studying for my economics test.

'I don't want to intrude,' said Miss Graham, 'but I know it's been a difficult term for you all. Do you think it's affecting your studies, Cass? Perhaps you should see the head of pastoral care.'

I sat and glowered while Dad went on about how our welfare was their first priority, how both of them were utterly supportive of my education, how keen they were that I should go to Oxford.

'I'm sure this is just a blip,' he finished. 'She's such a hard worker, aren't you, Cass?'

Just for a moment, I contemplated saying 'No'. I considered stopping trying to please everyone, working hard, trying to be a real Montgomery. Forgetting Oxford, and accepting that it wouldn't be a disaster to end up somewhere like Bristol or Exeter. Being *normal*. Getting As and Bs instead of A*s. Leaving school and taking a gap year and just messing around. Just hanging out and having fun. Like Aidan. Like Holly. Like the Cass I would have been if I hadn't got adopted by a couple of high-achieving, pressurising, middle-class ...

'I'm doing too much!'

Mum was looking into the distance, not really listening to the conversation. She came to with a little jump.

'What do you mean, darling?'

'I mean it's too much. A levels are a lot of work. I want to quit the extra stuff. Music and Duke of Edinburgh and being a prefect and all that.'

'But Cass, your personal statement—'

'I don't care about my personal statement!'

Dad looked around. 'Lots of people waiting to see Miss Graham,' he observed. 'Perhaps we need to discuss this with Cass at home. I'm sure she'll be back on track soon. Thank you so much, Miss Graham.' He dazzled her with his smile, teeth gleaming like a cartoon crocodile, and strode out of the room, Mum and I rushing to keep up with him.

People were looking. I knew it even though I couldn't see them. I couldn't see them because of the tears in my eyes.

'Out,' ordered Dad, even though we hadn't seen my history teacher yet. Mum murmured a faint protest, but he was holding the door open for us. We were ejected into the freezing night just as the headmistress arrived.

'Hello, Mr Montgomery! How very nice to see you!'

Mum and I shivered in the cold air, and she tried to put her arm around me. I shrugged her off. 'I'm fine! Leave me alone!'

Dad emerged at last. 'Come on,' he said. 'We need to talk. Let's go home.'

I really lost it then. 'You can't call it home!' I told him. 'You don't live there any more! Because of you there's a "For Sale" sign outside!'

'Well, we can go and sit in a restaurant and you can cry and shout at us in public if you prefer,' he said, smoothly. 'I honestly think it's better to keep things private.'

'Cass, be sensible,' said Mum. 'Of course Dad can come to the house. We need to have a talk, don't we?'

'No!' I said, but Dad just looked at Mum and said, 'I'll see you there.' Then he jumped into his BMW and we got into Mum's Mondeo, and I cried all the way home.

Mum pulled into the driveway, past the massive 'For Sale' sign, and handed me a tissue. I mopped my eyes and blew my nose and tried to think about tsunamis and earthquakes and World War Two and other things that would make my stupid emotions dwindle by their enormity.

'Oh, Cass,' Mum said, 'I'm so sorry, my darling. I wish we could have sheltered you from this.'

'I don't need sheltering!'

'You're bound to feel bad. It's so tough, what you're going through. I've been so bound up in myself, I've neglected you, I'm so sorry.' She had no idea. She had forgotten those weeks when she was a wreck, when she wasn't functioning, when I felt I was going to be left with no family at all. Just because she'd pulled herself together, that didn't mean everything was OK now. She'd shown herself as weak, and that was something I never wanted to see again.

'You haven't neglected me. It's just that I've got a lot on at the moment.'

Mum handed me another tissue. Then she said, 'Cass, do you think, perhaps, you should cut back on your social life? It's just – I can't help noticing – you've been spending a lot of time with that boy recently.'

'Which boy?' I tried to sound unconcerned.

'That boy. The one Ben knows. I can't remember his name. Kate said you went to Oxford with him.'

Mum was embarrassed, trying not to say the word 'black'.

'Oh. Will. What's your problem with him?'

'Well, people do talk, you know. Mrs Featherstone saw }you with him on the train. She couldn't wait to ask me about you. And I have noticed you've been out a lot. And then Mrs Thwaites said she'd seen you with him on the bus.'

The whole town is full of small-minded, bigoted old gossips. I could never take public transport again, but at least no one had seen us in our private experimentation places: the back of the shops in Walker Lane; the bomb shelter in the park. The car park at the library.

None of them were great, really. We'd been talking about finding somewhere warmer. Somewhere indoors.

'They should all mind their own business.'

Dad rapped on the windscreen. 'Are you two going to be in there all night?'

'No, we're coming,' said Mum. 'I know this feels strange, Cass, but we're determined to make it work in a civilised way.'

Dad being in our house was nothing compared to seeing Annabel going into Mum's bedroom, cooking in Mum's kitchen, coming out of the bathroom in Dad's bathrobe. I didn't say so, though.

We all sat round the kitchen table. Mum poured herself a glass of wine. Dad said, 'Better not, I'm driving.' No wine for me, I got offered juice or tea. I didn't want either.

'So,' said Dad. 'This is really quite serious, Cass. You've let things slide. I knew I should have looked at that essay the other day.'

'Look, I don't need you to police my homework, OK? I'm fine. I can manage.'

Thank goodness he didn't speak to the history teacher. I had only handed it in that morning, a full fortnight late.

'What's all this about you giving up your extra-curricular activities? You've always managed fine before.'

'I've got a lot more work now.'

Mum joined in the attack. 'Is the difference this boy? Because if he's disrupting your work, Cass, it's maybe not such a good idea.'

'Oh God! Why can't you keep your nose out! Nothing is happening! He's just a friend!'

'What boy?' Dad again. 'Why are you over-reacting, if he's just a friend? Who is he, anyway?'

It was one thing for Mum to ask questions; Dad butting in was completely, outrageously unacceptable.

'None of your business! I'm not having some secret affair, like you did!'

'Look, Cass, you can't speak to me like that. I'm still your father. I've got the right to interfere if you're messing up your school work, mixing with the wrong sort.'

'You don't know anything about him!' Mum tried to take my hand, but I snatched it away.

'Darling, I'm sure he's a very nice boy. Maybe you could bring him over for dinner one day?'

'He is not my boyfriend! You don't need to meet him!'

Ben came downstairs. He refused to have a babysitter – said he was too old – so when we were all out he was under strict instructions to stay in his room.

He looked alarmed when he saw us all sitting there. 'What's the shouting about? Why's Dad here? Is Cass in trouble?'

Dad ruffled his hair. 'How's it going, kid?'

'Bad, but not as bad as it was before half-term.' Typical Ben. 'How's Annabel?'

Mum's turn to wince. I frowned at Ben. 'Go away.'

'Why?'

'Because Mum and Dad are telling me off.'

'Why?'

'Because I'm not living up to their high standards.'

'Did they find out?' he asked, all wide eyes and innocence.

I froze. Had Will said something to Ben? Had he seen us?

It just wasn't possible to keep a look out all the time; we tended to get a bit distracted.

'Find out what, darling?' asked Mum.

'Shut up, Ben!'

But Ben didn't hear me.

'About Aidan. Cass found her other brother.'

25: AIDAN

Ellie-Mae runs her hands through my hair. Her fingernails scratch my skin as she massages my scalp. It's giving me a headache.

It's model night at the salon, and I came to see Mum, but she's not here. According to Ellie-Mae, Mum hasn't quit three weeks ago.

'I'd have thought you'd know,' she says, letting her finger tickle my neck. 'She wanted more time with her kids.'

'She didn't tell me.'

Ellie-Mae starts washing my hair, rubbing the shampoo into my scalp incredibly slowly. 'Dad wasn't too happy. She left us short-staffed. That's why he's moved me off reception. I don't like washing hair, it plays havoc with my acrylics.'

'Your what?'

'My nails.'

She rinses the shampoo off, wraps a towel round my head. She lets her hand brush my ear.

'Ellie-Mae,' I say, 'I don't suppose you could do me a big favour?'

'Of course!' She bats her eyelashes at me.

'I don't suppose you've got my mum's address?'

'Don't you have it? Can't you ring her?'

'I lost my phone. All my contacts wiped.'

She buys it.

'I might have it in the system . . .'

'I'd be very grateful.' I smile my best smile.

When I'm finished with the haircut and the photo, she slides a piece of paper into my pocket. Without looking, I know it'll have her number on it, as well as Mum's address.

'Ellie-Mae, you're a star,' I tell her.

'What's my reward?'

'I owe you a drink,' I tell her. She beams and I breathe, and I'm out of there.

I'll never go back.

I divert via Rich's bedsit and have a quick drink while he looks up Mum's address on his phone. 'It's not far,' he says, showing me the map. 'Just here, then here. Look. Number twenty-four.'

I drain my beer bottle. 'I'm going round there now. She's got to be in, with the kids and all.'

Rich looks dubious. 'Is that a good idea? Why not ring her or write her a note, or something? I'll help.'

'I've got to see her. She would've told them at the salon not to give me her address if she really didn't want me.'

'Yes, but, Aidan, she threw you out. And what about her old man?'

My throat tightens. My fists clench. 'That was years ago. I was eleven, for Christ's sake. It'll be OK now.'

'Why do you have to go round there? Look, Aidan, let me go for you. I can talk to her, arrange something for you. On neutral ground, like. I mean, she never minded you turning up at the salon, did she?'

'She won't mind me turning up at her house. Not when she hears what I've got to tell her.'

'You're going to tell her about Cass?'

I open another beer. 'Too right I am. She's going to be made up. All those years she didn't know where Cass was, how she was, and now I've found her.'

'Yeah, but what about Cass? Does she want your mum knowing about her?'

'Holly wants to have a tea party. Introduce everyone. It's a crap idea, I know. But it might work. Holly thinks so.'

Rich sighs. 'I don't want you getting hurt, Aidan.'

I throw a pillow at him. 'You big girl. I can take care of myself.'

I finish the beer. It's my third or fourth. I'm perfectly prepared for Mum, head just about clear, nerves nicely numb. Hair newly cut too, clean and shiny. I'll just go round there and knock on the door and say ...

'Rich, why don't you come with me?'

'OK. And if it doesn't go well, we can go for a drink.'

'Yes.'

We get slightly lost on the way so it's forty minutes before we get to Mum's house. It's a semi with a Ford Fiesta parked on the front drive. Just the one car – I hope that means she's not with her bloke, Keith, any more. I kind of forgot about Keith when I decided to come over to Mum's. I've blotted him out of my mind since he threatened to kill me.

Rich rings the doorbell. I bounce on the balls of my feet, getting ready to run if I need to. We notice too late that the curtains are drawn and none of the lights seem to be on.

Someone fumbles with a latch. The door creaks open a crack.

I smile. 'Hey, Mum!'

She's wearing her dressing gown. She's got slippers on. 'What the hell, Aidan?' she hisses, furiously. 'What time do you call this? Are you trying to wake the kids up?'

It's only about 10 p.m. She's making a big fuss about nothing.

'I just thought – I've got some news.'

She opens the door properly. 'What news?'

How many people have mothers who hate them like mine hates me? Luckily, Rich's parents were even more useless than mine and, besides, they're dead. Actually, my dad's dead, too. But I never knew him, and Rich was ten when he lost his mum and dad to a batch of bad heroin. It didn't really bother him much, because he was living with his Nan. When she had a heart attack a year later, that was when he got dumped in care.

'Can't we come in?' says Rich. 'It's kind of cold out here.'

She gives him the glimmer of a smile. 'Hey, Rich,' she says. 'I like your hair.'

Typical that she mentions Rich's stupid red hair, but doesn't notice that I've just had mine cut. She pecks him on the cheek. I get a quick kiss, too. Her lips are dry and cold.

'You're looking well,' he tells her. I keep quiet. She's looking rubbish. She's got no make-up on and her roots need retouching.

She leads us into their front room. Massive flat-screen telly, two black leather sofas, shiny laminate floor, a smoky glass coffee table. She's done well for herself.

She folds her arms. 'Lucky for you, Keith's out tonight,' she says.

So she is still with him.

I look around the room. Everything is sparkling clean. There's a huge picture on the wall, one of those photographs printed on canvas. Their kids. Hers and Keith's. Louis, the boy, must be eight or nine now. Scarlett, the girl, is maybe five. I can't bear to look at it. There's a black leather sofa right underneath and I sit down, so there's no danger that I'll see it. Rich sits down next to me, and Mum sits opposite us. She doesn't offer us a drink or nothing.

'How's Keith?' I ask. 'Still in the same business?' When I knew him, Keith was running a nightclub in Dagenham. I'd liked it, because he wasn't around that much.

'Yes,' she says. 'He's got a few clubs now. He's doing OK. Is that why you're here, Aidan? Looking for money?'

'I'm not looking for money,' I say, 'because I've got a job. And if I was looking for money, I wouldn't be asking Keith for it.'

'Don't get aggressive with me,' she says, though I didn't even raise my voice. 'What's the problem, then? In trouble with the police?'

'I've come to tell you something,' I say. 'Something that I think will make you happy. If you're capable of being happy, that is, you sour-faced bitch.'

'Aidan—' says Rich, but I wave my hand to shut him up.

'You always have to dig at me, don't you? You always have

to make out it's my fault. You never think that you abandoned me when I was six and then, when you thought you were finally ready to be a mum, you just couldn't hack it. If I'm screwed up, it's all down to you. It's all your fault. What happened to Louis, it's down to you.'

'Get out!' she says, her voice shrill with fury. 'Get out!'

'Mummy!'

The little girl's voice from the door shocks us. We all sit there, staring as she runs across the room and dives into Mum's lap.

Mum hugs her. 'It's OK, Scar. Did you have a bad dream?'

She's got Cass's red hair this Scarlett – she's well-named, actually – and Keith's brown eyes. She's peeking a look at me, and I have a brainwave. I dig in my backpack.

'Hey, Scarlett,' I say. 'I've got something for you.' I hold out a lollipop. I keep them on me for Finn's worst meltdowns.

Scarlett reaches over and grabs it. 'Thank you,' she says.

'She's brushed her teeth,' says Mum. 'Give it to me, Scar, and you can have it tomorrow.'

'It's sugar-free,' I tell her. Holly's very fussy about Finn's teeth. Scarlett shakes her red curls and says, 'I keep it safe' and I'm hit by a memory of Cass at around the same age, Cass hugging her teddy and singing and asking me for a story. I'd just started learning to read at school, and I used to remember books off by heart to tell them to her. There was a nice lady at school and she helped me with my reading. I could read then. I wasn't stupid, or confused, or dyslexic, or whatever happened to me later.

I blink. I'm going to have to be careful or the memories will set me off.

'What's your name?' asks Scarlett, and Mum says, 'Never you mind. He's going soon. Get back to bed now, darling.'

'She's got a right to know,' I say. 'I'm called Aidan.'

'Not now,' says Mum.

'I want a story,' says Scarlett, and again I remember Cass.

Mum kisses Scarlett's head. 'It's late now. Off you go.'

'Mum,' I say, as soon as Scarlett's out of the room. 'Mum, I'm sorry. I didn't mean to lose my temper. I just came to tell you something.'

But Mum had spotted Finn's baby wipes and stuff in my bag when I opened it.

'Aidan, what was that stuff in your bag? You've got a kid?'

'No,' I say. 'Leave it, Mum.'

'What do you want then?'

'Well, it's just . . . it's Cass. I've found her.'

Mum's face is a picture. Her cheeks are puffed out and if her eyebrows went any higher, they'd be hovering in mid-air above her head.

'What do you mean, you've found her?'

'Aidan found her,' says Rich. 'On Facebook. It's definitely her. She looks just like your Scarlett.'

'I've been in touch with her and met her and she wants to meet you,' I say, all in a rush, before Rich can tell any more of my story.

Mum's eyes are full of tears. 'Aidan? I can see Cass again? Oh, Aidan, you darling, darling boy.'

My mum hasn't said anything like that to me since I was eleven. Her birthday, actually. Keith had bought her some bubble bath and told her it was her present from me, and she'd made a big fuss of me when she'd opened it. I'd loved it. I remember thinking I needed to save and plan for her next birthday.

Three days later, she called social services and asked them to take me back.

And now, it's like I'm naked and shivering, and she's wrapped me in a blanket, a soft, warm blanket, the sort you could sleep in for ever.

'She's great, Cass,' I say. 'She's clever and she's pretty and she's doing really well at school.'

'Oh, Aidan,' says Mum. 'I'm so sorry – I didn't realise that was why you came. Thank you, Aidan. Thank you.'

None of us hear the key in the lock. None of us notice the door opening.

So it's a total shock when a bald, stocky guy – Mum's Keith, same as ever – grabs my shirt, sticks his face in mine and yells, 'What the hell are you doing here? I told you to keep away from my family!'

26: CASS

Mum said she was going to ban me from using Facebook.

'How are you going to police that?' I asked. 'Going to take my laptop, too? Because if so, I might as well give up on A levels right now.'

'I'll change the internet code.'

I snorted. She had to ask me for help whenever there was any problem with the router.

'I'm going to report him – Aidan – to Facebook. Surely there's a law against contacting minors on the internet.'

'I bet there isn't.'

'There should be.'

'Give me your phone, Cass,' said Dad. 'I don't think we can trust you with it.'

I kept a firm grip on it.

'I want to see any messages he's sent you,' said Dad. 'I want you to delete his contact details from your phone and your computer.'

'Who are you – Stalin? I'm nearly seventeen years old. This is completely ridiculous!'

'Give it to me!'

'No!'

Mum wiped away a tear. 'When you're eighteen, we can't stop you finding out about your birth parents, even being in touch. But then it'd be done properly. With support. You'd have counselling, and a social worker to help you through the process.'

'I don't need counselling! I don't need a social worker! I like Aidan, and it's good to be in touch with him, and I don't understand why you kept us apart all these years.'

'At least you haven't met him,' said Dad, grimly.

'I have met him!'

Collective gasp.

'You've met him? How irresponsible! You met someone who contacted you over the internet! Cass! Don't you realise how dangerous that could be? What were you thinking?'

'I took a friend with me so I was perfectly safe. I met him in a public place. We had a coffee together. He's my brother! I can't believe you're both being so horrible!'

Dad thundered as though he were back in the House of Commons. 'You took a friend with you? A friend knows about this? Which friend? The boyfriend?'

'He's not a boyfriend!'

'Grace? Megan? How many people know about this?'

'Oh, that's so typical of you! You only care about what other people think!'

'We care about your welfare!'

'If you really cared about that then you wouldn't be selling my home! You wouldn't have split up!'

'Cass! That's completely unfair!'

'Oh, no, it isn't!' *Bang, slam,* I ran up to my bedroom.

Ben was curled up on my bed, hands over his ears, tears pouring down his face.

'Oh, Ben! Don't cry!'

'It was all my fault! I thought you'd told them!'

'I shouldn't have made you keep a secret. I'm sorry, Ben.' I flung my arms around him, gave him a big hug.

'You're so angry all the time, Cass.'

I was angry. I had every right to be angry. I loved Ben, but right then I wanted to let myself be furious, not worrying about him.

'Ben, go to bed. It's late.'

'Will you stop shouting?'

'In a bit. But it's not your fault.'

Mum and Dad hadn't changed their stance when I went back into the kitchen. Dad was on the phone explaining to Annabel that he wouldn't make it back to London that night; Mum was on the internet, trying to look up how to ban me from Facebook.

Dad had cracked open a bottle of red wine. I hoped he'd get done for drink driving.

'Has Aidan asked you for money, Cass?'

Outrageous.

'No, he hasn't. What do you think of him? He's got a job, actually. He works in a shop.'

'Maybe we should call the adoption society ... the social workers ...' suggested Mum.

'No way on earth am I allowing social workers anywhere near my daughter,' said Dad. Just in case anyone thought that I was his priority, he added, 'Can you imagine if the press got hold of it?'

'Cass ... Aidan wouldn't go to the papers, would he?' Mum's face was pale, her voice shaky.

'To say what?'

'Of course he won't.' Dad's frown was ferocious.

'What's he like now?' asked Mum. 'He was such a beautiful child.'

'Why are you scared of him going to the press? What would he talk to them about?'

'He might exploit you ... his knowledge of you ... your family background. It wasn't very happy,' said Dad.

I gazed at him. He was hiding something.

'What are you scared of?'

'I met your mother,' said Mum. 'Just the two of us. She was very clear that it was the best thing for you to be adopted. It was very selfless of her. She accepted that she couldn't look after you, that she needed to get her life together. She trusted us to give you a good home. And we did ... we did ...'

Why was she crying? Dad put his arm around her. 'Don't blame yourself, Susie.'

'Don't blame yourself for what?' My voice was shrill and scared.

Dad cleared his throat. 'Cass, obviously we've kept from you some of the details of your life before we adopted you. It wouldn't have been appropriate to share them with you; we didn't want to burden you with everything. But perhaps now it's time for you to know the full facts. We were going to wait until you were eighteen, ideally until after your A levels, but it's clearly now more urgent.'

'Why is Mum crying? Why shouldn't she blame herself?'

'Well, of course the adoption process was quite drawn out, and we had to give you and Aidan time to get used to the idea that you wouldn't be living together any more. Time to say goodbye.'

'That's not true, Oliver,' said Mum. 'We owe it to Cass to tell her what happened.'

'What? What happened?'

Mum wiped her eyes, blew her nose.

'We were going to adopt both of you. You both came to live with us. But Aidan's behaviour was so challenging that we couldn't cope. We had to make the decision. It was so diffi-cult—'

People talk about out-of-body experiences: when they feel their soul leave their body and hover over it, watching them-selves from above. I swear I had that then. I was watching from a long way away, three people sitting at a kitchen table, talking about something so terrible, so dreadful, so unforgivable ...

'You gave him back?'

27: CASS

It reminded me of hearing the news that Grandad had died (a heart attack, very sudden, Christmas Eve when I was eight). All sad faces and hushed voices. And me, unable to believe what I'd just been told, numb and cold and angry.

'How can you even do that? Hand back a child when you've said you'd adopt him?'

Dad's voice was measured, professional, unemotional. It made me want to scream. 'It was quite early on in the process. We realised that Aidan had complex needs that couldn't be met in our family. The social workers agreed that they should find a family of his own.'

'That's ... that's disgusting. You separated us. I was all he had.'

'We tried so hard, darling. But he hated us. He didn't want to be part of our family.'

'He was only six!'

'Let me explain, Susie,' said Dad in his best persuasive

politician's voice. 'Cass, I believe in adoption. I've been pushing for it to be available to more children, at a younger age. To speed up the system, find families for children who desperately need them. You know that. It's one of the ironies of this whole situation that I've had to move off my family brief.'

'This whole situation!' I exclaimed, but Mum said, 'Not now, Cass. We need you to understand what happened.'

'It's probably the most important thing that we as a government can do. Saving children from neglect and abuse. Changing the balance in favour of the children's right to a decent home, not a parent's right to mistreat their children.'

'Dad, I don't need a speech. I want to know about Aidan.'

'He didn't want to be adopted by us, that's what it came down to. He constantly tried to disrupt our attempts to bond with either of you. He'd pinch you if he thought you were having a happy time with us. Kick you under the table. We'd try and give you equal attention, one-to-one time, but he'd make sure he got in the way if Mum tried to read you a story, or have a cuddle. I've never seen a kid so cold, so calculating, so determined to be completely unlovable.'

'Oh, Oliver, that's so harsh,' said Mum. 'We weren't enough for him, Cass. He needed so much love, so much reassurance … We let him down. We couldn't reach him.'

'You say that, Susie, but some children have just been damaged too much. I honestly believe that there is nothing more we could have done for Aidan.'

I think about Aidan, how he kisses Holly when he thinks no one's looking, how he cuddles Finn.

'He's not like that! He's so happy to see me again!'

'Can't you see, Cass? He's doing it again. He's trying to create a rift between you and us.'

'He must have missed you,' said Mum, but even she didn't sound very sure.

'Do you remember that day out, Susie? That day we realised?'

'We asked the social workers, and they suggested giving him more attention,' said Mum. 'So, one day, we asked Granny and Kate to look after you. You were so open to new people that you'd go to anyone. Actually, we worried about that. We wondered if you could form close relationships, or if everything was superficial.'

'Of course I can!'

'Of course you can. It was just a worry then. Look at you with all your friends. Anyway, we spent the day with Aidan. It was wonderful. He seemed much happier, better behaved. We took him to the playground, read stories to him, just had a normal, nice day. We felt like his real parents, began to see how it could be. And then when I put him to bed he said, "Can I go home now?"'

'He must have missed his mum.'

'He hadn't lived with her for years. She abandoned both of you. First with her mother, and then you went into care. She stayed with a man who beat her up rather than look after her children. It's a hard thing to believe, I know, but she made that choice. She gave you up because she couldn't leave him.'

I felt sick. 'My father?'

Dad shook his head. 'I'm sorry, Cass. We kept the details from you. Should we have told you? He was a very troubled man. He was violent, alcoholic … she left him eventually, but too late to keep her children. As far as I know, your father's been in and out of prison. We wanted to shelter you … we thought we'd wait until you were an adult … '

'I was four! I must have had memories!'

'You had bad dreams sometimes, but you settled so well with us. Especially when Aidan had gone – you hardly seemed to miss him at all. We thought it was better to dwell on the present and the future as you'd gone through so much pain in the past.'

How could I have forgotten Aidan so easily? There must be something wrong with me. I really was the Ice Queen. Right down to my frozen heart.

'Thank you for telling me,' I said. 'And don't worry about me and my work. It's just been a bit of a blip. I'm right back on track.'

Dad sighs. 'Cass, I can't let you go on seeing Aidan like this. We have no idea about his life … his state of mind … anything … '

'I'm nearly seventeen. In just over a year I'll legally be an adult. You won't be able to stop me.'

'Cass—'

'He's my brother. Just as much as Ben is. More, actually.'

Dad's face changed. He wasn't Oliver Montgomery, suave star of the government front bench. He was just a tired, middle-aged man, with lines on his forehead and bags under his eyes.

'Cass, my darling, your birth family, they have a claim to you, but they can't possibly love you more than we do. I sometimes think that being your father is my greatest achievement. We took on a little girl – a bright, beautiful little girl – who was being neglected and exposed to violence and all sorts of other horrors – real horrors, Cass – and we gave her the chance to turn into someone so wonderful, so impressive ... Please never, ever feel that Ben isn't your real brother, that we're not your real parents. It's just not true.'

Unworthy, that's how I felt. Fraudulent. And resentful that he presented his love in terms of success and achievement. What if I'd failed at being his daughter? Would I have been sent away like Aidan?

'I actually hate your birth parents,' said Dad. 'It's politically incorrect, I know –nowadays we have to understand and not condemn – but when I think about them, how they failed to care for you properly, put their own selfish needs first, I want to string them up.'

'Oliver, they're people with difficult lives, they have their own stories.' Mum put her hand over mine. I wanted to shrug her off, but I didn't have the energy. 'I met your mother, Cass. She genuinely wanted to do the best for her children.'

I pulled my hand away. 'She trusted you, and you let her down!'

Dad sighed, ran his fingers through his hair.

'It was you or him, Cass. Or let the whole thing break down. What would you have done?'

28: AIDAN

'Aidan? Aidan! Wake up!'

My head hurts. In fact, every bit of my body hurts. My eyes
are so crusty that for a moment I think they're full of superglue
and they're never going to open. My mouth's dry, my tongue
is as furry as Finn's favourite toy rabbit, and my stomach is
churning like a washing machine.

I made it home, but wasn't sharp enough to unlock the
door: I spent the night propped up against the sign Clive has
on the pavement. 'SALVAGE' it says. I'm beyond saving,
though. I'm damp, I smell, I disgust myself, so God knows
what Holly and Finn think.

'What's happened to Aidy?' says Finn, and I start crying again.

'Let's go inside,' Holly says. 'Come on, Aidan. Let's go
inside. Before Uncle Clive gets here.'

We go up to the flat. Finn's still staring at me, like I'm an
alien or something. Like he doesn't know me. I have to turn
my back on him because it hurts to look at his face.

I start babbling. 'I'm sorry ... really sorry ... I just had a few ... it was late ...' Holly's face is stony, though. There's no point. 'I know, I've totally screwed up. I'll go. I'm sorry.'

'Get yourself showered,' she says, pushing me towards the bathroom, 'and then we'll talk.'

The shower is good. Shaving is better. I wish I could shave away all the layers of things that I want to forget. The haircut is sharp. But the face that looks back at me from the mirror is nothing like the one in the photograph yesterday. There are bags under my eyes, a grey-green tinge to my skin, a split lip, a few bruises. No permanent damage.

When I come out of the bathroom, Finn and Holly aren't there. She must have taken him to the child minder. I'd better start packing. She won't want me to stay. You don't get too many chances once you screw up, and I'm always screwing up with Holly, I'm always getting it wrong, and now ... I'm trying not to panic. I'm trying not to remember all the other places I've moved on from. It's just that this was the best, this was home, this was ... I probably won't have a job any more ...

I sit down on the floor and take deep breaths and try not to panic too much. I'm eighteen. I ought to be able to take knockbacks, I'm certainly used to it. I grind my fists into my mouth and concentrate on a happy memory. The day after Holly and I got together and I went and got the word 'Hope' tattooed on my neck, because it was half of Holly's name all wrapped up in something bigger, something I hadn't had much of. She'd loved that.

But that meant without Holly there was no hope.

I'm so wrapped up in my own misery that I don't hear her come back.

'Hey.' Her hand brushes my cheek. 'Hey, Aidan.'

'Holly, I'm so sorry, Holly, I'm going, I won't stay, I'm sorry ... truly I am ... Can I just stay to say goodbye to Finn? Because people say it's better for the kids if they don't say goodbye, but it isn't, it's worse. Believe me, I know.'

'I'll make you a coffee,' she says. 'Come and talk to me.'

It takes some persuading to get me to sit down and drink her coffee, because I don't even want to look her in the eye. I know I've screwed up once too often and I wish that Finn hadn't seen me like that. Lying outside the shop like an old tramp. But she says I owe her an explanation, and I suppose she's right. So I plunge right in.

'I had to have a drink,' I say. 'Something happened, and I was upset and I needed a drink.'

'Did you get beaten up before or after the drink?'

I shrug. 'I don't know. I'd had a few.'

'Aidan, tell me the whole story. Please. I love you, Aidan. If you keep things from me then I can't help you. I don't want you to leave. I love you.'

Holly's too loving for her own good. If I were her, I'd throw me out. But I'm so lucky to have her. I can't tell her the whole story. I can't lose her.

'I went to see my mum. I wanted to tell her about Cass. It went OK until her boyfriend came in. He doesn't like me, and he went mental. It was kind of upsetting so I needed a drink. I had a few drinks. I tried to get home – I did get home – but I must've been more drunk than I realised. I don't remember much what happened after that. I'm sorry.'

If I had £1 for every time I'd apologised to Holly then I could buy us a weekend at a hotel by the seaside. It's a shame it doesn't work like that.

'He hit you? Your mum's boyfriend?'

'He shouted at me. Threw me out. He hates me. I didn't know he'd be there.'

'You should phone the police!' She lowers her voice, takes my hand. 'Aidan, love, did he beat you up when you were a kid? Was that why you went back into care?'

I hate it when she goes into social-worker mode. Like I can explain everything, just like that. Like it's all down to one bad person or one bad thing, when there's so much to explain that it'd take a book. A Life Book. I should have asked Mum if she still had mine.

'He just doesn't like me. He never beat me up. I just drank too much and ... I dunno. Stuff happened.'

Keith was all right before it happened. Really tried to welcome me into the family. It wasn't his fault that I missed Jim and Betty so much. Not his fault what happened to Louis neither. And I can't really blame him for hating me. If someone did to Finn what I did to Louis ...

'Why doesn't he like you?' she says, and just for a moment I think about spitting it out. Telling her what happened. This could be the moment.

But then I'd lose everything. Every last bit of hope.

'He's just a nutter.'

'Aidan, you need to stop drinking. You don't want to let it become a problem.'

'You drink, too,' I point out.

'I have the occasional glass of wine! I don't go out on benders and stay out all night, or pass out on the pavement!

I don't get into fights that I can't even remember and scare Finn by looking like a corpse on the doorstep.'

'Your life wasn't as shit as mine,' I say.

It sounds pathetic even to me. Holly ignores it.

'They have an alcohol counsellor at the practice. He's meant to be very good. There's a long waiting list but I could push you to the top. There have to be some perks to working there.'

I shrugged. 'OK, if you want.'

I've seen counsellors before, at school mostly. I liked it. I got to miss lessons and I had someone listening to me. They'd ask me about how things were and I'd tell them all the gossip – Denise's pregnancy, Neil up in court, Rich trying to top himself – and they'd tut and sigh and say, 'But what about *you*, Aidan, what's happening with *you*?'

I'd been drinking forever: I learned really young that if you're going to have to do stuff you don't want to do, it's easier to be drunk. It relaxes you. You might even start feeling that you do want to do it.

Of course, sometimes you don't know what's going to happen beforehand and you have to get drunk afterwards to block it out of your memory. That's not so good. And you've got to be old enough to take the alcohol. You've got to be twelve at least.

It's not a good way to grow up. You need someone bigger and stronger than you to keep you safe. I never had that, and I couldn't do it for Cass or Rich, but I want to be there for Finn. So if Holly thinks some counsellor can help, well, I'll try it. I'm doubtful, but I'll do anything she wants.

'I wish you'd trust me, Aidan. I wish you'd tell me all the bad stuff that happened to you in the past. I think it would help.'

'There's nothing to tell,' I say. 'I'm just a screw-up. I don't know why you put up with me.'

'Because I know that's not true,' she says. 'So, you told your mum about Cass?'

'Yes. She was happy. She wants to meet her.'

'Did you suggest meeting here? So I could meet her, too?'

I'm shaking with nerves just thinking about it. I'm going to have to trust Mum, that she'll give me a chance, that she won't tell Holly or Cass what happened, that she'll let it lie, that she'll be so grateful to me that finally, finally, she'll forgive me.

Forgive and forget.

'She's up for it. We just have to set a date.'

29: CASS

On the bus the next morning Will texted me:

- *I've got an indoor location for this afternoon. Are you interested and available after school?*
- *Where?*
- *I'll meet you round the back of Tesco*
- *OK*
- *You're not very enthusiastic. Are you OK?*
- *I'm fine*
- *Will you be able to stay for long?*
- *Yes*
- *Good*

I hardly glanced at him when he got off, him and his noisy group of friends. As the bus drove off, though, I did notice that he was walking with the pretty, blonde girl, stooping over to talk to her. Was his arm around her? The bus was too fast to be sure.

Well, so what if he was seeing someone else? We weren't

going out. We were just experimenting. She'd be good cover. I was sure Grace would tell me all about her sooner or later.

Will was waiting for me after school, leaning up against the back wall of the supermarket, reading a paperback. He was wearing an oversized red jumper and skinny jeans, with red Converses. I stood for a moment, just enjoying the view. I didn't know what was going on between Will and me, and I didn't really care. I just liked looking at him, anticipating the moment when we'd carry on with our experiments. And it gave me a buzz, thinking of all the people on the other side of the wall, doing their shopping, while we were meeting in secret just yards away. People we knew. People who'd be interested.

He looked up from his book. 'Hey,' he said. 'How long have you been standing there?'

'I just got here. What are you reading?'

He showed me. *Anna Karenina.*

'You're just a walking cliché,' I told him.

'You should read it.' He flipped to the first page. '"Happy families are all alike; every unhappy family is unhappy in its own way."'

'Ha ha, very funny.'

'I didn't mean it like that. You know I wouldn't make fun of you.'

'Good,' I said.

'You look quite different,' he said. 'I don't know what to make of it.'

Mum hadn't seen me that morning, which was why I'd got away with wearing a super-short skirt that had been lurking at the back of my wardrobe since I was twelve. Then, it had come down past my knee and was actually too big. Now, I could still wriggle it over my hips, and it was just about long enough to be decent. I'd worn it all prepared for another screaming row – they seemed to think I was a tart, I might as well dress like one – but Dad's car had gone in the morning and Mum had left a note on the table saying she'd gone to early morning Pilates.

I was beginning to realise that they were both quite selfish.

I'd got quite a few comments at school, as well. Miss Graham had told me that my skirt was too short and too tight and she didn't want to see me wearing it to school again. 'I'm disappointed in you, Cass.'

Grace told me she loved the tight black cardigan, and it'd be even better with a few buttons undone. 'You're sure to get his attention like that,' she said. 'Your make-up's gorgeous, too. Are you coming to Starbucks after school?'

'No,' I told her. 'I've got some important research to do.'

'I thought I'd change my style a bit,' I told Will, now. 'You told me I was boring.'

'I was talking about your colour palette,' he said, 'but hey, I'm not complaining.'

'Where are we going then?'

'My sister's flat. She's away on holiday and I'm feeding the cats and watering the plants.'

A whole flat to ourselves, with no chance of anyone seeing us. This was taking experimentation to new and dangerous levels.

Excellent.

My phone pinged with a new text. Dad had agreed in the

end that he couldn't confiscate it, that it would cause Mum too much hassle, worrying about where I was, plus I could easily buy myself a cheap pay-as-you go. A small victory. But they were still insisting that they had to meet Aidan themselves, and know about any plans to meet my birth parents.

Why couldn't they mind their own business?

The text was from Mum, wondering why I wasn't home yet.

After-school meeting for prefects. I texted.

When will you be back? I need to talk to you.

Not until late. Duke of Edinburgh volunteering.

Can't you drop it for once?

Just thinking about my personal statement. Don't you want me to go to Oxford?

'Finished?'

'Oh, sorry, Will. Just getting rid of my mum. I bet your parents don't bug you like mine do.'

'Oldest child syndrome. They used to bug my eldest sister all the time. Layla fought all the battles. Then Cleo and Hattie fought them all over again. By the time I got to puberty they were exhausted.'

'I wish someone had done that for me,' I said. Of course, that's what Aidan should have done. He could have been my older brother all my life. Everything would have been different.

'Cass! What did I say?' Will's arms were around me. I gulped, turned a sob into a laugh.

'Nothing – what are you doing? I'm fine.'

'You looked like someone had died – I'm sorry. I got it wrong. Are you coming to visit the cats, then?'

'Of course. It's a difficult job, feeding cats. You need some help.'

Will's sister's flat was in a small modern block, just off the high street. We walked quickly, avoiding the main road, hoping no one would spot us. The entrance hall smelled of furniture polish and bleach.

We climbed the stairs to the second floor. 'Here we go,' said Will. He opened the door. 'Alone at last. Apart from Lily and Barney, that is. Cleo got them from the cat shelter. Do you like cats?'

'I don't mind cats.'

'You're like a cat. Everything's on your terms. I'm much more of a dog.'

'You said it.'

Barney was a sleepy grey tabby, curled up on a cushion; Lily was a black and white bundle of nerves, who took a swipe at Will when he tried to stroke her. He fed them and refilled their water bowl while I prowled around the flat.

It was the opposite of Dad's bland pied-à-terre in London. It was full of colour: a bright pink shawl slung over a purple sofa; a mirror framed with tiny turquoise and gold mosaic tiles; a picture of skeletons dancing in a graveyard, grinning happily under Mexican sombreros. Photos everywhere, a whole wall of them, pinned onto cork tiles, some old family pictures in frames on the wall. One man – serious in a single-breasted suit – looked a lot like a retro-version of Will, except he was scowling into the camera. And I found lots of pictures of Will himself, always smiling, always happy, always surrounded by admiring women, it seemed. I assumed they were sisters, aunties, his mum, but one was definitely Ruby and that blonde girl was there too.

Will's sister Cleo liked candles – they were everywhere, in

various stages of meltdown. She had a jelly bean dispenser on her coffee table and a packet of Chi tea (whatever that was) on the kitchen top. She'd stuck postcards onto her fridge from Mumbai, Scunthorpe, Kingston, Jamaica.

She'd left Will a note, scrawled in red crayon on the bottom of a credit card bill:

Hey bro!

Thanks for feeding my babies! Lily will be feeling a bit needy so make sure you give her a big cuddle and make a fuss of her.

Help yourself to anything in the fridge and there's ice cream in the freezer if you want it.

No parties! Good luck with you-know-what!

Love you Cleo xxxxxx

Will was looking over my shoulder. 'Ah, ice cream. Cleo's good with the essentials. Do you want some?'

I only wanted him. 'No thanks,' I said.

He leant in towards me. 'It's different being here on our own, isn't it? Do you like it?'

'I don't know yet.'

But I did know. I just didn't want to tell him how much I liked it there, how different it felt to home, which wasn't really home any more; how the bright colours made me think of Aidan and Holly, young and happy and free and in love.

Just for a minute, I imagined being Will's real girlfriend. Meeting his sisters. Hanging out with his friends. Laughing and kissing and not worrying about gossips and standards and grades.

I wanted it so much that I couldn't risk messing it up.

He kissed me, light, teasing, promising. 'What do you think now?'

'Not bad. But I don't think a kitchen is really ideal.'

An hour later, we'd experimented in the kitchen, hallway and the bathroom, which was painted bright pink. I found I liked watching myself kissing Will in the mirrors that covered most of the wall space in it – a patchwork of mirrors – some big, some small, all of them showing us ourselves, entwined, my hair bright against his dark skin.

There was a very comfortable sofa in the living room, and we'd tried sitting on it and now we were lying down. I'd peeled off my cardigan, and he'd kissed all along the top of my camisole. He'd discarded the big jumper too, and our bare arms were skin to skin, sending little shivers of excitement all through me.

I pulled Will down on top of me. Curled my legs around him. Pushed my hand under his T-shirt, so I could feel more of his skin.

'Mmm,' he said. 'Wow. Mmmm.'

My hand went lower.

'Oh my God,' he groaned. We kissed again, harder this time, exploring each other's bodies.

I wondered how many other girls he'd brought back here.

'What's the matter?'

'Nothing.' Suddenly I felt foolish and awkward. Had he realised how much I was hiding from him? How hopeless I'd be at a real, close relationship? Maybe we were just doing this so he could laugh about me with his friends. I bet Ruby hadn't been uptight or weird.

'Something's the matter. You went all tense.' He kissed me again, just where the camisole ended and my bra began. I felt my shoulders hunch. 'What is it? You liked that before.'

'I know. Sorry. I just thought of something. It doesn't matter.'

'Yes, it does. Tell me.'

I wriggled around, so I was lying on top of him. On top of all of him. I kissed him, full on the lips, nudging his hand with the top of my thigh.

He got the message, all right. His hands were inside my camisole. His flies were undone. I could do this. This was fine.

We were ... we could ... we weren't.

'I'm sorry.'

I was mortified. I didn't know why he'd suddenly pulled away from me (was I meant to know? Had I done something wrong?) but I felt stupid and ashamed and angry. I pulled down my camisole, re-adjusted my skirt, moved to the end of the sofa where we weren't touching any more.

'That's OK,' I said, buttoning my cardigan with furious fingers. Barney and Lily were staring at me. I narrowed my eyes at them and they ran away.

'I'm ... it's just ...' For once I couldn't read Will's face. Was he embarrassed, or repulsed, or had he suddenly realised that I liked him much more than he liked me? 'I wasn't really expecting things to go so fast, and I thought we should, you know, at least talk first.'

'Oh, is that what you usually do?'

'You what?'

'When you bring girls here. I'm sorry. I didn't mean to rush you or anything.' I was back behind the comfortable veil of sarcasm.

'No, no, you don't understand—'

'Oh, well, I'm sure Ruby and Daisy understood perfectly.'

He looked at me, head on one side, an annoying smirk on his lips. 'Cass, are you jealous of my ex-girlfriends?'

'Of course not. Why would I be jealous of them? Daisy, she's doing a BTEC in beauty therapy, isn't she? And Ruby's a star at media studies, I hear.'

Will's mouth was a tight line. I'd defeated the smirk. 'Well, of course, we can't all be straight A students, can we?'

'Look, if you're intimidated, then back off.' I remembered that's just what he'd done. 'I mean, good, let's not do this any more. It was a stupid idea.'

'I thought you liked it.'

'You thought wrong.'

'I just thought we should talk about it. Before we ... you know ... stop pretending it was just an experiment.'

'It was just an experiment.'

'Well, I don't want to experiment any more. It's doing my head in. Look, I really like you, and I really fancy you. Can't we go out, you know, properly? I can be your boyfriend and buy you little presents and meet your friends and stuff like that.'

'And then dump me, like Daisy and Ruby and all the rest? I don't think so.'

'Cass ... you're getting it all mixed up ...'

'I'm not mixed up. It's you who's changing the rules.'

'Don't be angry! Why are you angry? I just want to stop sneaking around! I want everyone to know about us! We can drop all this secrecy, this experiment stuff, and be a couple. We'll be great together.'

'I'm not angry,' I lied.

'Why are you being like this, then?'

'I thought you liked what we were doing.'

'I do like it! It's because I like it that I want more – a proper relationship. I hate all the sneaking around, not telling people what's going on.'

'Who defines a proper relationship? The kids in Starbucks? It's none of their business. I don't want people knowing everything about me.'

He was silent. 'You don't want to be seen with me?' He'd lost his usual bounce. His voice was softer, more hesitant. 'You don't think I'm good enough for you?'

'No, don't be so stupid,' I said, but he'd got up, gone over to the window.

'What is it, Cass? I'm not rich enough for you? Or maybe it's because I'm not at the grammar school? It couldn't be the colour of my skin, could it? I'm sure you're much too politically correct for that.'

'It's nothing like that,' I said.

'I saw your face when we bumped into your aunt. You were horrified.'

I didn't have the time or energy to work out what to say. All I knew was that I'd been right. I couldn't get close to anyone. I was abnormal. No wonder my birth parents had given me away.

'I'm going,' I said. 'I can't deal with this now.'

'Cass, stay, please. We can't leave it like this.'

'Oh, can't we?' I said. 'Watch me.'

30: AIDAN

I've got two customers in the shop and I think they're thieves. They're doing the things that shoplifters do: picking up stuff and putting it down; talking in whispers and then breaking apart; one wandering around at the front of the shop, the other at the back.

One's a pretty girl, yellow curls tied back off her face with a scarf. The other is a black guy, dressed in grey trackies and a black hoody. I keep my eye on him when she approaches me to ask about some electronic keyboards we've got in. I know the way it works. One distracts, the other nicks.

Rich and I used to do it all the time.

I answer her questions as quickly as possible. Yes, we can deliver. Yes, there's a guarantee. Yes, even though it's second-hand.

'I'll think about it,' she says. Surprise, surprise.

The bell jangles. Perfect. Fantastic. Just what I need: it's Neil, glaring around him as though it's my fault that I've actually got customers.

He leans into my shoulder. 'Get rid,' he mutters into my ear.

I stand up fast. Just his hot breath on my cheek makes me feel dirty.

'We're closing up now!' I announce, but I can't see them. I just get a glance of her spotty scarf – a red flash – and the door slams. They've abandoned me, without even knowing it.

'Lock the door,' says Neil.

'My boss, Clive, might come back,' I tell him, but he shakes his head.

'Went off an hour ago, didn't he? With a nice empty van. Is he teaching you to drive that van, Aidan? Or is the written test too much for you?'

Bastard. I learned to drive ages ago, Clive paid for lessons, let me practise on the van. I could pass my test just like that if it wasn't for the written bit. I've tried and tried to learn it, but whenever I sit the test, the words start whirling around and I have to stop. It makes me feel sick.

'You got anyone watching you?'

I shake my head. There is CCTV, but it's in the yard. Metal gets a good price, especially copper, so we have to guard it pretty carefully. The walls have spikes and barbed wire. It's not helped keep Neil out though.

I'm breathing hard and my heart is thumping. I'm kind of used to it. I've been scared for so much of my life that the moments of calm are the unusual ones.

'I'm trusting you. You wouldn't lie to me, would you, Aidan?'

I shake my head.

'Remember Bobby? You wouldn't want your little boy looking like him.'

Bobby was a kid at the home, a bit younger than me. Neil and his mates decided to carve the letter 'B' into his forehead. I don't know why, and I don't know what happened to Bobby, and I don't know how they got away with it.

I just know that no one's ever going to do that to Finn.

'You're not going to hurt him,' I tell Neil. I look him in the eye. 'You listen to me – nothing happens to him, OK?'

'Not if you do what you're told.'

Neil locates a dark corner at the back, jerks his head. 'Floorboards,' he says.

I fetch a hammer, prise up the nails, lift the boards up. Neil opens his coat, pulls out a package. I know what it is. A firearm. A weapon. A gun.

'You do it,' says Neil. 'Put it in.'

I don't want to touch it. But I do what I'm told. Now my prints are all over the packaging.

At least he hasn't picked up on Cass. At least he's forgotten about her.

It's as though he can read my mind.

'Striking, that girl you had here the other day. Very striking. All that red hair. Natural, is it?'

'Yes,' I say, and he says, 'I suppose you've checked,' and gives me a nudge and a dirty laugh.

I want to kill him.

'Your girlfriend know you're running around with another girl? Looked like jailbait, too. You're a naughty boy, Aidan.'

'Can we just get on with it?'

'She's a bit posh for you.'

'Can we hurry up? Before Clive gets back?'

'Oh, don't worry about Clive. He's stuck in Colchester.'

'How do you know?'

'He thinks he's gone to pick up a load of copper piping, but when he gets there, he'll find nothing. Serve him right.'

'For what?'

'Oh, nothing. Don't bother your pretty head about it.'

My hand curls into a fist, and then uncurls again. We replace the floorboards, bang in the nails, cover them up with a rug that Clive swears is Indian and worth a fortune if he could only find a buyer.

'That's it,' I say, sucking my finger. 'I've got a splinter.' They won't be here long, will they, Neil? I'm not sure how long I'll be in this job.'

Clive's a great boss. Really understanding. But, just recently, he's been talking about needing someone who can take on more of the driving. 'I'm sorry, lad,' he said the other day. 'If you can't get through the test, then I'll have to consider the situation. I can't carry passengers. And, while I'm at it, you can stop helping yourself to the stock.'

'It was only a rabbit!' I said. 'For Finn. Its ears were singed, I swear.'

'Ask first,' he said. 'And get studying for that test. I can get a girl in to mind the shop – it's your muscle I need. I'm not a young man any more.'

Neil's voice brings me back. 'You going anywhere, Aidan? Not planning anything stupid, are we?'

'Nah. Just this job … it's so boring …'

'Stick with it,' he says. 'I need you here. For a few months, anyway. Agreed?'

'Yeah, well, yeah.'

There's no point in arguing with Neil.

He leaves and I know that I ought to open up the shop again, but I can't. I sink down on an armchair (salvaged from a flooded warehouse, slight water damage) and try and think my way out of this one. I could call the police. I could take the gun out, try and get rid of it. I could persuade Holly to leave London – take her and Finn off to Spain where her dad lives. Maybe he'd help us find jobs, somewhere to live. Maybe Keith would give me money to piss off out of London, out of Mum's life, out of Louis and Scarlett's life for ever.

No. I'm not asking him.

Maybe Cass could lend me money. She must have loads of money.

What am I thinking? I can't ask Cass, and I can't run away from Cass – I've only just found her.

I'm trapped. I'm caught.

I really, really need a drink. If I had any money, I would go to the pub.

I realise that it's kind of ironic that I'm thinking like this, as this morning was my first counselling session.

The counsellor was useless. He talked about his method, which is based on the twelve-step approach used by Alcoholics Anonymous. He said it was proven to work, that millions of people had been helped by it.

'You have to admit that you have a problem,' he said. 'You have to stop blaming other people for it. You have to accept that there is a higher power.'

'I'm not religious,' I say, and he says, 'You don't have to be. Just stop thinking that you are all alone and no one is looking out for you.'

'Is that it?'

'Eventually, you'll need to help other people tackle their addictions, just as I'm going to help you. But first you need to apologise to those people you've hurt.'

I got angry right away.

'What about all the people who hurt me? What about them? I haven't had any apologies from them!'

'This is about you and your actions, Aidan. Not other people's actions, hard as it is to accept.'

'I never hurt anyone!' I said, and he looked at me, but I couldn't meet his eye, so I sat and stared at my trainers, which I'd taken from Clive's shop because he had a whole container full of them – five-hundred shoes – and my old trainers had holes in them.

'Let's work on that next time,' he'd said in the end, after ten minutes of silence.

I really, really want to go to the pub. Clive wouldn't notice, would he, if I just borrowed some money from the till? Just twenty quid. He won't notice.

It's in my pocket before I have time to think.

31: AIDAN

Holly and Finn have made cornflake crispies, lemon drizzle cake, chocolate brownies. 'I think I'm going to do a batch of fairy cakes,' she says, 'just in case they don't like chocolate.'

'But then they've got the lemon cake.'

'I know, but Finn wants to decorate them.'

'Spinders!' says Finn, which I happen to know means those multi-coloured things you put on cakes. Sprinkles, Holly calls them.

I ruffle his hair and say, 'Spinders and cherries, if we've got any left.'

'Aidan, what if she brings her kids? So they can meet their sister.'

'She won't,' I say, and go off to tidy the lounge.

It's a tip. I put Finn's toys back in the toy box, sweep up all the crumbs and hairs and dust from the floor. I chuck out some flowers that have been mouldering in a vase for about a week. I open a window to make it smell fresher. I spray furniture polish on the table and make it shine with a duster.

'You're acting like my gran!' says Holly, carrying in the lemon cake. 'Cleaning every surface.'

'Hang on a minute!' I borrowed a tablecloth from the shop earlier, and it's in my backpack. It's white and lacy, just like one that Betty had. I spread it on the table. 'There!'

'It looks great, Aidan.'

'Shall we sit at the table to eat, or take plates and sit around the room?'

'Shall we just see what people want to do?'

'I want it to be ready, though.'

Betty used to make afternoon tea when her mum and sister came round. She'd set the table, and make sandwiches with no crusts. She cut them in little triangles. I used to help her. The teapot had flowers on it, and a bright pink, knitted tea cosy. She made scones with jam and cream, and we'd all have our own serviette.

'Have we got serviettes? We need them! Shall I go out and buy some?'

'You'll want doilies for the plates next!' Holly's laughing at me.

'No, but really Holly, I think we need serviettes.'

'I'll go and get some,' she says. 'Are you sure your mum won't bring anyone?'

'She won't. Holly, my mum's a bit odd. Don't pay too much attention to what she says.'

'How do you mean?'

'She might say weird stuff. Don't worry about it.'

'I'll go,' she says. 'They'll have serviettes at the corner shop.

You keep an eye on Finn, eh? I left him putting cherries on the fairy cakes.'

I open the door to the kitchen.

'Aidy! Look! Cakes!'

Finn has studded every cake with cherries, crusted them with sprinkles, piled chocolate chips and sugar roses on top.

'More spinders!'

'You've got loads of cherries and sprinkles. Let's put them on a plate.'

He watches me suspiciously as I pick up each cake and lay them out on a plate. The cherries look like massive tumours or boils, scarring the icing.

'Pretty cakes!' says Finn.

'Let's clean you up,' I tell him, getting a wet cloth to wipe his hands and face. But Finn scrambles down from the chair and runs away, laughing like a maniac, wiping his sticky hands on the sofa, clutching at the tablecloth ...

The lemon cake lands *splat* on the floor. A plate follows it, but I dive to catch it mid-air and end up on the floor, clutching the plate to my chest. Finn cackles with delight and gives the cloth another tug.

'Finn! For Christ's sake!' I bellow, as teacups tumble around my ears.

Finn watches open-mouthed as three cups smash onto the fireplace, and he bursts into tears. Good.

'Finn! Look what you've done! Naughty!'

I give him a quick slap on the bum. He needs to know that he can't act like that.

He howls. 'Aidy! I hate you!'

'I hate you too!'

The room is a complete mess. Any minute now Mum could arrive, Cass …

I'm sweating, my breath is coming in little pants. I wanted everything to be perfect and now it's all ruined.

Finn runs out of the room, wailing for Holly. I gather up the smashed china, try and save the lemon cake. But the sticky drizzle hit the rug. The cake is covered with turquoise fuzz, and the rug glitters with sugar. The chocolate crispies have disintegrated. There's a huge chocolate smear on the tablecloth.

The doorbell rings.

Oh Jesus. I don't know what to do. I try and sweep everything up into one big pile, but I accidentally kneel in a chocolate crispie and it looks like I've got dog shit all over my clean jeans.

The bell rings again.

I give up. I lean back against the sofa, stare at the ceiling, put my hands over my ears and pray for Finn to shut up and whoever is at the door to just go away.

Finn screams louder. The bell goes again.

Finn's gone quiet. The bell seems to have stopped. Maybe they've gone away. They've realised that this was a terrible, terrible idea, and they've gone away and left me. Holly and Finn and Cass and Mum.

They've left me alone, like everyone does in the end.

'Oh my God! What happened!' It's Holly's voice.

'Aidy hit me!'

'Finn! Did you make this mess? Aidan? What happened?'

I don't move. 'I didn't hit him,' I say.

'You did! On my bum!'

'Just a smack. He made all this mess on purpose, Holly. It's ruined. You'll have to tell them ... you'll have to ...'

Finn's staring at me. He opens his mouth and starts yelling again. 'My cakes! My spinders!'

'I'm going to put you down for a nap,' says Holly. 'I'll ... I'll leave you to it.'

'Oh, Aidan.'

That's not Holly's voice. Slowly I look towards the door. Holly and Finn have gone. But I'm not on my own.

'What a mess,' says my mum.

She doesn't say it in a nasty way. She sounds sad for me. She can see that I wanted everything to be nice for her, for Cass. I tried. I really tried.

'I wanted it all nice,' I told her. 'Finn messed it up.'

She comes and crouches down next to me, picks up bits of tea cup. 'It's only china, darling. Nothing that can't be replaced. No bones broken.'

I scrape up a mass of cherries and icing.

'Aidan, is he yours? The little boy? Why didn't you tell me?'

I shake my head.

'You've taken him on, though?'

'I've been around since he was a baby.'

Silence. She's thinking.

'You've taken on a lot, sweetheart. Are you sure you're ready?'

'I want to.' It comes out more fiercely than I expected.

'And everything's gone well?'

She's trying, I can tell, really trying not to upset me, to remind me of why things might go badly. She's on her best behaviour. I wish she could always be like this.

'Yes. It has gone well. Ask Holly.' I want to get down on my knees and beg her not to spoil it, not to say anything that would take Finn away from me. 'Mum, this really means a lot – if you wouldn't say anything to Holly, about - you know – '

'It's a big thing that you're asking me.' She pauses, looks round the room. 'You have made it nice here. I'm happy for you. I'm not going to spoil it for you, Aidan. Just make sure that little boy is safe and sound, you hear me?'

I'm so grateful. 'Yes, Mum.'

She pats my shoulder. 'Tell you what, I'll go out and have a fag and you can clear this up and forget it happened.'

I close my eyes. 'Thanks, Mum.'

She's gone.

32: CASS

I was a bit late getting to Aidan and Holly's flat. A whole hour late, in fact. It was incredibly difficult finding excuses to go out: Mum quizzed me the whole time about what I was doing, where I was going, and Dad phoned and texted the whole time about my homework.

In the end, I lied. I told her I was going out with Will, it was none of her business and I'd be back when I felt like it. We had a short, sharp little fight, and I succeeded in distracting her from the truth. But all the way to London on the train I felt like a bully and a traitor.

All Mum ever did was love her family, and one by one we had all betrayed her.

Maybe it was what she deserved. After all, look what she did to Aidan. Told him that he had new parents and then handed him back. I felt physically sick whenever I thought about it. I didn't want to hear their explanations. How could anyone reject a six-year-old boy because he didn't come up to scratch?

And that led me on to thinking about the mother I was about to meet. Why did she hand over her children for adoption? Or were we taken away from her?

I was so wound up when I arrived at Aidan's flat that I felt too nervous to go in. Instead, I stared into the window of the salvage shop. The display was children's toys: dolls lined up in a row, some furry rabbits. A dolls' house. I wondered where the stock came from, why some things ended up here. It all looked fine, good as new. Was there damage that couldn't be seen? Or was it all just surplus to requirements?

'Cass?'

I jumped, and looked round to meet Holly's eyes.

'I'm sorry – I just got here. I was about to ring the bell.'

'I saw you out of the window,' she said. 'You must be on edge – Aidan's been a bag of nerves all morning and I'm not much better. But she seems really nice, your mum. She's very good with Finn.'

I followed Holly up the stairs, thinking again how unlikely a partner she was for Aidan. He's so tall and good looking, laidback and ... well ... young. There was something a bit mumsy about Holly. It might have been her slightly dumpy figure or her minimal make-up, or the way her thin, flat hair was scraped up in a wispy bun. But I thought it was more about her air of anxious concern, as though she was constantly waiting for you to crumble onto her shoulder.

'Judgemental, much, Miss Montgomery?' said Will's voice in my head, and I felt intensely irritated. When would I stop thinking about him? He was making it easy enough – no calls, no texts – at least, there hadn't been any the last time I

checked my phone, which was when I came out of Camden Town underground station.

'Here we are,' said Holly, and opened the door.

Little Finn, building his train track again. Aidan on the floor, helping him. A plate of biscuits on the table – they hadn't gone to much trouble, which was good, because I'd been dreading some sort of formal, sit-down sandwiches and cake affair.

And her. Sitting on the sofa, drinking tea from a mug, which she put down as soon as she saw me, put down on the floor, so she could stand up and walk towards me.

'I'm Janette, darling. Your mum. I couldn't mistake you, you've hardly changed at all. You're the spitting image of my Scarlett, too.'

She was shorter than me, but she wore heels with her black skirt and white blouse. Her hair was a soft honey-blonde, brittle with spray. If she really was my mum, then a lot of work had gone into eliminating the ginger. She had on a lot of eye make-up – smoky, shimmering grey – and candy pink lipstick.

My hand was over my mouth. I made a little sound that wasn't quite formed enough to be a word.

'Here, have a look.'

She passed me her iPhone. Two kids smiled out from the screen. One did look like a younger version of me – not just the marmalade hair, but something about the eyes and nose as well. The other, the boy, had straight brown hair and a round face, and was squinting into the sunshine.

'They're lovely,' I said. My voice was shy, nervous. I didn't sound like myself. My voice was shy – less than, short of, its normal sound.

'They're my second chance,' she said, taking back the

phone. 'What can I say to you? I'm so sorry, darling. I thought I was doing the best thing at the time.'

'I understand,' I said, because I wanted it to be true.

'Come and sit down,' said Holly. 'Cass, would you like tea? A top up, Janette?'

'There are biscuits, too,' said Aidan. 'And there would have been cake ...'

I waited for the '... but the shop didn't have any' or whatever, but he left it at that and went back to Finn's train set. No hug for me. Barely a smile. Had this all been a colossal mistake?

'Here we are then,' said Janette. I couldn't think of her as 'Mum'. 'Here we are. After all these years.' A tear rolled elegantly down her cheek. 'What must you think of me? Abandoning you to strangers.'

'They're not strangers ... I mean, I've had a good life. They've always loved me and everything. It's just now ... things have got difficult. You know. But it was never like that before.'

'What's difficult, darling?'

Aidan must have told her about my dad – or hadn't he?

'My dad ... he's left ... I thought you knew.'

'Aidan didn't say.'

I was absolutely certain she didn't mean to criticise Aidan, but I saw his jaw clench and his shoulders hunch just a little.

'Cass's dad is in the papers,' he told her. 'The politician. You know the one.'

Janette gasped. She was a little odd, I decided. Everything about her felt like she was acting a part.

'Him? The one who's run off with a girl half his age?'

I dug my fingernails into my palm. 'Actually, she is twenty-three and he is fifty so, technically, he is more than twice her age.'

'How could he? The bastard.'

Bizarrely, I felt the need to defend him. 'He fell in love, I suppose. Mum said they hadn't really been happy for ages. And he hasn't run away from us ... from my brother, Ben and me. He's still a totally hands-on parent.'

My phone pinged with a text. My heart leapt for a second – *Will?* – but, no, it was Dad. Right on cue. Asking about my economics worksheet.

Holly handed out mugs of tea. Aidan glowered at his – he must be fussy about how he likes tea. His expression, all pout and crinkled forehead, sparked a distant memory. Aidan with just that frown, kicking a table. Kicking our table. In our kitchen. Scaring me, upsetting me, making me wish he would go away.

Did I ever tell him to go away? Did I reject him along with Mum and Dad?

Janette asked me lots of questions. My school, my exam results, my plans for university. Did I remember before I was adopted? She seemed sad, yet relieved when I said no, I couldn't remember anything at all.

'They were bad times.' She looked around at the flat. 'This is lovely. Aidan, you've fallen on your feet. Holly, I hope he behaves himself, I hope he's a good boy ... a good partner ...'

Holly blinked. 'He's wonderful. He's great.' Her hand rested on Aidan's shoulder. 'Finn and I, we're so lucky to have him.'

Aidan ducked his head down.

'I think he's the lucky one, aren't you, darling?' Janette

seemed like she was about to say something else, but no words came. We sat waiting for a long minute, until Holly passed around the biscuits.

'So your mum, Cass, she's having a hard time then?' Janette's voice was straining to sound sympathetic, but she didn't quite get there.

'She's coping. We're fine.'

'I met her, you know. When they first made the placement.' Janette's voice was husky, as though she was trying so hard to sound posh, say the right thing, that it was giving her a sore throat. 'Right in the middle of my troubles. They said it would help if I met her, it would put my mind at rest. She was lovely, you know. Well, of course, you know. And she did put my mind at rest. Told me how much she loved you already. Told me how clever you were – well, I knew that, didn't I? How you liked living out in the country. Has she been a good mum to you, darling?'

'Yes,' I told her.

'Because she was lying, that was the thing. I believed her and it helped me. But she told me the same about Aidan. That she'd love him too—'

'Shut up.'

Aidan's voice was so angry, so abrupt, that Holly spilt a little bit of tea on the sofa, and Finn asked, 'Why you cross, Aidy?'

'What's the matter, Aidan? Cass must know. She must remember. How did they explain it to you, darling? When they sent your brother back into care?'

I opened my mouth, but Aidan got there first.

'Shut up, Mum. No one needs ... this isn't important ... it was a long time ago ... '

'I didn't know,' I told him. 'I truly didn't know. I didn't remember and no one told me, no one explained. Only last week. They told me last week.'

Holly's mouth is round with surprise. 'Why didn't you ever tell me, Aidan?'

He tried to make a joke of it. 'If I told you about everyone who didn't want me, it'd probably have put you off.' No one laughed.

Holly turned to Janette. 'He came back to you?'

'Not then,' she said. 'Later he did. After I fought for him. They gave me a lot of guff about how they'd find him someone else, how he needed to be the only child, centre of attention. "Somewhere more suited to his cultural back-ground," they said. What a load of rubbish. He never even knew his dad.'

Her eyes went from Finn to Holly and back again. 'You got left in the lurch too, darling?'

'Finn's dad ... he wasn't ready for the responsibility.'

Aidan exhaled, somewhere between a hiss and a sigh.

'Aidan, please ...' Holly's face was worried.

'Why don't you tell them the truth? Finn's dad was never around. When I met you, you were with that toe-rag Don. I saved you from him. I told him to go away and he never came back. He hit her, but I saved her.' His voice was proud.

'You and Uncle Clive's solicitor and the restraining order,' said Holly. 'Not that I think it's anyone's business.'

Aidan turned away. I felt terrible for him. All he wanted was for Holly to acknowledge what he'd done for her, say thank you for protecting her. She'd managed to make him sound in the wrong.

Janette's eyes were sad under all that make-up, and her mouth might have been sad too, if it hadn't been drinking her tea.

'Let's face it,' she said, putting her mug back down on the floor. 'A good man is hard to find. I'm lucky, I've found one now. But I chose some monsters in the past.'

'I don't actually know anything about my dad,' I said, cautiously. 'Just that he couldn't cope and left.'

'He couldn't cope. Well. That's one way of putting it. What a bastard he turned out to be.'

I winced, but she didn't notice.

'Took it out on me and Aidan, whenever anything went wrong. Jesus, he hated Aidan. Aidan tried to stand up for me, you see, get in the way when Mac was angry.' A tear escaped her eye, and she brushed it away with a brisk flick of her hand. 'First I sent him to my mum. Then we all went. But Mac followed us, wouldn't leave us in peace. So we went to the refuge.'

'Were you ... we ... were we safe there?'

'Sweetheart, you're never safe anywhere. And I was my own worst enemy.'

'It must have been so hard for you.'

'He loved you.' I couldn't work out if Aidan was angry with me or not. His voice was harsh and his face unreadable. 'He loved you, Cass. He did really bad things, but he never hurt you. That was the one good thing about him.'

Janette ignored him. 'I was in love, understand? I was dazzled. I thought it was my fault when he got into a temper. I thought if only I could get it right, he was the only one who could bring me happiness. I lost sight of what was really happening. I'm so sorry, Cass, so sorry.'

'You don't need to say sorry to me, really.' My cheeks were hot with embarrassment. She was apologising to me because I'd had a great life, full of love and privilege and holidays and presents.

Aidan stood up. 'How about me, eh? Where's my apology? He never touched Cass.'

Finn was watching and listening to all this and although he couldn't possibly understand, his eyes were wide and his lip was trembling.

'Finn, do you want to show me your room?' I asked, and he nodded and took my hand and we went and looked at his bed, his toys and his books. Holly is a great mum, I thought. It couldn't be easy for her, but she'd given her kid everything he needs, and even a really caring substitute dad.

Finn and I could hear raised voices from the living room, but we couldn't hear what they were saying, until the door opened and the voices were right by us.

Aidan was nearly shouting, 'I told you this was a bad idea. I told you it was a mistake. I can't take it any more.'

And Holly, 'Just stop and listen, calm down. Let's talk.'

Then the front door, *bang, slam.* Twice.

33: CASS

Finn wasn't happy, and I didn't know how long Aidan and Holly were going to be, so I took him back into the living room, where Janette was sitting, gazing into space. 'Why don't you pick out a DVD, sweetheart?' she told him. We all three sat and watched penguins shuffling around in the snow.

'The male Emperor penguin incubates the egg in the coldest winter weather, while the mother is searching for food.' David Attenborough's voice boomed out.

'I'm dying for a cigarette,' said Janette. 'Do you think they'd mind? Tell you what, pass me that saucer, I'll use it as an ashtray.'

There's a broken saucer just poking out from under the sofa. I was surprised to see it there – Finn could have hurt himself on the sharp edges.

She offered me her cigarette packet.

'No, thank you,' I said.

'Don't smoke, eh? Clever girl.'

She lit her cigarette, inhaled deeply, let the breath go in a cloud of smoke. Strangely, it reminded me of Mum doing yoga: her shoulders relaxed, her forehead unpinched itself. 'I've thought about you, worried about you, wondered about you so much over the years. It's marvellous to see you so grown up and beautiful. My little girl.'

I cringed inwardly, but hoped it didn't show. I reminded myself that she knew me much better than I knew her; she knew about a part of my life that I couldn't remember at all.

'My dad – Mac? Can you tell me anything about him? Now Aidan's not here.'

She took another breath in, smoke out. I tried not to cough.

'He was a bad boy. It took me a long time to realise. I thought it was me, thought as long as I didn't make him angry ...' She waved her cigarette in my direction. 'Got a boyfriend, darling?'

'No.'

'Pretty girl like you? I'd have thought you'd have loads of admirers.'

'I prefer to concentrate on my school work,' I said, and then spent the silence that followed thinking about how prim and stuck up I sounded. *Urgh*.

'I wasn't sensible like you. I messed around at school. Only had eyes for the boys. I liked being noticed, liked the attention. And then Ray came along. I was swept off my feet. I was only fifteen, darling, younger than you. He dazzled me.'

'He was Aidan's dad?'

'Good looking, like Aidan. That wicked smile, that was Ray. His granddad came from Trinidad, that's where he gets his colouring from. Oh, how I loved him. And he looked after me, too. Helped me find somewhere to stay when I fell out with your nan. Gave me money to help with the baby.'

'Oh. Why ... what happened?'

'Went off to war. He looked gorgeous in his uniform. Went to Kosovo, to fight other people's battles for them. He was a hero. Of course, the British Army didn't want to know about me and my baby that hadn't even been born yet.'

'That's terrible!'

'Yeah. Everything went to his wife.'

'Oh.'

I didn't like to ask if Ray and his wife had children, children that were Aidan's brothers or sisters, just as much as he was mine. I imagined our family like a daisy chain, spreading out on a green lawn. Some of the linked stalks were strong and firm, but others were wilting and withered, falling to pieces or failing to connect in the first place.

'So I was in a bad place when I met your dad, Cass. I needed someone to lean on. And he was so strong, Mac. That's what I thought. A strong, protective man. But he had a terrible temper. I left him three times when I was pregnant. Aidan stayed with my mum for a while. But I kept on going back. I loved him, you see, and he loved you. He loved you so much. I didn't feel I could take you from him.'

'Do you think ... should I find him?'

Finn's DVD came to an end, and he came out of his penguin-induced trance.

'Where's Mummy?' he asked.

'She'll be back soon,' I told him. He gazed at me, trying to work out if I could be trusted. Then his lip trembled. 'I want Mummy! Want Aidy!'

'They'll be back soon,' I promised again. 'Do you want to choose another DVD?'

Janette waited until Peppa Pig had started, then she ground her second cigarette into the saucer and said, 'No point looking for Mac, darling. You're better off without him. He sent me to the hospital so many times. Every time he swore it was a one off. Aidan's arm got broken, I covered up for Mac. Said it was an accident. But then things got really out of hand. So I talked to the social workers, and they said they'd find you a new family. And I honestly thought it would be the best thing. For both of you.'

'I think it was, for me anyway. I mean, I've had a really good life so far. I appreciate that chance.'

'Do you? Did I do the right thing?'

I was saved from answering by Finn.

'Where's Mummy?'

'Let's try ringing Aidan,' I said. 'I bet they'll be back soon.'

Aidan's phone went straight to voicemail, so I texted him.

Will you be back soon? Finn asking.

'Let's find you some supper, Finn,' said Janette. She looked at her watch. 'I hope they're back soon. I need to go. Keith's taken the kids out to his mum's in Harlow for the day, but they'll be back by eight.'

'I need to go, too.' There'd be a big row waiting for me if I was very late.

We looked through the kitchen cupboards and found some pasta. Janette boiled the kettle, found a saucepan. 'Ketchup, sweetie? Cheese? Why don't you show me where the bowls live?'

Finn was grizzling, his little fists rubbing his eyes.

'He's tired,' said Janette. 'Have your tea, darling, and then we'll put you to bed. Oh, he does remind me of Aidan at the same age. I was sure he was the dad. It'd be just like him to have a child and not tell me.'

'Why ... you don't really get on, do you?' I was being as tactful as I could be, but she was offended. I could tell by the way her shoulders hunched as she drained the pasta.

'He's impossible. I'm sorry to say it, but it's true. There's a side to him ... he turns people away. He's had so many chances. I'm not surprised your parents found him too much to handle. Do you know, I fought for him for years, fought to get him out of foster care, get him back home again, and then he let me down. He let me down so badly.'

I gave Finn a spoon to eat with, but he threw it onto the floor and picked up the pasta twirls one by one with his hands, which soon became sticky with ketchup. So did his face. He wasn't crying, though.

'How did he let you down?'

'My Louis – he was only small. Only about the same age as little Finn. Aidan was a big, tall boy of nearly twelve years old. As tall as me, he was. I'd worked so hard to make a home for him, Cass. I met Keith, and he's a good man, Keith. He works so hard and we have a good life, and we were happy with Louis. But I couldn't forget Aidan and you. There was nothing I could do about you, but I fought and fought to get Aidan.

Those foster parents, those social workers, they wanted to keep us apart, but I won. I won!'

She wiped away a tear. 'All those years of being judged, thinking I was a bad mum. I can't tell you how it felt. How happy I was. But Aidan didn't want to know.'

'Why?'

She shrugged. 'He's an angry boy. He fought us, he was rude, he turned away. Wouldn't kiss me, cuddle me. Every single day he told me he hated me, hated Keith, hated Louis. Tried to run away a few times. I was at my wits' end.'

I wondered what Aidan was like when he lived at our house. Was he so angry all the time? Is that why they rejected him? I never used to get angry. Never thought I had anything to get angry about. After all, my life was perfect. But now that it wasn't perfect, I felt angry all the time and that scared me. Could it be that I thought I'd disappear if I got angry? Just like Aidan?

'I thought things were getting better. He stopped running away, seemed to calm down. But then, one day, Louis did something to annoy him. He lost it. Lashed out. At a little kiddie, Cass. Just like Finn here.'

I found a tea cloth, wet it under the tap, cleaned Finn's face and hands. He started to cry again. 'Mummy!' he wailed. 'Want Mummy!'

'Keith wouldn't have him in the house after that. I was pregnant again, and he said we couldn't trust Aidan.'

'Couldn't you have given him another chance?' I lifted Finn out of his chair. 'Come on Finn, time for bed, eh?'

Finn's crying was getting louder and I had to strain to hear Janette's soft voice.

'You don't understand—'

'Mummy!' Finn had heard the key in the door. I lifted him out of his high-chair and he rushed to the front door.

'Cass, listen to me.' Janette put her hand on my arm. 'Aidan didn't just slap Louis. He blinded him.'

34: AIDAN

'She hates me,' I tell Holly. 'There's only so long I can take it. I'm sorry, I thought I could do it, but I can't.'

We're sitting by the canal, legs dangling over the water. I didn't expect Holly to come after me when I walked out on the tea party, and I kept telling her that she should go back to Finn, to them. But she stuck with me. 'They can look after him for a bit. He'll be OK. You're important, too.'

So now we're sitting here, shivering a bit, but we're alone and it's quiet and I feel I can talk. Perhaps I can even explain.

'Why would she hate you? She's your mother. Aidan, you've got it wrong. There's nothing to hate about you.'

'You don't know the whole story.'

'You can tell me.'

How can I tell her? She's going to hear what I did to Louis and she's going to look at Finn, his beautiful face, his perfect eyes, and she's going to tell me to get out and go away and never come near them again.

'The thing is, I was really happy before she took me away. I loved living with Betty and Jim. They were ... they were safe, Holly. They gave me a home, and I thought it might be for ever. They said ... they were talking about ...'

I never talk much about Betty and Jim because I get too choked up. But now I can't stop myself.

'They seemed to really love me, you know? And I don't think they would have got rid of me. They'd done a lot of fostering and they knew ... they seemed to know what I needed ...'

'We could get in touch with them,' says Holly. 'They'd be happy to see you again, wouldn't they?'

I shake my head. 'I screwed it up. I don't know how, but I did.'

She leans against me, plants a kiss on the back of my neck, just where I've got the tattoo that tells the world that I had hope. A tattoo I can't see. And I'm glad of that. Because I'm not sure that I could take being reminded of it, day after day, if this doesn't work.

Finn is my hope. Finn is my chance. Finn is everything to me. And Holly as well, of course. I love her. I really do.

'You're not going to screw it up with us,' says Holly. 'I don't think you know how much we love you.'

Holly and Finn come together, that's the thing. She gave me an instant family, and that's what I wanted, that's what I need, that's what I can't risk losing.

'I'm not ... I try ... I do love you so much, Holly.'

'I wake up in the morning and I see you in my bed and I think, what did I do to deserve you, Aidan? You're the best thing that ever happened to me. You're ... I don't think you realise what a failure I felt up to the point where we got together. Failed as a daughter, failed at school ... university ... got pregnant like a loser, by a man who didn't want to know. And then Don – that bully – I had to be supported by my family. Didn't even have a job. And then you came along. You changed my luck. I pinch myself sometimes, to make sure it's real, that you really are mine.'

'I'm nothing special, Holly.' I don't like it when she goes on like this. She sees the outside me, she ought to know that it doesn't match the mess inside.

She wrinkles her nose. 'You are special. You've got that ... that look. People notice you.'

Whatever that look is, it's brought me more trouble than good. I used to pray for something – spots, maybe – that would put people off. Stop them wanting me, because they wanted me in a bad way. But if Holly likes the way I look, I suppose it's worth having.

She's not finished. 'My mum was disappointed in me; my dad doesn't give a toss. I was always near the bottom of the class at school. I always felt like a failure. But now I've got you.'

'I'm nothing much. Not like Cass.'

'You haven't had her advantages. She's great, but she's a bit scary isn't she. So cool and confident. I'd have been terrified of her at school.'

I put my arm around her. 'Remember that day? When Finn was staying at your mum's?'

Don't ask me when I got the idea of getting with Holly. We'd been flatmates for a few months, and we were kind of used to each other. We liked some of the same things – folk music, quiz shows, hot curries – and we both loved Finn. I was doing more and more stuff for her, babysitting and shopping and all that crap, and I loved it. We were playing houses. We were pretending to be a family.

And then I started fancying her. She'd walk out of the bathroom, wrapped in a towel, and I'd feel turned on. Her arm would brush against mine, and I'd want to grab her, kiss her. I started staring at her lips, wondering if I could, if she'd ... But I never did anything. I just worried she'd notice the staring.

Rich and I had had a drink one night, and I'd told him about it, and he'd laughed at me. 'You're crazy! Of course she'd be interested. Who isn't interested in you?'

'That's really not helpful.'

'She'd be grateful! I mean she's not all that ...'

'Don't talk about her like that.'

Rich looked at me. 'You really do like her, don't you?'

'She's my friend. I do really like her.'

'Tell her.'

'I can't. It's too much of a risk. She might think I was being weird and inappropriate. She might throw me out.'

Rich patted my arm. 'You can come and live with me in my beautiful home.'

And we'd laughed a lot, because he'd just moved into the bedsit, which was seven foot by ten, and he went out drinking every night he could afford it so he wouldn't have to sit and look at the same four walls.

Anyway, I'd gone home and I was tiptoeing around, because I hadn't wanted to wake up Finn or Holly, but when I made a coffee and took it to sit in front of the telly, there she was. Sitting in the dark, wrapped in a duvet, surrounded by sad little heaps of scrumpled tissues.

'Holly? What's the matter? Is Finn OK?'

She'd blinked at me. 'Aidan? Oh, I'm sorry. Nothing's the matter. Finn's staying at Mum's. I just got thinking ... about stuff ...'

'You've been crying.' I was only stating the obvious, but it set her off again.

It was the perfect excuse. I wrapped my arms around her, and she cried more and more, but then I very gently kissed the top of her ear, so if she didn't like it she could move away and we could both pretend it hadn't happened. But I worked out she did like it, because she tilted her face towards mine, and I kissed her eyebrows, and she didn't even try to stop me, so I kissed all over her face, licking away the salty tears, and she stopped crying altogether. And I made her happy. And she made me happy, and we'd made each other happy, more or less, ever since, which was a bloody miracle in my life.

She still cried for no special reason sometimes, and it was more awkward if Finn was around, but I could always kiss her, and we both remembered that night, and sometimes it helped her feel better.

'You're so kind,' she says now. 'So loving. You're everything to me. I'm very lucky.'

I take a deep breath.

'Holly, I ought to tell you about when I lived with Mum.'

'Tell me.'

I can't find the words. She kisses my neck, holds my hand. 'Come on, it can't be that bad.'

'I hated being there. I wanted to be with Jim and Betty. I tried to get back to them, but I couldn't ... I was eleven, Holly, and no one listened to me ...'

She waits. 'What happened?'

'I can't explain it. I remember once – round about this time of year, when everyone wears those paper poppies for the soldiers—'

'Yes . . .'

'My mum had one of those and I thought, that's what I'm like, all black and evil inside.'

'Oh, Aidan. You were only a kid. You can't have done anything that bad.'

Under my feet the water of the canal is still and dark and welcoming. It's getting late. I can hear traffic and people laughing and water and the beating of my heart.

I'm going to have to tell Holly somehow.

'I was only eleven,' I start, but my phone buzzes, not for the first time, and she says, 'Is that Cass texting you? We've been out ages. Finn doesn't really know them.'

'We'd better get back,' I say. 'Finn needs us.'

We scramble to our feet. Holly's still holding my hand.

'What were you going to tell me?' she asks.

I'm trembling. I want to tell her, to trust her, but I can't. I can't. She'd throw me out and I'd have nothing. I can't let that happen.

'Oh, nothing. My mum, she's just a bit difficult, that's all. Makes up things. Bad memory. Don't believe all she tells you.'

Holly looks confused, but her mind is on Finn, and deep down, I think, she doesn't want me to tell her bad stuff. She doesn't want to spoil her vision of the perfect boy in her bed. I do that enough as it is, every time I get drunk.

So, we go home.

35: CASS

Aidan apologised to me when he got back. To me, and to Janette. He was sorry for walking out. He'd got overcome with the emotion of it all. 'It's not easy,' he said.

Janette kissed him – how could she? – and said, 'It's all right, darling. I know how it goes.' Then she gave me an unexpectedly fierce hug, enveloping me in the scent of smoke and hairspray. Her body felt thin and fragile, easily breakable. So different from Mum's warm strength. But even Mum could crumble. Maybe the whole idea I had of a mother – someone to protect you – was wrong.

She left and I didn't know what to say to Aidan; I could hardly look at him. 'What did you do to our brother?' I wanted to ask him. 'How could you do that? How do you live with yourself?' But I couldn't bring myself to ask him. I didn't know him well enough.

When I saw Holly cuddling Finn, singing him a song to get

him to sleep, I wondered if I should tell her. She couldn't possibly know. Why would she let Aidan anywhere near her son? But surely it was up to Janette to tell her? 'I honestly don't know what to do about that girl,' she'd said to me. 'Should I tell her what Aidan did? No wonder he never came clean with me, never told me about the boy.'

It wasn't my story. It wasn't my business. So I said goodbye, smiled, pretended everything was fine.

When I got home, Mum was on the phone and Ben was already asleep. So I didn't have to talk to anyone.

The next day I got up early for school and caught the bus so I'd be there in good time for the prefects' meeting. My hair was back in its usual neat ponytail. I wore a white shirt and a black skirt. No make-up. I wanted to get back to normal; I had a lot of studying to catch up on.

It took until lunchtime to realise that Grace was upset about something, and it took Megan to tell me.

'What's wrong with her?' I was sure it couldn't be anything much. Just an essay crisis or a boyfriend disaster, something Grace thinks is important, but isn't really. I was bored just thinking about it, but she'd been trying so hard to be there for me, I knew I had to reciprocate.

'I don't know what her problem is,' said Megan. 'She wants to talk to you, but she thinks she can't because you've been so secret squirrel about Will Hughes.'

I'd been quite happy eating my spaghetti bolognaise, but right then it turned into a writhing plate of maggots. I dropped my fork. 'What? What did you say?'

'Oh, come on, Cass, it's the worst-kept secret in town. Abigail Ellis saw you two walking through the park, and

Isabella Thomas said she saw you going into some house in Denton Road. Her grandma lives there—'

'We were just going to feed some cats,' I said. 'He runs a business. Pet care and private investigations. I might be going to work with him.'

'Pet care and private investigation? Really?'

'There's a lot of money in it,' I said, brisk and smiling, so she could think it was a joke if she wanted, but she wouldn't realise that I was dying inside. 'He's quite an entrepreneur. I might invest. Where is Grace, anyway?'

'She's out by the pond.'

The pond is outside the science labs, and it's where the Year Sevens watch frogspawn turn into tadpoles and frogs. In the summer, lots of people take their packed lunch and go and sit on the benches and pretend they're on the beach by sunbathing as many bits of themselves that they can expose.

In the winter, though, there was just Grace, sitting moping on a bench, throwing her sandwich bit by bit at the one lonely duck. I sat down on the bench next to her.

'You're not meant to do that. It'll ruin the pond's eco-system, and I don't think they eat peanut butter.'

'Like I care.'

'Well, Miss Worth will care, and it's not really fair to the biology department. Or the duck.'

'Oh, that is so typical, Cass. You're more bothered about a stupid duck than about me! I'm meant to be your best friend, but you've hardly spoken to me for weeks.'

'I've just had a load of work to do.'

'Yeah, right, whatever, Cass.'

'What's going on with you? Come on, Grace, you can tell me.'

'I'm not telling you a thing. You don't tell me anything.'

'Oh God, it's not a game, Grace. It's not, "I'll tell you and you can tell me." My parents have split up, OK? It was all over the newspapers. Isn't that enough for you?'

'I don't believe you. I know there's something going on with Will. And you've just been so . . . so . . .'

'So what?' I snapped.

'So closed up. Like, if I ask you how you are, I'm intruding. So I feel I can't tell you anything, or ask you anything, and we're meant to be friends, Cass. I don't know what's going on.'

I was about to feed her the pet care and private investigation story, but then I paused. Maybe she was right. Maybe I did push people away. If families were so unreliable, maybe I needed my friends.

'I'm sorry. There has been loads going on. So much that I don't even know where to start.'

'Try me.'

The bell rang for the end of lunch. Saved by double history. Grace stayed put.

'Come on, we've got to go.'

'I'm not going.'

'You've got to come. We're going to miss history.'

Grace put her lunchbox back into her bag. The duck nibbled a bit of crust and then swam away fast.

'If you walk away from me now, that's our friendship over, Cass Montgomery.'

'You've gone mad! Can't we just talk after school?'

Grace pouted. 'No.'

'What's up with you, anyway?'

'Liam dumped me.'

Who's Liam?

I improvised. 'Oh, no, Grace, that's awful. The bastard. What happened?'

She snorted. 'That so proves you don't pay a blind bit of notice to anything I tell you. Who's Liam, Cass? I've never heard of him.'

My face was hot. 'Oh, well, if you're going to play tricks on me, I might as well go to history.'

'Go on, then. Run along, Little Miss Perfect.'

To my horror and surprise my eyes filled with tears. 'I don't know what I'm meant to have done.'

'You're meant to be my best friend, but you never talk to me. You don't let me in, Cass. You've gone through so much with your mum and dad splitting up, but you don't talk to me at all, don't even let me come round. I feel like you don't value me or our friendship at all. I can't tell you stuff if you don't tell me anything.'

I was blinking back tears, torn between guilt – she wasn't wrong – and fury. How dare she make me cry at school! I'd be a laughing stock.

'I told you all about Leon – that's his name, by the way – that day in Starbucks, and you just nodded and smiled and went on total auto-pilot, and I thought never mind, actually it's quite sweet because she's looking over at Will and he's looking at her, and that's just what she needs when everything's been so rubbish for her at home . . .'

'Oh! No . . . Grace—'

'And you never asked once about how it went—'

How what went?

She read it on my face. 'The audition! Duh!'

'Oh right, the *audition*.'

'For the drama production. Joint with the boys' school. Oh, Cass.'

'I'm sorry, I'm sorry, I'm sorry,' I burbled. 'You are right. I am wrong. I've been a terrible friend. How did it go?'

'Hopeless. I got Lady Macbeth, but Leon didn't get Macbeth. He's Banquo. We hardly have any scenes together.'

'Oh, well, but Grace, there's not a lot of scope for romance in the Macbeths anyway.'

'Shared rehearsals. Practising lines.'

'I bet you can do that anyway.'

'If he's interested. It's all right for you, Cass. You play it so cool all the time that all the boys see you as a challenge. I'm sure I just come over as desperate.'

'No, you don't, because you're not desperate. Leon's probably just shy because so many boys like you.'

'I am desperate. I'm desperate to stop feeling like a reject just because I haven't got a boyfriend. I wish I could be as self-sufficient as you, Cass. You're so confident. You don't need a boy's approval to feel good about yourself.'

'I'm not so confident. I don't even know who I am any more.'

The school was quiet, everyone was in class. I supposed if anyone saw us they'd assume we had a free study period.

'My life is one big mess,' I told her. 'I still can't believe Mum and Dad have split up. I hate him so much, but I still really love him, too. And I'm dreading having to move house. I feel like I've got so much security bound up there. It's stupid, I know, but I sometimes think I care more about the house than anything else.'

'You don't really, though,' said Grace. 'I mean, it's probably easier to feel upset about the house than about your parents.'

Which parents, I want to ask. My parents now, or my parents then? The mother I hardly know any more. The father who kept secrets from us. And Janette - what about her? And Mac, violent, scary Mac?

'And then my brother ... he contacted me. Not Ben, I mean my birth brother. I hadn't seen him since I was really little.'

'Oh my God! Cass! How did he contact you?'

'Facebook.'

'How do you know it's really him? It could be some paedophile!'

'No, it's really him. I've met him. And it's the strangest thing ... it's great actually, but it's turning everything around. It's making me question everything about my life. I can't explain it ... it's making me think about who I am and what I want, and I just don't have any answers, Grace.'

'What's he like, your brother? Have you met him?'

'He's ... I don't know. He's different from anyone I ever met. He seems nice.'

He seems nice, but he attacked a little child. And I'm not sure if his girlfriend knows. And she has a child, exactly the same age ...

'I can't believe you didn't tell me!'

'I couldn't. It was all a secret. I didn't even tell my parents or Ben, until, well, last week and I didn't want to then. It all just came out.'

Grace seized my hand, gave it a squeeze. It was the sort of

gesture that I'd have pulled away from normally, but I didn't mind this time. It was cold, sitting on the stone bench, and I appreciated the warmth.

'Oh, Cass, I am so here for you.'

'Thanks, Grace.'

'And what about Will? I know there's something going on.'

I wasn't going to say anything about Will, because, frankly, what was there to say? Nothing was going on. We'd messed around a bit, but I hadn't heard from him for ages. I'd avoided the bus, and the one time I'd spotted him in town, he'd been with the blonde girl. I was almost sure he'd moved on.

'There's nothing going on,' I said, completely and totally accurately.

'Are you sure? Because everyone says ...'

That's when I surprised myself. 'There's nothing going on,' I insisted, 'because I've totally messed up.' Suddenly, stupid, unnecessary tears were pouring down my face. 'And I don't know what to do!'

Grace patted me on the knee. 'Trust me,' she said. 'Tell me the whole story.'

36: AIDAN

She knows. Cass knows. I could tell by her face when I walked in the door.

That's typical Mum. She makes me think that everything's OK, that I can trust her to keep my secret. And then she spills it to the one person whose opinion I care about as much as Holly's. To the one person who might tell Holly, as well.

I can't decide what to do. Tell Holly? I was going to, out by the canal, but now I'm here, back in the flat, holding Finn in my arms, I can't bear the idea of losing everything.

Should I ring Cass? Go and see Mum? It's tearing me apart. My mind is all over the place. Which is why I overslept. Which is why Clive's pissed off with me.

He starts right away. Why am I late? What's going on?

'I'm sorry! I'm sorry!'

'You only live upstairs! What's going to happen when you're further away?'

I freeze inside.

'What do you mean?'

'I'm thinking of putting the flat on the market. I mentioned it to Holly the other day. I can't afford to keep it on, not at the rent you two pay. I'm sorry and all that, but I've given you a pretty good start. Now you'll have to find somewhere new. I'm sure it'll be fine. You can always stay with Juliet in the interim. She's got plenty of room, she's rattling around in that house.'

Holly's mum lives in Primrose Hill and true, her house has room for all of us, and more. But every time I've been there, she's been as cold as the house – which is permanently freezing, because she doesn't ever put the heating on.

The minute I walk in, she's fussing about dirt on the floor: 'Can you just take your big boots off, Aidan?' and criticising my manners. 'Would you like a spoon with your pasta, Aidan?'

And then she starts with the awkward questions and the snarky comments.

'So, Aidan, did you actually get any qualifications at school? None at all? Not even the easy kind?'

'So, Aidan, when did you enter the care system? You were five? How tragic.'

'So, Aidan, do you think you'll want to spread your wings one day? You're very young to be tied down to a partner and someone else's baby.'

'So, Aidan, it must be hard to adjust to family life when you've never really experienced it.'

The worse thing is that Holly can't even hear it. If I say one thing afterwards, then Holly tells me I've got it wrong and her mum is just trying to get to know me and understand, and actually she's dead impressed at how hard I work to overcome my difficult past.

That'll be why Holly hasn't told me about the flat. She'll be working out how to persuade me to stay at Juliet's. Or she's planning to move in there, just her and Finn. She just hasn't got around to telling me yet. She's just going to move out one day and I won't even get to say goodbye ...

'Wakey, wakey!' Clive's clicking his fingers in front of my face. 'What's the matter? You knew the flat wasn't for ever. Don't worry, we'll sort you out with something.'

He's off on another job. 'You can study for your written driving test while I'm out,' he says, shoving the book in my hand. 'Time's running out, Aidan. You've got a new test coming up next week. You'd better pass it.'

I'm never going to pass it. The job's going to end. Holly's going to leave me. I'll never see Finn again. And the flat ... the flat ...

Clive goes out into the yard. I'm not meant to use my phone when I'm in the shop, but it's ringing and it's Rich and I haven't spoken to him for ages.

'Hey, Rich?'

'Hey! Long time, no speak!'

A little bit of my brain registers his bright, happy tone. I'd better call in about a week to check he's OK. That's how the cycle usually goes.

'You sound good, how's it going?'

'Oh my God, Aid, I'm in heaven!'

'Well, you've tried to go there enough times.'

He ignores the dig. 'This is The One! I can't tell you!'

He's going to anyway.

'What's his name?'

'Brendan. I told you about him before.'

266

I'd probably zoned out. There have been so many Ones over the years.

'Rich, don't get too excited. Remember Tom ... and that little shit, Joel ... and Hans didn't work out too well, did he?'

'Aid, you're bringing me down! Shut up! Brendan's different.'

'How?'

'He's like, he's really caring. We talk. He's introduced me to his parents.'

'What? When? Why?'

'Last weekend. They were so lovely, Aid. His mum gave me a hug and said she hoped I'd feel part of the family. Said she'd never seen Brendan like this about any other guy.'

I swallowed. 'That's great, Rich. What does he do, this Brendan?'

'He's so cool. He's a student.'

'A student of what?'

'Dance. He's all muscle and stubble and curls.'

'Oh. Well. I just hope he's not like the others.'

'He's totally not. He really loves me. We're talking about moving in together. He's got a flat in Walthamstow.'

'Oh, right. Well, I'd better go. I'm at work. Can't sit around talking all day.'

'I've got a job, too. That's how we met. I'm working at an organic café in a dance studio in Crouch End. It's such a cool place, and I get free food, and that's how I met Brendan, because he teaches zumba there, three times a week, and he came into the café for a smoothie and we just looked ... we saw each other ... and I've never felt like this before, Aidan. This is it, he is The One.'

'Got to go!' I say. 'Customer! Bye.'

I don't know why I feel so sad and empty. I ought to be happy that Rich is in love, right? He deserves to find someone: we all do. It's just that I'm about to be homeless and loveless, and he's going to be living in bliss in Walthamstow. He won't need me any more. I'll be all on my own.

The bell jangles. I look up, startled.

'Well!' says Neil. 'Good morning to you.'

37: AIDAN

'Go away, Neil.' I do my best to sound strong and tough. 'It's not a good time.'

'Expecting someone, are we? That girl, maybe, with the hair. Ginger. What was her name? Cass?'

'I don't know. She's not really a friend.'

'Cass Montgomery. Daughter of Oliver Montgomery. You've heard of him, haven't you, Aidan? Oh, no, hang on, I forgot. You don't read much, do you? Probably missed the news about how he's been caught with his pants down.'

I hold my breath. Had Neil worked out that Cass was adopted, that there could be a connection? No. He didn't say anything. I shrug. 'She could be anyone. You know what it's like.'

Neil smirked. 'I'm sure you have a lot of success with the ladies, Aidan. Maybe your girlfriend would like to hear about this Cass, how you got off with old Monty's daughter. How you're mixing with the rich and famous.'

He's so off-track that I actually laugh. 'You've got to be joking.'

'Maybe the papers would like to know about it?'

'You're just scum,' I tell him. 'No one's going to listen to you.'

'You're very cocky,' he says. 'Think your girlfriend's so into you that you can get away with anything? Well, I suppose a single mother is grateful for anything she can get. She's looking a bit old for you, though, Aid. Old and knackered. No wonder you take the chance to get some posh totty when you can.'

'What the hell do you think you're doing in my shop?' Clive's bark shocks us both. I nearly fall off my chair. 'I know you, don't I?' Clive's not scared of Neil. He's right in his face.

Neil's always had a bit of a swagger about him. But now he's chewing his thumbnail, staring at his boots.

'You only lasted here two days. Had to let you go. Fingers in the till, wasn't it? What's your name, again?'

Neil mutters something under his breath.

'Neil, weren't it? I remember you, Neil Johnson. Seem to remember telling you not to come back here again.'

'Aidan asked me. Said he needed help with something.'

'This true, Aidan?'

I don't know what to say. I want to tell him no, no it's not true, but Neil's there and he's looking at me, and kind of squinting his eyes and I know the kind of thing he'll do if I don't lie for him. Broken fingers is just the start of it.

'Yeah. Sorry, Clive. I didn't know.'

Clive's eyeballing Neil. I never knew he could look so scary. 'You listen to me, lad. My niece is Aidan's girlfriend and if I ever hear you speak about her with less than total respect, you'll feel the consequences. I let you off with a warning, last time, remember?'

Neil mutters something so low that I can't make out if it's actual words or just the kind of growl that a cornered dog might make.

'What? Speak up!'

'Yeah,' said Neil. 'But it was Aidan who—'

'What's that?'

'Yes, sir.'

'That's better. Now, you get out. And I never want to see or hear you near this place again, got it?'

'Got it.'

I am amazed. My mouth is hanging open. One minute Neil was big and scary and had so much power over me that I was like an ant under his Timberlands, the next he's shuffling out like a little boy. All from a telling-off from Clive, ordinary Clive in his sweater from Debenhams, with his bald head and his little paunch and his glasses. Clive who looks like every dad in every crap Christmas advert you've ever seen. Boring old Clive who's straight as a die – whatever that means – and doesn't even swear.

Clive, who's looking at me like I'm a stranger.

'Did I hear right? That toe-rag Neil is your mate? You were slagging off our Holly, laughing about her?'

'No, Clive, wait, that's not right.'

'You've been having it off with a bit of posh totty, in secret?'

'No, no, Clive, that's all wrong.'

'You bet your life it's wrong. You bet your life it's very wrong. What's Holly going to say when I tell her?'

I'm scared witless. I just stare at the floor.

'How d'you know Neil Johnson?'

'From the children's home. Clive, it's not like he said—'

'My brother, Bernie, and me, we went into those homes together. Barnardo's. None of your private rooms and televisions and en suites in those days. We were all together in dorms. It was a hard life. You kids today, you're soft. You have no idea.'

I open my mouth. I close it again.

'Me and Bernie, we came out, we were both determined to make something of our lives. I did it the legit way; Bernie, not so much. That's why he buggered off to Spain. Costa del Crime, you know. Holly, bless her, she's got no idea. Don't want you telling her, neither.'

'I won't ... I didn't do anything, Clive.'

'I thought you really cared for her. God knows, she's not had it easy.'

'I do – I do really care.'

'Well, watch it. Don't invite your friend here again.'

I want to explain that Neil's the last person I ever want to see again, but the words are flying around in my head, the way they usually do on the page.

Clive's getting nearer. His head is getting bigger. I can smell aftershave and alcohol – although it's coming from my breath, not his, I had an emergency can of lager for breakfast – and all I can think of is Mac, his big, red face, and the way he shouted, and the sudden smack of his hand on my ear or my head, and the way that anything I did, any sound or movement or just looking at him could set him off ...

I flinch away from Clive, so suddenly that I fall off my chair for real. I can't breathe. I'm gasping for air.

'Whoa!' he says. 'What's going on?'

I can't speak.

'What's the matter? Are you ill?'

'I'm ... I'm OK. I'm all right. I'm sorry.'

Clive's shaking his head. 'Someone's spooked you bad in the past, eh? Take a moment. Calm down. Want to take a break? Go up to the flat?'

'I'm OK.'

He leaves me alone for a bit, makes coffee, comes back and hands me my mug. He's remembered I take two sugars. He's put some ginger nuts on a plate.

I hate how badly I've let Clive down. I've let Neil hide a gun in his shop. I owe him so much, and I've done this terrible thing. The coffee nearly chokes me. I can't take his biscuits.

'What's the problem, Aidan? What's going on?'

'Nothing. He's ... Neil ... he's not a friend of mine. He just came in the shop. Honest.'

'He's scum. You don't need to associate with trash like that. Call the police if he comes back, tell them he's shoplifting.'

'OK.'

'You thought I was going to hit you?'

'No ... not really ... you just reminded me of someone.'

'Listen, son, you got the chance of a new life. Bad stuff has happened to you in the past, but that's gone now. You pick yourself up and you start again. You've got a chance here, you make the most of it.'

'I will ... I am ...'

'You got nothing to be scared of, Aidan, as long as you treat Holly and Finn right and keep out of trouble. Work hard and stop stealing from me. If you need new trainers, just ask me. Think you can do that?'

I wish it was as easy as he seems to think it is. 'Yeah, Clive.'

'Good lad. Right, time for you to go and stack the new boxes in the yard.'

'Yeah, OK.'

I feel better with the coffee inside me, but as I stack the boxes all my troubles come back, rolling around my head.

Neil's not allowed to come into the shop, but I still have his gun.

Clive's going to sell the flat.

Holly might already know what I did to Louis. Cass almost definitely does know.

I'm losing everything.

I might lose Finn.

38: CASS

Ben's birthday. Always a problem, every year, but this year it promised to be a disaster.

My birthday parties were easy. All my friends at our house. We used to play party games and eat jelly and ice-cream. More recently we'd eat pizzas and watch DVDs. For my sixteenth I'd had a proper party – a disco in the church hall. For my seventeenth – well, it was months away. I had time to decide, and I felt I was getting a bit old for birthday parties. But Ben never had enough friends for a party. One year Mum invited a load of kids anyway, and watched as they played football in the garden while Ben sat in his room, headphones on, reading *The Hobbit*. Dad shouted at him to join in and Ben cried. After that, we'd made a new birthday tradition. Just family. A film, or bowling, and a meal out.

But this year, Dad wasn't really part of our family any more. And Ben had ideas of his own.

'I want to invite people and I want a barbeque.'

'It's November,' I pointed out. 'Not exactly barbeque weather. And who's going to barbeque?'

'Dad.'

Dad always took charge of our barbeque. I'd forgotten that was another part of family life that had ended, *bang, smash,* just like that.

'Dad doesn't live here any more.' Time to be brutal.

'He'll come for my birthday!' Ben looked amazed that I even thought that perhaps this year Dad could be missing from the birthday celebrations.

'Look, Ben, things are different now.'

'He'll come. It's my birthday!'

I talked to Mum and she agreed that it was hard for Ben to be expected to celebrate without Dad. 'Besides, it'll be his last birthday in this house. It's nice that he wants to have a party. Do you know who he's inviting?'

I did not. Ben was very secretive about it. It was only when Mum started asking how much food she should buy that I got the list from him.

Dad

Annabel

Annabel's sisters, Imogen and Rosie

Aunt Kate and Granny

Emily and Phoenix and Sebastian

Will Hughes

'Ben!'

'What?'

Where to start?

'Ben, you can't invite Annabel, let alone her sisters. How would Mum feel?'

Ben considered this for a few minutes, frowning as though he was working out a tricky maths problem.

'Mum might like them. They're all nice. Rosie has got a toy poodle called Apricot. She could bring her.'

'Ben, Annabel has ruined Mum's life! She stole her husband! You can't just start expecting everyone to get on!'

Ben's mouth drooped. 'But it would be better if everyone did get on, Cass. The vicar said . . .'

'No one listens to him! Who are Emily, Sebastian and Phoenix? And what's Will Hughes doing on this list?'

'I love Will. He found my friends, Emily and Phoenix and Sebastian. We all like *Lord of the Rings* and *Doctor Who*, and Emily plays chess and Phoenix is teaching me to program, and Sebastian like bowling, and we're all friends now, and it's all thanks to Will. I love him and I thought you were his friend.'

'He found you all those friends?'

'I actually like going to school now, because I've got friends. And none of them play football. And we all like barbeque.'

'But maybe Will won't want to come to a twelve-year-old's party.' I was panicking now. He wouldn't turn up, would he? If he did, I'd have to thank him, because finding friends for Ben . . . I mean, no one had ever been able to do that. It was the best thing that anyone could possibly have done for our whole family and when I thought about Will doing that, really thinking about Ben and caring enough to bother, I felt warm and tingly. I nearly phoned up Grace to ask her advice, should Will turn up. But he wouldn't, I was sure. He'd forgotten all about me. I just hoped he wouldn't see Ben's invitation as some cringingly clumsy attempt engineered by me to get back together with him.

Anyway, Mum looked at the list and said, firmly and bravely, that Ben must be allowed to pick his own guests. In the end, though, Annabel, Imogen and Rosie sent him cards and letters saying how much they would have loved to have come, but their step-brother was getting married and they all had to go to his fiancée's hen weekend at a spa hotel in Cornwall. Imogen and Rosie sent him gift tokens, and Annabel said, 'I'll give you your present when I see you!!!!'

So I only had Dad and Will to worry about, and Will probably wouldn't turn up. Surely he'd realise it wasn't appropriate?

He didn't. A good hour after everyone else, there he was on our doorstep, holding a lumpy parcel.

'Oh. Hi. Is that for Ben? I'll give it to him, I said, which wasn't at all the polite, dignified, serene welcome that I'd planned that morning.

'Hi, Cass.' Will wasn't smiling, which was so unusual for him that he felt like a completely different person: someone who'd had a personality transplant, or a terrible tragedy in his life. Maybe something had happened. Maybe someone had died, or had an accident or something? He wasn't wearing his usual colourful clothes either. He was in jeans and a black hoodie, no Dora bag, no fake glasses. On Will, this looked liek a funeral suit.

'Are you all right?' I asked him.

'I'm fine.'

'Oh. Good.'

'And you? How are you, Cass?'

'I'm absolutely fine.'

I quickly turned my back on him because I had a massive lump in my throat, and led the way through the house.

'Ben's in the living room. Here.' I showed Will the door. 'The barbeque's in the garden, but it's really cold, so we're bringing the food into the kitchen. That door there. But you might not want to stay that long. I mean, it's mostly just Ben's Year Seven friends, and family.'

Will paused at the door to the living room. 'I'll stay as long as you want me to. Not long, I suspect.'

I opened my mouth to reply, but he'd gone. I heard squeals of delight from Ben and Emily and Phoenix and Sebastian over the rumblings of the DVD of *The Fellowship of the Ring*, and then the door closed in my face.

Mum and Granny and Aunt Kate were making salads in the kitchen, and I really didn't want to be quizzed about my A levels, so I went out into the garden to see how Dad was getting on. At least it wasn't raining, although it was so cold that I could see my own breath.

'Trust Ben!' said Dad. 'A barbeque on the coldest day of the year so far. Oh well. I suppose I'm lucky to be on the guest list.'

He did that thing, the waggling eyebrows thing, and instead of feeling irritated and angry and full of hate, I remembered when it was the funniest joke in the world that my dad could waggle his eyebrows. When I was about six and I'd stopped having nightmares and I'd almost forgotten – had forgotten, really – that there was ever another Mum and Dad, that there ever was an Aidan, that once upon a time I lived in a very different sort of home. I had a new Mummy and Daddy and I loved them and they loved me and everything was all right and we were going to live happily ever after.

Dad looked at me, and he must have seen something in my face because he said, 'I'm sorry. I'm so sorry, Cass. I never meant to hurt you. I think this divorce is harder for you than anyone.'

I actually gasped out loud. 'What the hell? What about Mum?'

'The way it happened was terrible, I admit that. But we haven't really been happy for years. Not as a couple. We both knew it, but we never addressed it. We were too busy putting on a brave face, thinking about you children.'

'Mum's lost everything! Her home ... her job ...'

'She didn't have a job.'

'Being your wife was a full-time job!'

'Yes, and she never let me forget it. Cass, we were a good team. But the magic went out of our relationship a long time ago. Maybe it's inevitable when you've been married a long time. But I know I'm happier now, and I'm convinced your mum can be happier, too. But can you be? What about you, Cass?'

'What about Ben?' My voice was a growl.

'Ben's blossoming! He's made friends, he's really taken to Annabel. Your Mum and I agree that he's coped surprisingly well. Ben isn't too involved in other people's emotions. And that's actually helped him cope with all of this.'

'Oh, so you did it for Ben's sake?'

'Try not to be childish, Cass.'

I felt childish, that was the problem. I wanted to shout and scream and stamp my foot. But that was unthinkable, with Mum and Granny and Aunt Kate just metres away. With Will Hughes in my house.

'Is he here, the boyfriend?' asked Dad, expertly rolling the sausages over. 'I'd like to meet him again.'

'He's not my boyfriend. He's Ben's peer mentor or buddy or something.'

'He found all these friends for Ben, I gather. Took them all bowling. Seems like a nice lad.'

How did Dad know all this stuff when I didn't? Obviously I'd been too busy moping to notice anything that was going on around me.

Mum came out into the garden. 'Any food ready? If you put the sausages into this dish, Cass, I can keep them warm in the Aga.'

'Just a few minutes,' said Dad. 'Susie, thank you for including me in this. I appreciate it isn't easy.'

'It wouldn't be the same without you,' she said.

I exploded.

'How can you say that! He's smashed our family to pieces! We're having to sell the house! It's never going to be the same again!'

'Calm down, darling, remember we've got guests,' said Mum.

'I don't care!'

A cough. Will's cough.

'Umm, I just came to say goodbye. Thanks for inviting me.'

Mum and Dad looked at me – red-faced, fighting back tears, furious – and Will, an unbouncy, frowning, almost unrecognisable version of Will.

SALVAGE

'Won't you stay and have some sausages?' said Mum.

Will looked at me. I couldn't speak.

'I'd better go,' he said.

I heard the faint sound of the doorbell. I ran to answer it.

There standing on the doorstep was the last person on earth I expected to see.

Aidan.

39: AIDAN

Holly knows. Holly can't look at me. She tells Finn to hush and watch Peppa Pig when he shrieks 'Aidy!' and rushes to hug me after work.

I pick him up and breathe in his smell – ketchup and baby shampoo – and rub my face on his fuzzy hair and think about carrying him down the stairs, jumping on to a bus, running away and taking him with me.

But Finn can't be without Holly. He needs to be with her. Just because I didn't get much of my mum when I was growing up doesn't mean I can take Finn away from his.

'Aidan, we need to talk,' she says, over Finn's head, once he's settled in front of the telly again.

'Is it about ... is it bad?'

'Of course it's bad. You must have been so scared that I'd find out.'

Just for a moment I think that means that she understands. That she's kind enough to give me the benefit of the doubt.

Then I catch her eye and there's no love, no warmth, nothing left for me.

'I wanted to tell you – I tried.'

'But you didn't try hard enough.'

'Who told you? Mum?'

She shook her head. 'Not your mum, no. You'd have thought she would. She should understand how a mother ... how I'd feel ... why I needed to know.'

So it must have been Cass.

Betrayed by my sister.

'Holly, I'd never hurt him, you know that. You must know that.'

Finn stirs, turns, looks at us. 'Aidy?'

'It's OK, Finn. Nothing's happening. Aidy and I are just going to the kitchen to make a cup of tea, OK?'

His thumb is in his mouth. 'OK,' he says.

In the kitchen she lets the tears go. I want to hug her, kiss them away. I can't. She wouldn't let me.

'Holly, it was an accident, I swear. I was only eleven. I never meant to hurt him.'

'You blinded a little boy!' She's shaking. 'You did that and you never told me! You came into my life, and you – I let you! – be a dad to Finn, and all the time you had this awful secret ... it was only seven years ago ...'

'I was a kid.'

'I'm trying to understand. I'm trying Aidan, but it's a shock ... such a shock ... I wish you'd told me right at the start. You kept it secret!'

'Because I knew you'd be like this! And I didn't *blind* him, it was only one eye ...'

'I can't believe you think that makes it better!'

'I'm just trying to explain … how it was—'

'What else haven't you told me, Aidan?'

What else haven't I told her? I take a deep breath.

There's the life I led before I was taken into care. Not just Mac, but the filthy places we lived, and the parties, the way people came in and out of our house, strange people, sick people. Sleeping in my clothes because I was cold, and I had no pyjamas. All that stuff. Cass is lucky she doesn't remember.

There's the day Mum gave us up for adoption.

There's all the stuff that happened to me at foster homes and in children's homes, the people who touched and hit and made me feel like I was nothing.

How it felt to be rejected again and again and again.

There's the fear I carry, day after day, that she's going to stop loving me.

And today's the day.

'I'll go,' I say. 'Just let me say goodbye to Finn.'

'Aidan, I just need time … to take this in. To understand. I need to think …'

But I don't stop to listen to her. I go into the living room, lift Finn up into my arms, hug him as tight as I can without hurting him.

'I've got to go, Finn, but I will see you again. I promise I will. I love you and I will always love you and you never did anything wrong, OK? You never did anything to stop me loving you. I'm going to go now, but it's not down to you. Take care. Look after Mummy for me.'

He's screaming and crying and I'm crying too, and I can't stand to hear it so I don't even stop to pack anything. I just put him down again, and brush past Holly. I grab my backpack and I go.

I tumble down the stairs and then I think of the gun. How can I leave it in Clive's shop? What if the police find it? Then he'd know and Holly would know that I was weak and bad and dishonest. And they'd tell Finn that, and he'd believe them.

So I open the door to the shop and I get Clive's tool kit and I prise up the floorboards. I pick out the gun and I push it right down to the bottom of my bag.

Then I help myself to some things that might be useful. A hoody. Some jeans. A toothbrush – Clive just had a load of stuff in from a burned down pharmacy in Wembley. A rabbit, to remind me of Finn's.

I get all the way to Rich's bedsit and I'm thumping on the door before I remember Brendan. Bloody Brendan and his flat in Walthamstow. Rich'll be there, all loved up, thinking he's going to live happy ever after.

There's no such thing as happy ever after.

I pull out my spare key and in I go. It's empty. No more posters on the wall, no duvet, no cans of cider.

It's like Rich is dead. This is what I feared I'd find, all those times. But he's not dead. He's allowed himself to hope. He should know better. I should've known better.

I slide my hand round to the back of my neck and I remember how it hurt, the needles going in and out, marking my skin, writing my happiness onto me for ever. What a stupid thing to do. What a joke.

I sit down on the bed, and I stare at the walls and I think about the gun in my bag.

And I think about Cass. She has everything and I have nothing. And she took everything away from me.

40: CASS

'Aidan? What are you doing here? How did you know where I lived?'

'I got a train. Then, I dunno, I just walked around. I asked people.'

There was something wrong with him. He wasn't smiling, or looking me in the eye. He was mumbling, twitchy. His eyes were bloodshot, his face pale and unshaven. Drugs, said a voice in my head. Drink. Danger.

'Look, it's not such a great time—'

He laughed. Aidan laughed. But it wasn't the sort of laugh that meant he was happy, or he thought something was funny.

'I remember this house, you know. I remember that clock. I never saw anything like it again.'

The clock is eighteenth century and it belonged to Mum's great-grandfather. It's a quite rare sort of pendulum clock, with a pattern of stars on the clockface and a mahogany case. It's beautiful. I'm not surprised he remembers it.

'Look, Aidan, maybe we'd better go and get a coffee in town?'

'I just need to ask you something. It won't take long. I just need to understand.'

'We could go to Starbucks or somewhere,' I said. Then I thought of all the people I might know in there, seeing me with Aidan, and I cringed a bit. And then hated myself for it.

'I won't be long.' He looked around. 'It's so weird to be here.'

'Cass?' It was Mum's voice. 'Who was it, darling? The food's ready.'

I was frozen. Should I invite him in?

Ben and his friends burst into the hallway. Phoenix, with his camouflage trousers and his ponytail; Emily, little and plump, wearing glasses so thick they look like swimming goggles; Sebastian, who had a woolly hat and stripy shirt just like *Where's Wally*. They gathered behind Ben like a freaky little welcoming party.

Aidan blinked. 'I didn't know you ... your parents ... they foster kids?'

'No ... it's just ... '

'Hey!' said Ben. 'Who are you?'

'I'm Aidan.'

Ben totally took this in his stride.

'I'm Ben. Are you Cass's brother, Aidan? I'm Cass's brother, too. Have you come for my birthday?'

Aidan blinked. I realised I hadn't warned him about what Ben was like.

'Not really,' he said. 'I'm sorry. Cass. I just—'

'Come and have barbeque! Mum said I couldn't have any because it was November and too cold, but I said we could get

Dad to come home and make it, and he has. And we're going to eat it inside and there is cake, as well.'

'What's the hold up?' Mum appeared at the kitchen door. 'Come on, get your food while it's hot.'

Ben and Phoenix and Emily and Sebastian ran past her.

'Come on, Cass,' she said.

Then she saw Aidan.

'Oh! It's ... Aidan, is it you? Is it really you?'

Aidan swayed a little, and I thought he was going to fall. He put his hand on the doorframe to steady himself.

'Susie?'

She laughed, a funny, choking little laugh. 'You always called me Susie. Oh, Aidan, it is good to see you.'

'It is?'

'Cass, can you go and see that everything is all right? And ask Dad to come out here, too? I think we need to talk to Aidan, don't we, Aidan?'

'Susie,' he says again. 'I remember this house. I lived here.'

'You did live here, Aidan, you did. For three months. We need to talk to you, Aidan.'

'I need to talk to Cass.'

'We can go to Starbucks,' I said, and then I realised that Will was standing in the hallway. His mouth was actually wide open as he looked from Aidan to me and back again.

'Bye, Will,' I said quickly.

Will scrunched up his eyes. 'Cass – I just thought ... if I could have a word?'

'Look, another time, OK?'

'But it's really urgent now.'

'It's just not a good time, as you can see,' I said.

Aidan was staring at Will. 'I've seen you before,' he said. 'I know I have.'

'No, Aidan, you can't have,' I said, but then remembered how Will had been there the first time I met Aidan. 'Look, I can explain. Will was just there to keep an eye on me. Just in case, you know, you were some dodgy internet person. But you weren't.'

'Cass – I – look, maybe I will stay a bit longer,' said Will. 'Those sausages looked awesome.' And he went back into the kitchen.

'Aidan, dear, won't you join us? We're just about to eat – Ben's party, you know ...'

'I don't want ... I just wanted to tell Cass something—'

'We can go in the study,' I said. 'We can talk there. Just you and me. We could take some food in there, if it's OK with you, Mum?'

Mum's usually a bit strict about not eating anywhere except the kitchen table or the dining room, but she said, 'That sounds like a good idea. You go along and I'll bring you some food. And then we can talk later, Aidan? I know Oliver will want to see you again. How tall you are! Oh, I'm sorry, what a stupid thing to say ...'

'This way.' I showed Aidan into the study, and shut the door behind us. 'Look, you sit there and I'll grab another chair.'

But Aidan just sank to the floor, sitting with his back against the wall, and after a moment or two I did the same. Side by side. Brother and sister. Maybe we sat here together like this twelve years ago.

Aidan was thinking the same thing. He stared at the wall

where I'd put my revision whiteboard. 'There used to be a picture there. A man and a ship.'

'Dad's great-great-great uncle. He served with Nelson.' Dad took the picture with him when he left. A little bit of family history that the new baby's going to have. It doesn't matter to me, I suppose, but I feel upset on Ben's behalf. Nelson should belong to him.

'Oh,' he said. 'I think I remember.'

'Aidan, are you all right?' Stupid question. He obviously wasn't.

'Cass, I needed to say ... to say that you mustn't feel bad.'

'Sorry?'

'I understand. I think I understand. I've been staying at Rich's, two days now, and thinking, trying to work out ... I'm not as clever as you, Cass, and maybe it takes me longer.'

'Don't say that, Aidan, please—'

'I just couldn't understand why you would do that. Why you would tell Holly. But you did and I see it was probably for the best because she had to know sometime, and for all you knew I'd told her anyway, and that's what I should have done.'

I tried to untangle this statement. 'I'm not sure I under-stand ...'

'You told Holly about Louis. About what I did. Mum told you and you told Holly and now she's angry with me, because I never told her. And I just came to tell you not to feel bad, and not to feel guilty and I'm still so happy that I met you again.'

He took a deep breath, looked up at the ceiling.

'Aidan—'

The door opened. Will, carrying two plates full of burgers, sausages, salads, bread. It seemed excessive, somehow, all this food. I remembered Aidan's idea of a tea party – a few biscuits on a plate.

Here we were, showing off how much we had.

'Thanks,' I said, scrambling up to take the plates from him. 'Look, Will, it was kind of you to come for Ben's party, but I need to talk to Aidan now—'

'We need to talk.'

Was he winking at me? What on earth was going through his mind? I was seriously rethinking any ideas I still had about trying to make things up with him. The boy was socially inept.

'Look, it's not the right time.' Of course, he wanted to tell me he was seeing that blonde girl. That was why he'd come to the party. Well, he'd have to wait.

Will leaned towards me and I got a whiff of that sweet Will smell, and I was slightly overwhelmed with wanting to throw my arms around him. Luckily, I was carrying two plates of food and couldn't.

'I think he's got a gun.'

Will's whisper was so soft, and directed straight at my ear, so his breath tickled it, and for a second I was so distracted that I thought I'd heard wrong. I must have heard wrong.

But Aidan heard too. And Aidan reacted. He grabbed his bag and he pulled out something that was definitely a gun.

A gun.

A real gun. Here in my home, with a houseful of people. My brother with a gun.

And the gun was pointing at Will.

41: AIDAN

I don't know what's going on any more.

I've spent so long thinking about Cass and why she might have told Holly, trying to make it OK, so I don't have to hate her; trying to make it so I can just do what I need to do and not hurt anyone, not make her feel bad.

That's the problem when you care about people – you care about what they feel, and I don't want to care any more, I just want it to finish, because I can't take the pain any more, of being told goodbye, of never feeling at home, never knowing when the end's going to come.

This is how Rich must feel. I've never felt it before.

I thought and thought about Cass and why she told Holly, and I thought she must know the right thing to do, being so clever and all, going to Oxford University, and I can't even read, but now I don't know what to think.

Because she's with some guy who's got to be working for

Neil. He was there in the shop, I remember now. He was dressed just the same, in a black hoody. I thought he was on the steal, but he wasn't, he can't have been, he just sank into the shadows when Neil brought the guns. They must've been together, they must've been working together, and now he's here, he's with my sister – you can tell they're together by the way they look at each other.

Neil's following me, he's on to me, the sooner I do it the better, and then he can't hurt me no more, no one can hurt me, and I can't hurt no one else.

So all I have to do is turn the gun around, turn it around, so it's pointing at me, and not him, and fire.

But what if this guy is Neil's way of getting at me through Cass?

And what about Finn? What if he finds out? And he thinks I didn't care about him; that I didn't care enough to stay around? He won't remember me saying goodbye, he'll just think I didn't care enough.

After all, my dad didn't care enough to stay around for me. Every story Mum tells about him is different. Every story she tells is a lie. I asked Jon, my social worker, outright one day, and he found out for me. My dad killed himself. He was in the army – my mum hadn't lied about that – so it was kind of an easy thing to do. He shot himself. Maybe he'd just heard that Mum was expecting.

I hate him for it, but I hate Mac more. Better to have the kind of dad who kills himself than the kind who kills other people. Mac killed some random guy and they put him in prison for a long, long time. And that told me that some random guy mattered more than Mum and me.

'Aidan,' she says. His daughter. Mac's daughter. 'Aidan, put the gun down.'

Mac loved her. I was safe if I was holding her, holding the baby. I used to carry her around like a lucky charm. I thought she'd bring me luck again. But instead she's destroyed me, and I might have destroyed her. Neil might destroy her.

'Aidan, I didn't tell Holly. I didn't tell her anything. Why don't we ring her, Aidan? Why don't I talk to her?'

I shake my head. 'My phone's dead.'

'I can charge it for you! Or give me her number.'

'I can't talk to her.'

'Aidan, put the gun down, please, and then we can talk properly. We can sort this out. Holly loves you so much.'

'Not any more.'

'I don't believe it!'

'I'm not telling lies.'

She's lost her cool confidence, my sister. She's pink and scared and there are tears in her eyes. I don't want her to be scared. I hate her being scared.

But Neil's man is here. He'll want the gun. He's the threat.

'Cass, this guy, he's a gangster, he's a criminal, he's going to hurt us.'

The guy squawks, 'No – I –' but I lift up my hand with the gun, to show I mean business.

'Aidan, he's not, really not – you're mixing him up with someone else. He's called Will and he's in the sixth form, and he's really a very nice person.'

The guy nods, 'It's true! Honest!' and I don't know what to think.

'You were in my shop. You were with Neil.'

'Was he the guy who made you hide the gun? I was there. I'm sorry. I was spying on you. But I wasn't there to help him. Don't you remember? I had a girl with me.'

'What girl?' Cass sounds like she's going to cry.

'Just a friend - honest, Cass, she's just a friend. Katie. She's at Bonny's. She helps me out with jobs sometimes. We've been friends – just friends - for ever. You've got to believe me.'

I don't believe him.

'You're working for Neil. He's got you spying on me, spying on my sister.'

'No, really. I'm nosy, that's my problem, and I was worried about Cass, and I thought I should check you out. She said she'd met someone dodgy there, and I thought I could find out who he was.'

'Aidan, truly, he's not working for whoever you think – he is nosy, Aidan, please ...'

The guy is sweating. 'I'm sorry! Please will you put the gun down?'

I'm weak and weary and I can hardly hold the gun any more, it's so heavy. Maybe he isn't Neil's man. Maybe Cass is safe.

But if she really didn't tell Holly, who did?

Cass is still holding two plates of food, and I'm starving hungry and all I want is to eat and sleep, but obviously I can't, not now. Not now I've scared them. There's no place for me here. There's no placde for me anywhere!

'I'll go,' I say. 'I'm sorry.'

But Cass shakes her head. 'Aidan, give me your phone. We need to call Holly.'

42: CASS

Aidan was slumped against the wall, breathing heavily, as though he was in pain. His eyes were closed. The gun dangled from his hand. I slid down the wall next to him again. I thought about grabbing it, but decided against it. What if it went off as I took it?

'Why don't you go and find my dad?' I said, as softly as possible to Will. He nodded, and left the room.

I leant my head against the wall. Now that he'd had a gun pointing at his head, what was the likelihood that Will would ever want to see me again? Zero.

Aidan was crying now, big, gulping sobs, but making no noise. It was the saddest thing I'd ever seen. It was as though he'd taught himself to cry in silence, so no one would hear him.

I put my arms round my brother. He moaned, but didn't move. 'It'll be all right, Aidan, I know it will. It'll be all right. I never said anything to Holly. I trust you, Aidan. And I've seen you with Finn. You'd never hurt him.'

He put his head on my shoulder and we just sat there, side by side. And I remembered. I remembered crying, and Aidan rocking me in his arms. I remembered Aidan carrying me. I remembered Aidan telling me not to worry, he would get me back to Mum and everything would be safe. He would take care of both of us. He'd protect me. He'd protect Mum.

I'd found my big brother again. I'd found myself.

The door opened. I thought it would be Will, but it was my dad. He looked down at us like a bemused giant.

Then he sat down on the floor right in front of us. Next to the gun. If Aidan realised, if he panicked – anything could happen.

'Well. This takes me back.'

'How?' Aidan wasn't crying any more, but he was shivering, like a scared greyhound.

'The two of you. You used to huddle up like that when you were little. On the floor. Under the table, sometimes.'

Now I was the one crying. Tears, streaming down my nose.

'Aidan, I've been talking to Will. He's told me that you need my help.'

Aidan made a noise that wasn't quite a word.

'He told me that you've found a firearm and very responsibly you've come to me, as a government minister and friend of the family, to put it in the right hands. Is that correct?'

Aidan blinked and nodded.

'Very good. That is the gun in question?'

Aidan let out a deep breath and nodded.

'Perhaps you'd like to give it to me? I will pass it to one of the ministerial protection officers and I can assure you that they won't take any action against you. '

No response. Aidan seemed to be processing everything incredibly slowly.

Dad waited patiently, and then changed tack. 'Will also seems to think that you're in some sort of trouble? With your partner?'

'She won't ... I need to explain ... I can't ...'

'I thought we could ring her,' I said.

'In my experience, it's never a good idea to rush into these things when you're in an emotional state,' said Dad. 'Better to talk it out first here, and calm down. What's your girlfriend's name, Aidan?'

'Holly.'

'What's happened with Holly?'

'Someone's told her something ... something that I did. That I never told her. And now she thinks bad things about me, that I'm going to hurt her son, maybe her, and I wouldn't, I really wouldn't ... but she won't listen.'

'Have you ever hurt her? Or her son?'

The look on Aidan's face is so painful that I can't bear it.

'Of course he didn't!' I tell Dad. 'Just look at him! He loves them both so much!'

'I want Aidan to tell me, Cass.'

'I would never hurt them. They're everything to me.'

'So why would Holly think you could hurt them?'

'I did something bad to my brother. When I was eleven.'

Dad's voice is coaxing, persuasive. The gun still dangled from Aidan's hand. 'Tell us, Aidan. If you can tell us, it'll be easier to tell Holly.'

'I was – it was when I went back to live with my mum. I didn't want to, I was happy where I was before. I had foster parents who wanted to adopt me. But she went to court and got me back.'

'She must have loved you very much to do that.'

Aidan thought about this. 'I wish she didn't love me then.'

'We can't change the past,' says Dad. 'And we can't always control our emotions.'

'She'd had another baby by then. Louis. He was about two.' His voice wobbled. 'About the same age Finn is now.'

'What happened to Louis?'

'Louis was bothering me. Wanted me to read to him. I couldn't read. Ever since I'd left Jim and Betty's, I'd been rubbish at my new school. I couldn't get the words together. I told him no, and he shouted at me.

'I lost it. It hadn't happened for ages – Jim and Betty really calmed me down, but I was so on edge, missing them and scared of Keith. I'd never known my mum with a man who didn't beat her or me, and I was waiting all the time for the moment when he went on the attack.

'But it was me who lost it first, not Keith. I swiped Louis across the face. I never meant to hurt him, honest to God, but I had a biro in my hand, and it caught him. In his eye. He screamed, this scream that went on and on and there was so much blood and I just wanted him to be quiet, but he wouldn't. He couldn't. And then it came true what I'd feared because Keith did shout and shout and when the ambulance had come and taken Mum and Louis away, he smacked me, hard. The strange thing was, I felt better then. It was better being hit than being scared, waiting for it. And it was like . . . Keith had been nice to me, but I was waiting, always waiting for him to show what he was really like. And I'd made him do it.'

Dad shook his head, just a little bit. I tried not to make any noise at all.

'The social worker came the next day. My stuff was already packed. Keith did it for me and loads of things got left behind. Things from Betty and Jim. Their address and phone number. Mum was still at the hospital with Louis. She never even said goodbye.

'Keith talked to the social worker and told her I was not welcome there again. But I didn't care because I thought ... I thought ... ' Aidan's breath was shallow and his face was pale, and for a moment I thought he might be going to break down altogether. 'I thought I would be going back to Jim and Betty, you see? To my foster parents? But we didn't go there. We went to the children's home and she took my bag out of the car, and I asked her, and she said ... '

He trailed to a halt.

'What did she say, Aidan?'

'That Betty and Jim were looking after a baby, so it weren't appropriate, it weren't safe ... I weren't safe.'

'Oh, Aidan, that's so unfair.' I squeezed his hand.

'I didn't believe it. I still don't. They wanted to punish me. Or Betty and Jim, they heard what happened and ... I'd let them down, you see. They didn't want me any more.'

I can count on the fingers of one hand the times I've seen my Dad cry. He's old-fashioned and he's very English and he just doesn't do it. He didn't cry when he told us about Annabel and he didn't cry when he packed up his stuff and left. But when Aidan said that, a big tear trickled down Dad's face.

'It's tough, isn't it, when all you've known is rejection,' Dad said. 'That's why we need to make sure that Holly hears this story from you, just as you've told it, so she understands that it was an accident. Nothing but an accident. A child loses his temper in a stressful situation. Understandable that Keith and your mother were very upset … although in my opinion, nothing justifies violence towards a child … But Holly has nothing to fear from you. And nor have any of us. That's right, isn't it, Aidan?'

Aidan looked at him, his eyes huge and almost childlike, and then he handed Dad the gun. 'Can you really just get rid of it for me?'

'I know someone who can. Now, Susie is very keen to hear all about your life, and Ben is desperate to meet you, and you look as though you need some food. Could you bear some family time before I drive you back to London?'

Aidan nodded, slowly. He and Dad stood up. I stayed where I was. I'd hardly breathed for about half an hour, and I felt too weak to move.

'If you want,' Dad continued, 'I'll come with you and stay with you while you talk to Holly … if you think that would help? To make sure she understands the whole story. And if things don't go so well, you can come and stay at my flat, and we'll figure things out. You're not alone, Aidan. We let you down once, and I'm truly sorry for that, and we're here for you now.'

I didn't know whether to be grateful to Dad for being so kind and helpful to Aidan, or angry with him. Because he was doing it out of guilt, I know. And he had a lot to be guilty about.

Or maybe he was doing it for me?

Dad looked down at me. 'Come and join us, Cass, when you're ready.'

They left me, and I cried for a bit longer, and then I blew my nose and scrubbed at my eyes and felt thankful that I wasn't silly enough to wear mascara because it would have been all over my face.

The door opened again. I thought it might be Mum, but it was Will. Of course. Will and a piece of birthday cake, and me with piggy pink eyes and a scarlet nose.

'Hey. I thought you might not be up to crowds of people.'

'I missed Ben blow out his candles?' Oh, no. Tears again.

'He'll live. He's really happy with all his mates here. It's nice to see.'

'It's thanks to you.'

'Not me. He did all the hard work of actually making friends. I just introduced them.'

'You did more than that. I don't know how to thank you.'

Will offered me a tissue. 'It's totally clean, honest.'

I accepted it gratefully. 'I'm sorry. I don't know what's the matter with me.'

'It's OK. That was pretty scary. I've never had a gun pointed at me before.'

'I'm sorry! I'm so sorry.'

'That's OK. It was nice of you to speak up for me. I'm glad you think I'm ... what was it? "A very nice person." That was special.'

It was my moment.

Naturally I screwed it up.

'I don't know if you're making fun of me or not.'

'I wouldn't dream of making fun of you,' he said. Then he took my hand. 'Cass, can we try again?'

Obviously, most girls would have just smiled and laughed

and fallen into his arms, and that's what I wanted to do. But I had to make sure what I was doing.

'When you say try again, what do you mean, exactly?'

Will grimaced and said, 'Did you ever think of studying law? Because I think it might suit you much better than history. What I *mean* is anything you want. If you want to go on sneaking around in secret, that's fine. If you want a full-on, official, devoted boyfriend, then let it be me. I can't stop thinking about you, and I miss you so much and I really want to get it right. Just let me know what you want, Cass Montgomery, and I'll do my best.'

I didn't know what to say, so I pulled out my phone. Clicked on the Facebook app, found my profile.

'Look,' I told him, as I clicked the keys.

'"In a relationship with Will Hughes",' he read. 'Blimey. When you make your mind up, you really go for it.'

'Is that OK?' I wasn't sure if I'd just made a monumental fool of myself. Looking again at the phone in my hand, I saw that five people had already liked my changed status.

'It's a lot more than OK,' he said, as his nose bumped against mine and finally, finally . . .

The door burst open one more time and I heard Ben's amazed voice. 'Cass! Why are you kissing Will?'

43: AIDAN

It was Neil who told Holly. He made up all sorts of lies about it, all sorts of stuff that made me sound like a monster, like a mutilator. Once Cass's dad took me back to the flat, and we sat down and talked, it got sorted out. It was OK. He was actually really helpful. A bit like a counsellor or a social worker. Better.

Holly understood. She believed me. And we started talking in a different way. Because once she knew the very worst thing about me, I believed she'd stay with me, I believed she loved me, and that made me feel completely different about myself. I began to see how I could stop drinking. And then I did it. I stopped, just like that. Stood in the pub with Rich and ordered a Coke. It felt strange and stupid, but I did it once and then I did it again.

Even though it's Christmas Eve. I've set myself the target of an alcohol-free festive season. I actually think I can do it. I just say no, again and again and again, and every time I feel stronger and proud of myself. And if I don't feel strong enough, then I call Cass's dad and just talk it through a bit with him. He promised he'd be there for me, and so far he has been. I like him a lot. I haven't mentioned my benefits, though. Just in case.

Kicking the drinking really helps with the reading and writing. My brain seems clearer, the words stay still. I think I'd underestimated how much alcohol I'd been having and what it was doing to my brain.

I'm still seeing the counsellor. Still picking through the past. It's like when I'd help Betty unravel her knitting wool. Sometimes it'd go fast and easy and sometimes there'd be knots to untangle. I was good at that then, and I'm discovering I can do it now.

I asked my social worker about Betty and Jim and he contacted them for me. I got a letter from Betty, all wobbly handwriting and lavender scent. They missed me, she said. They always wondered how I'd got on. They'd love to see me again. I didn't have any trouble reading Betty's letter, not the first time, nor every time since then. They want me to go and visit. They want to meet Holly and Finn.

I can't believe how much difference a letter can make.

So I'm writing one of my own. Rich is here to help me with it. Rich's new boyfriend is great, never gets jealous, never minds if I come over to see Rich, never hits on me, really seems to care about him. It's a weight off my mind.

Brendan's gone out tonight, and Holly's at zumba class, so it's just me and Rich babysitting Finn. I'm going to drive Rich home when she comes back. No more late buses for us, now I've finally passed my test.

'So,' he says, 'you talk, I'll write. Who is it to?'

'Louis,' I say. 'My brother. You know.'

'"Dear Louis,"' he says, writing it down. 'Go on.'

'"I am your half-brother. I am called Aidan and I came to live with you when I was eleven and you were two. I didn't want to be there. I was angry all the time because I wanted to be with my foster parents, Jim and Betty. They were like my real mum and dad. Not your parents."'

'Slow down,' says Rich. 'I can't write that fast. I'm not sure how great my spelling is, either.'

'Spelling doesn't matter so much,' I told him. 'Susie said that. Cass's mum, you know. She said that what matters is communicating. Relationships break down when you stop. It doesn't matter how you do it.'

'Now you're sounding like a social worker,' says Rich. 'Carry on with your letter.'

'"I am sorry. I am sorry that I hurt you. I didn't mean to."'

'You did mean to,' says Rich.

I think for a moment. '"I didn't mean to hurt you so much. I didn't mean to hurt your eye like that. I just lashed out because I was angry and there was a pen in my hand and it caught you at just the wrong place. I never planned it, I never did anything like that again, and I have felt bad about it for years and years and years."'

I'm all hot and sweaty. Rich looks at me and says, 'Are you really up for this?'

'I am. Keep going. "I know your dad says he can never trust me, but I am different now. I've gone through a lot. And I've got a family of my own now, and I can understand how your dad feels because if anyone hurt my little boy, then I'd hate them too."'

'That's good,' says Rich. 'What about your mum?'

'"I never got on great with my" – no, make that "our" – "with our mum, but I think it's better now. A lot of time has passed. I'm sorry it's taken so long to say sorry."'

'That doesn't sound right.'

I'm exhausted. 'Just put, "Have a happy Christmas and new year. And maybe I can see you one day. I'd like to know you. But only if your mum and dad say it's OK."'

Later on, when Holly is home and I've delivered Rich to Walthamstow and I've parked the van outside our new flat – Clive decided to invest in a conversion in Kentish Town – I pull out my phone and I ring Cass. She answers right away.

'Hey,' I say. 'Happy Christmas.'

'Hello.'

We're getting past that day. We haven't seen each other since. We're just talking on the phone, gradually putting it back together again. It might take months, or years. I want to make it happen.

'What are you doing for Christmas?' she asks.

'We're going to Holly's Uncle Clive,' I tell her. 'He invited us. Her mum's going to her sister in Birmingham and she wanted us to go too, but then Clive said we should come to them. I haven't done it for years, that big, family Christmas thing.'

One day, I think, I'll make a massive turkey dinner for everyone in my life. For Holly and Finn and Clive and his family. For Cass and Will and her brother, Ben. Rich and Brendan. Even Mum and Keith and Scarlett and Louis. Maybe even Jim and Betty. And everyone can have serviettes and everything will be perfect.

Cass seems really happy with this guy Will. She says they

might take a gap year between school and university, travelling, doing some volunteer work. 'And I might not go to Oxford after all,' she told me last time we talked, 'I might look at other places. And I don't think history's for me. I'm looking at law courses.'

'I'm going to start college,' I told her. 'Clive said he'd sponsor me to do a course in accounting. He wants to train me up, give me more responsibility. I'm not sure if I can do it, but I'll give it a try.'

'Of course you can do it,' she told me. 'You'll be fine.'

Now she's going on about Christmas, about how she's going to miss her dad.

'It's going to be different this year,' she says. 'I can't believe my dad's not going to be there. It's going to be strange. But Will and I are going away for New Year. His sister's in pantomime in Newcastle, so we're staying up there.'

'Every year it's different for me,' I tell her. 'You get used to it. As long as the turkey's there, it works.'

Then she laughs and I laugh and it's good. It's OK.

Sometimes I think we all get too worked up about families. I mean, we're all related somehow, aren't we? What is a family, anyway? Is it Cass and Ben and her split-up parents? Is it Rich and Brendan, happy-ever-after in Walthamstow? Is it Cass and me? Holly and Finn?

I always wanted a perfect family, but I'll settle for a normal one.

I'm full of hope.

ACKNOWLEDGMENTS

Jacqui and Karen. Thank you for sharing your experience and wisdom, without your help this book would never have been written.

Anna found my Kindle in a busy shopping centre and her husband and son, Russell and Michael, turned detective to return it to me. Then Russell told me about his shop – The Salvage Store in Burnt Oak, north London – and I had a title and a setting for the idea that I was hoping might turn into a book. Thank you!

Jenny Savill, so much to thank you for, I'm very lucky to have you as my agent.

Sam Smith, your devotion to *Salvage* was above and beyond anything I could have expected. And thanks to everyone else at Atom, for making me feel so welcome, especially Kate Agar.

Anne Joseph, Amanda Swift, Anna Longman, Lydia Syson, Jennifer Gray, Becky Jones, Fenella Fairburn, Keris Stainton, Tamsyn Murray, Luisa Plaja, Susie Day, Cat Clarke and Sophia Bennett, thank you for your support, advice, and the laughs. Special thanks to Fiona Dunbar and Valerie Kampmeier who read multiple versions of *Salvage* and gave me excellent critiques.

Thank you to my family: Mum and Dad, Deborah, Alun, Jeremy, Josh, Avital and Eliana. Phoebe and Judah, you will see more of me now, I promise. Most of all, thanks to Laurence, love of my life. Twenty years, who'd have thought it?